# House of Light

———❦———

# House of Light

*a novel*

Joyce Carol Thomas

HYPERION *New York*

Library of Congress Cataloging-in-Publication Data

Thomas, Joyce Carol.
    House of light / by Joyce Carol Thomas.—1st ed.
      p. cm.
    ISBN: 0-7868-6606-3
    1. Afro-american women healers—Fiction.  2. Oklahoma City (Okla.)—Fiction.  I. Title.
PS3570.H565 H68 2001
813'.54—dc21                            00-047107

FIRST EDITION

10  9  8  7  6  5  4  3  2  1

*For*
*the living saints*

# Acknowledgments

I thank my diligent agent, Anna Ghosh, who welcomed my work into her keeping and delivered the manuscript to my meticulous editor, Leigh Haber, who said "Yes," and gave this novel a room in her house of books.

I thank my persistent Muse, my very own architect of the spirit who lives in the house of my mind, who oversees the changes each page whispers, and who dances ever in my sight, inspiring the shaping as I play within the circle of words.

To Anna Ghosh and Leigh Haber; to this book's listeners and readers; to my many supportive friends, family, and especially to my aunt, Corine Coffey, these three gifts: Solace. Sanctuary. Peace.

jct

# House of Light

This book is a work of fiction

*Abide with me*
*in light asymmetry*
Abyssinia

A bench baby is rocked on the first pew. Is looked after when death flies in the window, lest the living forget about life.

The faithful keep their eyes on tomorrow when they kiss her face.

Abyssinia.

Gazing at her, the preacher delivers his sermon.

The testimony service is one long poem, with each saint reciting a stanza.

Abyssinia is in the basket on her bench, channeling the spirits. Sifting pain. Studying joy.

She watches the curve and tremble of a left, palsied hand.

She hears the desperation trapped in a stricken throat.

There is a whisper that should have been screamed, which Abyssinia folds into an echo.

The spirit chants her name, and she stands up.

She calls to the earth, to the birds in the wild wheat fields, to the wreckage swirling amid tornadoes.

A glory light dances round her head from dawn to dusk.

The days spiral into years. As she blooms into a healer, the music of saints calls her to her own name again and again and again:

"Abyssinia."

And she answers.

Zenobia of the wild copper hair and lithe body sings and plays guitar nightly in the small Oklahoma City nightclub called the Green Apple. Word of mouth quickly spreads the story of the sultry, young woman who calls herself Miss Z, whose repertoire specializes in blues numbers.

There are those who swear she can make a song walk, can make the guitar cry whenever she wants to.

"Sing it!" they chant at first, then as the smoke-clouded room—reeking of whiskey and stale wine—fills, they hush. The audience listens for every twist and turn of note above the frosted glasses tinkling with ice, and through the ribbons of double-strength tobacco smoke they study Miss Z's every move.

"Reminds me of Bessie Smith," a tray-balancing waiter sighs.

"Billie Holiday's daughter and Mahalia Jackson's cousin mixed," a chunky woman declares after downing a gin fizz.

"Got to be kin to Aretha Franklin. It's some gospel in the woodpile somewhere. I know what I'm listening to!"

Sad-voiced, blues-struck, and good, Zenobia gets lost in her music, forgetting her audience, especially when she comes to her finale, her signature piece, and the crowd's favorite, "The Thrill Is Gone."

When she sings the last note of the first act, the lights shimmer off her copper hair. "Man, oh man, look at that!" the waiter exclaims each night.

The audience stomps, claps, and hollers their glee. The manager, Mr. Mason, all business, short and nattily dressed in his pinstriped suit, helps her off the stage after her finale.

The crowds gather nightly to hear the woman with a voice they think reminds them of someone famous, but it is Miss Z's style that mesmerizes them.

"Her phrasing is like nothing you've ever experienced. It takes your breath away," the major music critic—an advocate of blues music—writes in the *Oklahoma City Herald*, the largest circulation newspaper in the state.

After the newspaper review headlines the entertainment section in the Sunday edition, more people come rushing to hear her for themselves. They sit in the dimly-lit bar, head soaked in Miss Z music, heart jumping, feet twitching to the hard-to-keep-still rhythms that have them ordering trays of drinks, to the delight of Mr. Mason, the club owner.

Zenobia sings "The Thrill Is Gone," and every night the crowd multiplies. For the first time, Mr. Mason has to turn away customers.

"We'll have to add another set," he tells Zenobia.

"Then you'll be doubling my pay," she replies.

"I'm already paying you top dollar."

"Twice the work. Twice the money," Zenobia counters.

Mr. Mason gleefully imagines doubling his nightly income.

"Robbing me blind," he mutters under his breath even as he agrees to Zenobia's demand.

The second set proves to be as successful as the first. And still more customers squeeze in.

One blue-black man swears that Miss Z makes flames leap from her guitar strings. The guitar follows her voice faithfully into uncharted musical terrain that only she can negotiate. She takes the audience with her to places nobody else has ever been. Miss Z gives everything she has.

Offstage, Zenobia doesn't allow anybody to touch her or her guitar.

Both are virgins.

Zenobia's reputation as a blues singer continues to grow, and Mr. Mason thinks of expanding the building so he can accommodate more customers. Visitors from places as far away as Tulsa, Boley, and Stillwater go searching for the Green Apple Blues Club. Once there they start lining up as early as dawn, just to be able to hear Zenobia sing.

One Thursday night in her dressing room as she prepares to go on stage, she hears a strained voice shouting.

"I save my money to come all the way up here from Arkansas, and you're telling me I can't get a seat? Man, I took two days off from work just to see the woman. My uncle over in Langston saw her and told me, 'Drop everything and go hear you some Miss Z!'"

"I'm sorry, sir," Mr. Mason says. "But . . ."

"You let me in!" the traveler insists.

He pleads so desperately that the rowdy crowd, a perverse bunch, feels it is their business to keep the poor man out.

"You stand in line just like the rest of us, and if you don't get a ticket, get a rain check!" one woman wags her finger.

"I heard that man from Arkansas. Let him in for the next set," Zenobia says to the manager when he stops by her dressing room.

"I can't do that. It would make the other customers angry," Mr. Mason tells her.

"If that man don't get in, I'm not singing," she says sitting herself back down at the dressing stool.

"The hell you ain't!"

Zenobia wonders aloud, "What kind of unchristian folks out there anyway, let a person drive hundreds of mile and don't show a little charity?"

"That ain't your business. Your business is to sing."

She leaps up, quickly sticks her guitar in its case, and begins throwing clothes into her suitcase.

"Where you think you're going?" Mr. Mason barks.

"Don't feel good," Zenobia says.

"I got a packed house out there come to hear you sing and play. I pay you up front what you ask for every single week, now you go give them people some music!"

"Can't do that, don't feel good," Zenobia says stubbornly, now locking her suitcase.

"These folks about ready to riot, already they're saying they're not leaving 'til they hear 'The Thrill Is Gone.' "

"Guess you got yourself a riot," she says, lifting the suitcase off the couch.

He grabs hold of her arm.

"Take your hands off me, Mister! I already played one set, so I'm taking half the money. The rest is on the dressing table."

He sees the greenbacks stacked there, but the sight of them just makes him madder.

His mouth curls down meanly. "You ain't no bigger than a minute."

"Yeah?" Zenobia answers. "No bigger than a minute all right. This minute'll make you ache some awful hours."

Mr. Mason looks back and forth from her to his investment stacked on the table and grabs her again, digging his fingers roughly into her arm.

"I said . . ." he starts.

Before she can even think about it, it is a lightning reflex really, Zenobia picks up the closest thing she can lay her hands on, in this case, a brass lamp off the dressing table and hits Mr. Mason with it.

Thwop!

He slides to the floor.

A king-sized knot rises on Mr. Mason's mashed head.

He tries to stand up.

Wobbles and droops back down.

Before he can collect himself and get back up, Zenobia picks up her guitar, grabs her suitcase, and takes off for the back door.

A loud, crazy noise stops her in her tracks.

It is the sound of the predicted riot breaking out in the main room.

"You got what you deserved!" she says to Mason before slamming the door behind her.

When he finally pulls himself up and stumbles to the stage entrance, he looks out on an uprising of unhappy customers.

"Good God," he moans.

P*earline,* her buxom body clad in pajamas at her kitchen table, works past midnight typing the church bulletin. She has just finished the line announcing that Abyssinia Jackson-Jefferson, M.D., and her lawyer husband, Carl Lee Jefferson, J.D., will be hosting a tea during the fellowship hour on Sunday. She has started the "Sick and Shut-in" list before slumping over the typewriter. Sound asleep.

A screech owl hoots and wakes her. Her head, covered with jet-black ringlets, jerks up from the cool metal keyboard. She turns off the lamp, stumbles to the bedroom, and crawls under the covers.

She tosses and turns all night until a loud, chiding voice from the clock radio drowns out the blue bird sounds of morning.

"Put your hand on the radio and get your blessing!" a preacher wails through the static coming over the airwaves. Pearline lifts her head from the pillow, which might as well be a rock. Her head throbs with thought-stuttering pain.

"I say, everybody within the sound of my voice. Put your hand on the radio!"

Pearline throws back the sheet and raises her full-figured body from the squeaking bed.

"I say, lay your prayer cloth on the radio and get your blessing!"

She limps over to the dresser next to the radio, sticks a brown hand in the drawer, and pulls out the linen-white hand-kerchief sprinkled with holy oil.

"Now, ask whatever you want in God's name and it shall be done!"

"Just make Isaiah leave me alone," she groans as she bows her head.

"Amen," the minister says in a know-it-all voice.

Then he goes on to preach, talking about first one thing then another. He chides, "Some of you women don't know how to hang your head around a man. Always looking him dead in the eye! Got to learn how to hang your head so a man can get his act together. Don't know how to be a helpmeet. Now the Good Book say . . ."

Even as he speaks, Pearline thinks, *If I hang my head around Isaiah, I might not ever be able to lift it again.*

When Pearline reaches for the knob with one black and blue arm, her whole body aches. She turns off the radio.

Maybe the reverend can't help her. Whether she is holding her head up or hanging it down, Isaiah still hurts her. Maybe the season of miracles belongs only in the Bible.

"Blasphemy," she says, ashamed of her defiant thoughts.

That afternoon, she holds clothespins between her teeth as she stretches a strapless bra up next to a black negligee.

Isaiah leans from behind the peach tree.

"Who you go be wearing those sexy things for tonight?" he asks in a controlled, even voice.

She jumps.

"Who you getting ready to screw now?" he yells.

He leaps from behind the thick green limbs and branches and proceeds to beat the daylights out of her, the entire time saying, "I knew it! Knew you been messing with somebody else!"

Pearline trips on the clothesbasket when she tries to run.
"I'll kill you! I'll kill you dead!"

The sweet, sun-fragranced wash tangles her up in embroidered skirts and lacy crocheted blouses. They don't cushion the ensuing blows.

After Isaiah finishes, he roars away in his old Pontiac.

Weeping Pearline crawls through the grubby red dirt into the house. She picks up her handkerchief and blows her nose and suddenly stops crying. The handkerchief is a wedding memento, with two hearts, one embroidered with Isaiah's name, the other with hers. She winces as she remembers how proud she had strutted on her wedding day. Hadn't she held onto Isaiah like a swimmer drowning in a swift current holds onto a lifeguard? He was her lifeguard. Now he threatens her life. Maybe that is the problem, she figures. A lifeguard, when you give him power, can save your life, but he can take it just as easily.

"Never leave yourself at the mercy of anyone's benevolence or malevolence," her Grandma Vennie always counsels. "Otherwise you're asking them to play God."

Now she doesn't hesitate, she quickly twists the Off knob when the preacher hollers, "Put your hand on the radio and get your blessing!" The prayer cloth lays lonesome in the bottom of the dresser.

A blessing? All she gets lately is the backside of Isaiah's hand. Although he has taken up with another woman, he still stops by routinely to give her a regular whipping.

In the middle of washing the dishes or crocheting, she reaches desperately for the joy she used to feel, but she can't find it. It's as though something heavy inside her spirit has fallen down and broken. At night she cries into the balled-up sheet, catching her breath in jagged gasps.

The next morning, she pokes her head out from behind the

drawn curtains and watches the postman put something in the mailbox at the edge of the road. She waits a few minutes until she is sure he has gotten out of speaking range. No sense in trying Isaiah's patience unnecessarily.

She wonders what the mailman has left. She tells her heart to stay still, but it won't. Each day she hopes. Each day she finds no magic envelope, no notice she has won a million-dollar sweepstake or a trip that will take her to some exotic place where she can leave Isaiah far behind.

She walks, looking nervously all around her as she approaches the box. Inside she sees a genuine letter addressed to her in vaguely familiar handwriting.

Her fingers tremble as she tears the envelope open so hastily she rips the letter. She places the two pieces side by side until they fit. The words are so unbelievably welcome and wrenching that she has to hear herself say them out loud:

*Dear Pearline,*
*I'm tired of this big city life. Can I come visit next Friday if it's all right?*
*Your long lost friend, Zenobia.*

Pearline reads and rereads the letter. In her excitement she forgets about her limping pains and hurries up her porch steps.

The next morning, Pearline almost leaps up from her bed when the telephone rings.

"Can't talk long," Zenobia says. "Did you get my note?"

"Yeah, girl. Can't believe you're coming. I'm separated from Isaiah."

"Separated? You went and got married?" Zenobia asks.

"Big mistake," Pearline says. "Looks like we need to catch up on the news. And all the gossip in town."

"Well, I'll be there on the five-o'clock Greyhound," Zenobia says.

"When?" Pearline asks.

"How's Friday sound? A week from tomorrow."

"I'll be waiting for you at the bus stop!" Pearline replies.

The week passes with days steeped in hope. No sign of Isaiah. Surely that is a good omen. Pearline says her bedtime prayers now with more devotion than she has mustered since she prayed for a husband.

Friday comes and Pearline washes and rinses the white sheets for the sofa bed and shakes them 'til they pop. For once she feels almost safe. She pins the bedding on the slack line strung between the blackjack tree and the peach tree and thinks about the days when she and Zenobia were teenagers in Ponca.

Back then, in Attucks High School, Zenobia was famous for whipping any boy who dared touch her without her permission. Junior Brown, the burly football star, took the challenge and lost. When the teacher sent Zenobia to the office, she glared down the vice principal who blinked nervously and stuttered, "Z-Z-Zenobia, g-g-g-o on 'long home now."

After the football star incident, nobody messed with Zenobia, except the feeble-brained and those with short memories who had a reputation to make, those who had committed some act of cowardice they wanted to try to make up for. Tackling Zenobia was a shortcut to instant heroism if the challenger won, but no one ever did.

Zenobia would wheel into her assailant like a Bible belt tornado. When the dust cleared and she stood up, she would whisk the clay dirt off her blue jeans and strut away.

"Lord, Lord, Lord, them was the days," Pearline sighs.

Zenobia is coming on the five-o'clock Greyhound.

Now she sings bravely, as bravely as she and Zenobia used to sing in the church choir, her voice rising over the sheets and towels and pillowcases flapping in the humid breeze:

> *Don't want no man*
> *Hair and nails long as mine*
> *Don't want no man*
> *Hair and nails long as mine*
> *If I wanted me a female*
> *Buy me a doll at the five and dime.*

Isaiah accuses her of seeing somebody else, but she can truthfully say that not one man hovers on the horizon. After the divorce is final and with Zenobia here, maybe then she can direct her attention to Arthur Ray Cleveland, handsome Arthur Ray who has been watching her so closely. But 'til then she doesn't dare lift her head in greeting to a male diaper-wearing toddler, let alone a man fine as Arthur Ray Cleveland.

If Isaiah even hears of her saying, "How do?" to a man as she did that last time to Widower Parsons, he would come creeping around her windows trying to see if "somebody was wearing out the couch." He is bent on discouraging any chair pullers, flower senders, door openers, and hand kissers with his bare fists, but there never is anyone there. Now if he doesn't trust her around no-tooth Parsons, whose billy goat odor she can smell a country mile away, what chance does a serious courting caller have?

She has a hard time understanding Isaiah. Before they separated, sometimes he would stay out all night and tip in just before the rooster crowed.

"Where you been, Isaiah?" she would ask.

"In the alley with Sally, waiting for Sue to get through."

Pearline remembers something her Grandmother Vennie had said.

"A jealous husband always scared another man's gonna do his wife what he's sneaking 'round doing to other women."

Oh how she wishes she had listened to Grandma Vennie. The old lady had told her, "Pearline, don't you marry that man!"

"Why, Grandma?" she asked.

"Won't have anything to do with his folks, that's why!"

"Must be a reason," Pearline had answered in Isaiah's defense.

"A reason. Uh-huh," Grandma Vennie said. "And I don't and you don't know what it is!"

Pearline paid no heed. She was seeing herself marching down the aisle.

Grandma Vennie continued, "When you choose a husband, pay most strict attention. Close your ears to all the sweet talk and look at what they do. Disregard everything but their actions. I'm telling you, honey, they'll lie all the way on up to the altar. Don't be like some of these women who just have to have *a* husband. Now, that Isaiah can't be no good. Even the Hag Squad talk about him bad." Every gossip in Ponca City knows that the Hag Squad consists of those women reportedly so ugly they welcome all single males with open arms, disregarding any faults a man might possess from a bad case of laziness to falling-down drunk alcoholism.

But the caution ringing the loudest in Pearline's head this morning is her grandmother's warning, "A jealous husband always scared another man's gonna do his wife what he's sneaking 'round doing to other women."

Still, there are ways of handling Isaiah and other menaces to women. After she got tired of hearing about Sally in the alley and waiting for Sue to get through, she went up town. She told her lawyer, Carl Lee Jefferson, to file divorce papers and he did.

Now she sings in a high voice as she sticks the wooden clothespins on the last terry cloth towel, picks up the clothesbasket, and heads back to the house.

> Don't want no man
> Hair and nails long as mine
> Don't want no man
> Hair and nails long as mine
> If I wanted me a female
> Buy me a doll at the five and dime.

Inside the house, smelling of Pine Sol from the scrubbing she gave the floors, Pearline looks in the mirror and notices that her week-old bruises are just about gone. Her reflection tells her she is still a mighty fine looking woman. "Prettiest eyes in Oklahoma," Isaiah used to say when they first courted years ago.

"Well," she says, smoothing down her eyebrows as she studies her reflection, "I guess they still are."

Where, oh where, has love flown, she wonders as she turns away to dust the coffee table.

If he had courted her, she had courted him. First came the pies, scrumptious peach, dewberry, and apple-deep wonders. She followed these mouth pleasers with homemade vanilla ice cream as they snuggled on the screened porch.

One night when lightning bugs flew so dense it seemed God was putting on a special show just for the couple, she near about invited him to her bed. He reluctantly kissed her goodnight before leaving the porch very late.

They married too quickly. And then the spirits in a bottle of Jack Daniel's intruded. At first he took little sips, every now and then, upon his return from Conoco, the Continental Oil Company.

The sips became swallows.

The swallows became guzzles.

It was when he began finishing whole pints that the imps came to him. Two of them, looking wasted. They filled his head, he thought, with strange proposals. One night it got so bad he watched, shaking, as the two imps battled and wrestled with two angels. In this contest, Isaiah was the judge, only he could declare the winner. In the struggle between good and evil, it wasn't hard to tell who had the upper hand. He whipped Pearline on a regular basis until she had no choice but to file for divorce.

Lost in thought, Pearline adjusts the crocheted doilies on the arms of the chairs and sofa. Then she stands back and surveys the room with a satisfied sigh just as the ticking clock brings her back to the present. Four-thirty. Time to walk to the bus stop.

She starts down Loganberry Road walking as tall as she did when she was in high school and pretty and all the boys told her so.

She passes the Ponca City Carpentry Shop where Arthur Ray Cleveland sits cooling himself in the shade on his afternoon break. She walks on his side of the road, so close she is aware of the short, rough stubble on his square chin.

"Why, he's tall as an Oklahoma cypress," she whispers to herself. Muscles barely contain themselves under his clean blue Levi's shirt.

"Good afternoon, my dark lady," Arthur Ray says.

"How do, Arthur Ray." With this greeting she flashes a smile that lights up the two bright candles of her eyes.

Arthur Ray's answer is a row of strong white teeth flashing. Lord, help mercy, when she looks at him with those dark eyes, his whole body responds.

The encounter is not lost on any of the town gossips.

"Can't wait to tell Isaiah," one busybody says.

When Isaiah leaves the Continental Oil Company late that evening, every tongue will want to be the first to wag the news. Waiting is like an itch they can't quite reach.

*They don't know Zenobia's coming*, Pearline thinks. *They don't know help is on the way.* She holds her head high and struts like a cheerleader on the sidelines of the Attucks High football stadium on Homecoming Day.

Suddenly she finds the courage to do something outrageously wicked. All the way up until she reaches the bus station, she winks at every man she sees.

As Pearline nears her destination, she imagines what it will be like seeing Zenobia after so many years. The first hug. The catching-up talk going on from early in the evening into the wee hours of the morning. In the midst of her longing and anticipation, she hears a bus's loud gears winding down and realizes she is almost there. Picking up speed, she hurries around the corner just in time to see the five-o'clock Greyhound grinding to a halt.

She scans the bus windows for Zenobia, but she can't pick her out. Travelers are already standing in the aisle and filing off the bus and into the arms of waiting family and friends.

*What if Zenobia changed her mind and didn't come?*

Pearline wraps her arms across her waist and stares at the gaping bus door.

*What if she didn't change her mind, but missed the bus?*

A lump of fear bobs up in her throat. It hurts to swallow.

*What if . . . ?*

As the bus becomes almost empty, her hopes dim.

*She's not coming*, Pearline figures.

Disappointed, her head down, her shoulders hunched, Pearline turns away.

"Pearline, girl!"

Pearline catches her breath and looks over and up into Zenobia's grinning face.

Zenobia steps off the Greyhound carrying a tan leather bag, its seams bulging. Across her back hangs a guitar case. Here and there a small sign of aging, a wrinkle on the forehead, a few strands of rainbow ribbons add more highlights to her sleek copper hair.

"Zenobia, Zenobia, you haven't changed a lick!"

Zenobia puts down her guitar and bag for a moment. The two women hug and step back. Pearline picks up Zenobia's luggage and Zenobia, retrieving her guitar case, says in that voice husky as women's voices after screaming and running in a baseball game, "And you haven't either."

It's a lie and they both know it, but it sure sounds good.

They turn the corner and start walking down Loganberry Road on the way back to the house. They take their time, stopping here and there to identify old landmarks.

"There's Mrs. Parsons' house. Remember the window you knocked out playing baseball that time, Zenobia?"

Zenobia laughs. "And old lady Parsons come running out cackling like a hen whose nest been robbed of eggs, her hair strewed all over her head, caught in the middle of pressing it, one side straight, the other nappy, screaming, 'Your mama's gonna pay for this, you little careless witch!' "

"And you told her to stick her wig on her head if she wanted to have straight hair and stop burning her brains out."

"I was something mean all right."

"Except when you sang in the choir."

"Kept me from getting punished more than once. 'Fraid I didn't know what respect was."

"Old lady Parsons is dead now."

"Gone to glory. Probably the stench of old man Parsons got to be too much for her. She got a good whiff, the stuff knocked her into a coma and killed her."

"How'd you know? She did die in a coma, but it was a stroke took her on away from here."

"Smelling him is worse than being struck."

"Stroke."

"Whatever."

"Grandma Vennie claims old man Parsons smells like a man ought to smell. Ain't no man got no business smelling like flowers."

"Guess it makes a kind of sense, what Aunt Vennie said. That woman always strikes me as making sense."

"Struck me the same way," Pearline says. "Speaking of being struck, once we get home I got to tell you about Isaiah. I mean, girl!"

They walk on, stopping to study the old pecan tree they used to climb and shake until it yielded its crunchy delights. In younger days they picked up bags of brown nuts, shelled them, and baked rich pecan pies with melt-in-the-mouth crusts.

"Never guess what I been fixing," Pearline says.

"What?"

"Ready to bake."

"Don't tease me now."

"Pecan pies."

"Woo, Pearline!"

"Sure enough."

As soon as they step inside the house, Pearline pops the pies in the oven, small ones like tarts, individually and lovingly prepared.

"Rest yourself. Put your suitcase in the closet when you're finished unpacking."

"It's so restful just being here," Zenobia says as she places her guitar on the floor near the couch.

"And take a bath if you like."

"A bath! Just what I need after riding that long dog Mr. Greyhound," Zenobia says.

From a basket hanging over the oval tub, Zenobia selects lemon soap from Pearline's assortment of herbal bath bars. In the kitchen, Pearline warms up the tomato, corn, okra, and onion dish. By the time Zenobia steps onto the linoleum and hangs up her fluffy towel, the sausage and biscuit roll is piping hot. Pearline hums, "Don't want no man . . ." as she places the dishes on the table.

Zenobia, dressed in her down-to-the-toes rainbow robe, stands in the kitchen doorway, and takes in the bountiful array of food on the table.

"Talk about a feast for a queen!"

"You look like one in that long robe."

Zenobia grins. "I do, don't I. Um-hmm. Queen Zenobia."

They eat a while in appreciative silence, savoring the taste of Pearline's soul food, while the baking pecan pies sprinkle the air with nutty aromas.

Zenobia sighs, "Ummm. Ummm! Has this Isaiah gone and lost his mind or what that he'd leave such good cooking behind?"

"Gone crazy all right. Crazy with jealousy."

"Naw."

"Uh-huh."

"Somebody else?" Zenobia asks, arching her eyebrows.

"Me? No. Not yet."

"Not yet, huh?" Zenobia eyes her mischievously.

"Well, Isaiah got a serious problem. Every time he'd get ready to leave for work, the man would take his broom and sweep around the porch. Come home, first thing he'd do is check out the dirt. If there were any tracks, chicken or human, I'd be in trouble. If a traveling salesman stopped at my door, I was suspect. No explanation ever satisfied him. If a dog crossed the yard, he'd think some midget'd come to town on all fours just to mess with me."

Zenobia throws her head back and laughs in that rich timber of hers. Pearline joins in too, but soon says, "We laughing, but it ain't funny. I'm still suffering from that last beating, and he gave that one to me *after* the separation."

Zenobia stops tittering and screws up her face, narrowing her eyes to slits. "Well, now you just relax. I ain't scared of him. I'll make him run off and leave both his shoes. Make him call for his Mama and his Grandma come messing 'round here when Z's in town. I wish he would!"

Pearline says, "Lord knows I needed you to stop by here!"

"And I need another helping of sausage biscuits."

As she puts Zenobia's refilled plate on the table, Pearline thinks she hears a sound at the window.

"Did you hear something?" Pearline asks.

Zenobia listens.

"Just a dog barking. Don't be so nervous," she says.

"Want some coffee?" Pearline asks.

"Uh-huh."

"Cream and sugar?"

"Sugar. No cream."

"That's right, you prefer yours black."

"Like my men." Zenobia stirs the sugar into her coffee and says, "Old cock-eyed coon. Isaiah? Mess with me I'll skin him like a rabbit. What do he look like? I'd like to see him. Come messing around after I left, huh?"

"Yeah."

"What do he look like? Never mind. It don't matter. I'll know him by his ugly attitude. Ugly ain't he?"

Pearline lifts the pies out of the oven and places them on the dessert saucers.

Zenobia inhales, momentarily distracted by the intoxicating aroma of brown-sugar bubbling pies, chock full of nuts.

Pearline finally answers, "Way he acts I suppose you could say he's ugly as sin. Nothing at all like . . ."

"Who?"

"Never mind."

"Who?"

"Another fellow up the road."

"What's his name?"

"Arthur Ray."

"Arthur Ray who?"

"Arthur Ray Cleveland."

Just then a blue shadow flashes by the window, and the sound of glass breaking and curtain rods crashing to the floor makes the moment seem unreal. Then Isaiah Spencer busts through the curtains and into the kitchen.

"Yon he is Zenobia! Yon he is!"

Zenobia picks up her chair and whips it at the shadow. *Swoosh.*

Then the full man comes into full view.

"Huh?" Zenobia looks up, seems her neck can't stretch back far enough. She takes in the sight of Isaiah Spencer. All six-feet-four of muscle, bushy-hair, long gray fingernails, devil red eyes burning with rage and a fiery red tongue to match, and *clunk,* she drops her chair weapon.

Isaiah looks down at tall Zenobia like she is a new specimen of ant, and then he knocks the shiny silverware onto the floor.

Forks and spoons hit the linoleum with a *k-ching-k-clang-k-chang*. With one swipe of his hand, the fringed tablecloth follows the path of the utensils and covers them like a skirt in a heap. He reaches down and uprights Zenobia's turned-over chair. He stretches across to the stove and with his other hand grabs dessert. Then he sits in Zenobia's place at the table, scoops up the steaming and crunchy pecan tart with his bare fingers, and chunks the whole thing in his mouth.

He glares at Zenobia while he chews with noisy gusto.

Zenobia bolts for the door. She takes off running. Leaves her guitar on the floor and her shadow in the chair. When he finishes eating, Isaiah wipes his mouth and whips Pearline again.

On her front porch Vennie Walker sways in her rocking chair, her plump dimpled arms folded and her feet propped up on a stool.

Her neighbor, Arthur Ray Cleveland, opens his screen door and steps outside. "Miss Vennie!"

He salutes her, holding up a frosty champagne glass. The near full flask is tucked under his other arm.

"Come on over and celebrate," he says in a voice made louder by sparkling wine.

"Not tonight," Vennie says. "Got to rise up and get to work early in the morning. Just getting up is a job for these old bones."

"Youngest old bones I ever saw," Arthur Ray says with a playful wink.

"You do have good eyes, Arthur Ray," Vennie responds, with a smile.

"Forget about work, Miss Vennie. It's party time! Today I am a year older!" he bubbles. Inside his house, the record player blasts Aretha hollering R-E-S-P-E-C-T. Aretha's music shakes and dances through his windows.

"Well, happy birthday then!"

"What you need," Arthur Ray says, pausing to take a long swig from his glass, "is some of this liquid lightning to loosen you up. Just one drop is guaranteed to put some pep in your step. Some glide in your stride. Some ease in your knees. Little of this grape dew will see anybody through."

"I must decline even your good wine."

"Why you want to decline good wine?"

"If I drink too late, the only thing rising in the morning will be my swollen head."

"What?" Arthur Ray asks.

"I said . . ."

At the quick patter of footsteps running down Loganberry Road they both stop talking and peer into the gathering dusk.

"Who's that?" Vennie asks.

"If that don't beat the rag off the bush! Looks right like a raspberry in a rush," Arthur Ray answers, then drains his glass.

"No, it's not. It's just the way the colors swirl. It's . . ." Vennie cranes her neck trying to see as dusk, the color of charcoal, screens the evening.

"Who goes there?" Arthur Ray calls out. "Whooo! Whew! Ha! Ha!" laughing when he gets no answer. "It's a rainbow running down Loganberry Road and it ain't even been raining."

Vennie peers at the vaguely familiar figure, furry slippers on flying feet looking like two squirrels in a hurry.

Finally she says, "Judging by the wild copper hair, reminds me of a young Zenobia. But it can't be. She's not even in town. Whoever it is, wonder if she's exercising?"

"Exercising? In her robe?" Arthur Ray asks.

"Well, we know she's not sick. Anybody running that fast got to be in good shape."

"Uh-huh," Arthur Ray says as he heads for the door.

"Unless . . ." Vennie says.

"Unless what?" Arthur Ray asks, pausing with one hand on the screen door handle.

"Never mind."

"No. What were you going to say?" Arthur Ray asks.

"Maybe she's running from somebody."

"Whoever she is, I'd hate to meet her in the alley. She's so fast, she can outrun a haint!"

Arthur Ray takes another drink, and then starts singing along with the record.

"Oh, a little respect, all I want is . . ."

Still singing with Aretha, he pushes his door open, and goes inside to finish preparing for his party.

"C *an't* believe I'm running again," Zenobia says to herself. "Why?"

The most recent answer is a single name: Isaiah.

But this time, she figures there ought to be another way. Fighting is in her blood. She knows the importance of protecting herself. But she is tired of fighting, and she is tired of running.

Norman, the setting sun burnishing his blond hair, sees Zenobia running down Loganberry Road. She has run on out of the colored part of town and on into the white.

"Woman in distress," he says as he slows his truck down. Startled, Zenobia turns to hear country music swinging out of the truck window.

"Hop in," he says.

She does and crouches uneasily on the edge of the faded vinyl and cloth seat, ready to spring out the door any second.

*"Stand by your man,"* Tammy Wynette sings in sweet seduction.

Norman sings along with Tammy's trademark country voice.

"Music's too loud," Zenobia says. She reaches over and switches off his radio.

"That's my favorite song," he says.

"Um-hmm."

He drives on. "What's the matter?"

"Nothing."

"You sure?"

"Nothing. Nothing. Nothing."

"Something must be the matter, you running down the road like that in your bathrobe."

She leans far to her right, almost hugging the door, just in case she has to jump out.

"Where you want me to drop you off?" he asks.

"I . . ." she starts.

Her breathing comes in snags. She looks at the man sideways. Try something smart, she'll snatch the hoe out of the bed of the truck, chop through his pale scalp, and make meat loaf of his mind.

*Slow down, Zenobia*, she tells herself, *maybe he don't mean no harm*. Minutes pass before her breathing is almost normal.

And then again he could be one of those men who takes women to some secluded place and does horrible things . . . It is quiet a long time. Nothing between them but the droning truck motor and an elaborate silence.

Finally, she says, "I don't have anywhere to go."

"You're welcome to stay at my place 'til you find somewhere."

"We'll see."

Before long he pulls up in front of an isolated wooden house and the dog that belongs to it yelps noisily and runs to meet the truck, jumping up all over the man as he climbs out.

"Get down, Fetch. Sit." But the dog doesn't obey. Dances on him with his paws, wags his fuzzy tail, and grins his happy tongue at him. "All right, then. Come on."

Zenobia doesn't know if he is talking to her or talking to the dog, but she gets down out of the cab of the truck and follows him on into the dark house, her alert eyes picking out possible weapons: a shovel leaning against the porch, a metal poker inside the front door.

He switches on lights, and dust and unswept floors assail her nose and eyes, making her sneeze and her eyes itch. Racks of shotguns line the wall over the stone fireplace. She follows him on into the kitchen. Plenty of knives.

He takes a butcher-wrapped package out of the refrigerator, and unties three fresh pork chops. "I don't know about you, but I'm hungry."

"How do you want these fixed?"

"Anyway you want. Potatoes in the cupboard. Vegetables in the bottom of the fridge."

"Fix it? Where?" she asks, as she surveys the sink of dirty pots and pans and plates spilling over to the top of the stove. There isn't a clean dish or counter in the kitchen. An army of ants patrols in crooked columns across the floor, up the sides of the cabinets, and onto the sticky dishes.

"Start? Where?" she repeats.

He shrugs and sits down on a stool.

*Looks like no woman's been near this place for years*, she thinks. She eyes the stained coffee mugs, picks one up and sees mold, like a beard, growing inside and on the rim. A shiver of disgust goes down her spine, but she finds a box of Tide. Hot sudsy dishwater fills the sink. She looks over at the stool, at the man eyeing her, at the dog eyeing him.

"Hey," he says, "what's your name?"

"Zenobia."

"Zenobia," he repeats. "Mine's Norman."

Zenobia. He likes her name. Her voice. Her feisty spirit. Her looks. And he realizes that for the first time in a long time, he is smiling inside.

"I think you can just about wear her clothes," Norman says.

"Whose clothes?" She knows the answer the moment after the words leave her lips. "Where's your wife?"

"Gone," he says.

"Gone? Where?"

"She . . . died."

*Maybe he killed her,* she thinks.

And her blood runs cold.

$T$$his$ morning, when Pearline opens the refrigerator for milk, she finds an empty carton. "Vegetables so gray and limp they belong in the graveyard." Everything smells rancid and sour. And so does she. She has not bathed since. . . . When was the last time she ate?

As if in answer, her stomach growls, and she heads for the door. The red bricks on Loganberry Road look like red waffles swimming up to her as she lurches ahead.

At the store's checkout stand, she fumbles in her purse for some change to pay for her purchases and comes across Dr. Abyssinia Jackson's appointment card.

"Hurry up, Pearline!" the impatient shopper behind her urges.

She finishes paying and moves to the side.

She is so disoriented that the date on Dr. Jackson's card swims before her eyes. She searches her memory but can't recall even making the appointment.

"When?" she asks herself.

Her mind reels as she tries to focus her attention on the day and hour, but the words blur even more.

After what is only a few seconds, but seems like ten minutes, the type on the card shifts into focus. She fingers the raised letters spelling out Abyssinia Jackson, M.D., squints at the time through swollen eyelids.

"Why, it's today. But when did I make it?" Her whole world is topsy-turvy. She drops her bag of groceries more than once as she leaves the store.

An hour later, she wobbles down Loganberry Road toward the doctor's office. Her mind starts and stops in jerks, trying to remember what she already knows about the House of Light: Mother Beatrice Barker's old dwelling. Bequeathed to Abyssinia Jackson. Now renovated into a sanctuary for the afflicted. A lighthouse.

B*efore* she knows it, Pearline is at the edge of a neat green lawn, gazing at the loganberry bushes and studying the brick walk lined with lobelia and irises. Hanging from the porch the shingle reads ABYSSINIA JACKSON, M.D. 1028 SOUTH LOGANBERRY ROAD.

No official sign identifies the building as the House of Light, but that is the name they all know it by. The welcome house, painted white, trimmed in lapis lazuli.

Glazed clay pots of golden chrysanthemums and baby roses line the windowsills.

Pearline looks like a wilting flower on the path leading to the entrance, and her orange dress catches Abyssinia Jackson's eye as she looks up from her office desk to see her patient hesitating in front of the walk.

Abyssinia sets aside her prescription pad and studies Pearline. She knows that Pearline is getting a divorce, represented by Abyssinia's husband, Carl Lee. The very sight of Pearline is a study in physical abuse and spiritual neglect. "So glad you came before it's too late," Abyssinia whispers.

As Pearline pushes open the gate, Abyssinia makes mental notes of the sad lines etching the woman's face. *The beat down look*, thinks Abyssinia. The tired-to-death look, shoulders stooping from warding off so many blows, and here and there the telltale bruises.

By the time Pearline's feet hit the House of Light steps, Abyssinia starts to hum and sing under her breath.

*I see you coming*
*All dressed up in pain*
*I see you coming*
*All dressed up in pain*
*Took a lot of courage to get here*
*You're not the kind to complain.*

The sound of Abyssinia's voice is humble and healing. So muted you would have to be standing right next to her to hear it.

"Good morning, Pearline," the receptionist says. Pearline's hair looks like a tornado has snatched at it and twisted it every which away, then just dropped her hunched-down body inside the office.

In contrast, the receptionist's patent leather hair ripples back into a pincushion bun. Hairpins and hairspray keep every midnight black strand from straying. Pristine in her white uniform, she is a study in neatness. She peers over her half-frame reading glasses at the distraught Pearline.

"Good morning, Miss Lacy," Pearline whispers.

Pearline is as confused as she was in the grocery store when she couldn't remember making the appointment. Must've been at church.

Janet Lacy is such a committed receptionist for Dr. Jackson, that she even takes her appointment book to church.

This is Janet Lacy's writing all right, Pearline decides as she again studies the appointment card.

Abyssinia stands up when she hears Janet Lacy knocking at her door. She takes Pearline's folder, straightens her coat of snowy linen, and walks to the treatment room.

"Hello, Pearline." She stretches out a hand in welcome.

Pearline mumbles.

"What's that?"

"Good to see you." Pearline fiddles, uneasy.

"It's all right. You'll be fine."

Abyssinia's touch relaxes her somewhat.

"Could you undress, put on this gown?"

When Abyssinia examines Pearline's body, she finds bones that have broken and knitted themselves back together again. She finds bruises and scars, some old, some fresh.

"What happened to your arm?" Abyssinia asks.

"Well . . ." Pearline begins with much hesitation. "I . . . uh . . . fell down . . . slipped on the floor . . . when I was carrying some clothes in from the line. And the floor was a little wet . . ."

"Uh-huh. That must have been some fall."

They both take a deep breath. Abyssinia waits.

"You can tell me whatever's on your mind, Pearline," Abyssinia says gently. "You can trust me. I promise. You have my word."

Pearline hears the compassion in Abyssinia's voice, sees its subtle flash in her eyes.

"Uh, I don't know where to start," Pearline says. "It's very hard for me to talk about this."

"I know," Abyssinia says, reassuringly. "It's all right."

From somewhere deep and difficult, Pearline heaves a sigh so full of pain that it chills Abyssinia's spine.

Pearline begins, "This is what really happened . . ."

Norman doesn't try anything scary with Zenobia, so she relaxes around him. He tells her that his wife died of natural causes. "Or unnatural causes," he says, "if you consider breast cancer an unnatural cause."

Day after day, she continues to wash dishes. Finds them everywhere all over the house. Under the bed. Outside in the yard.

She is working on another pile of found dishes, pots, and pans.

"What did you do?" she grumbles, "go out and buy more dishes every time you ran out of clean ones?"

He nods, shame-faced.

"You can help," she says, as she shakes a dish towel at him.

He abandons the stool in one glad hop. Something about the woman splashing the dishes around in the sudsy water reminds him of his late wife. But that doesn't make a lick of sense. His wife had been a drugstore blonde with hair so platinum it looked white; this woman's is as coppery as a new penny. His wife's legs and arms were like cream; this woman's are like molasses.

While they do the dishes, he casts side-glances at her. She is efficient: glasses first, silverware, plates, pots and pans last. When he isn't looking at her, she is studying him. *Mangy*, she thinks. Hair needs cutting. Dirt under the moons of his fingernails.

Smells right ripe. Rate he's going, looks like he might stay a widower forever.

"How come you were running down the road like that the other day?" he asks.

"My business. Tend to yours. Leave mine alone," she huffs.

"I was tending to mine, driving on home, wasn't I, when I stopped and picked you up?"

Zenobia smiles in spite of herself.

"Well, you know, some of these men . . ." she says, voice rising, then ringing like an alarm clock. The panic in her voice startles her, and she gets quiet again.

The dishes shine, neatly stacked. The three pork chops sizzle in the frying pan. Potatoes bubble, boiling in their pot. String beans snap, singing in their kettle.

"You like Ponca?"

She nods. "Just got back. Been gone for years. Oklahoma City."

"The Big O, huh? Left the big city for this little bitty place?"

"Found out the Big O was all a big F. A failure. At least for me, anyway. I found other things like friends and how you treat people more important, so I came on home." She stirs pork chop drippings into the gravy skillet.

"Were you born here?"

She nods. "Left right after high school. Folks dead. No reason to stay. At least that's what I thought at the time."

When the food is ready, she fills two plates.

"I been meaning to tell you, don't forget Fetch's plate."

"What?"

"I usually feed him, but it'd be good if you did also."

"Yeah? Feed him what?" She hasn't noticed any bags of dog food.

Norman points to the stove.

"You mean the dog eat what we eat? Well, where's his bowl?"

"Use the same dishes we use."

"What?"

She stoops down, looks way back up under the cabinet, finds an old beat-up pie pan, and fixes the dog a plate, all the while mumbling, "Ain't no hound human."

She sets the dog's pan on the floor. The dog looks at her as though he expects her to place it on the table.

*No*, the man thinks, *she's not quite like my wife. She's not the obeying kind. Why, she don't mind a-tall.*

Still, the food is good, and he says so.

"Could be better," she says. "Meat smelling too gamey, and you don't have the right seasonings. Salt and pepper looking like two orphans in your spice box. Gravy tasting like paste."

He takes another bite, doesn't speak again until after he cleans his plate. Wonders what "better" might taste like.

"Well," he says, "you can be in charge of buying the food."

She looks at him and stands up to take the plates away. She puts the dog's pan outdoors, turns on the outside faucet, and lets the water run over it. The Fetch dog looks up at her with pleading eyes, still expecting something.

"Guess you want a glass of water next," she says to Fetch dog. "You ain't eating out of the same dishes as me. Understand?"

She comes back in the house, finds an old plastic bowl with dents in it where somebody has left it too close to the flame on the stove, and fills it with water, which the dog quickly laps up. He wags his thankful tail at her.

After another hard day's work, Vennie's telephone rings. She swings her feet off the porch stool and goes back inside.

"Hello. Widower Parsons . . . ? What . . . ? Yes, I thought

about it and this is my answer: No . . . That's right. No. What
do I need to marry you for? With my arthritis and your heart
trouble what we go do? Buy a house, convalescent home on one
side, a mortuary on the other? We both get sick, all they got to
do is wheel us on out the door, one going one way, one going
the other. No, Sir. No, thank you . . . Mr. Parsons, I wouldn't wish
myself on nobody and you shouldn't ought to either. What . . . ?
Don't rang my phone with no more of this foolishness. See you
in church next Sunday. You're welcome . . . No, I ain't gonna
change my mind!"

She places the phone back on its cradle. Then, as has become
her habit more and more, she turns into bed early.

"Never thought I'd see the day I'd be going to bed same
time as the lightning bugs come out."

The fireflies tease the dark, then sparkle and fly through her
thoughts, illuminating the dilemma of her life as she reflects on
the cost of living and doing day work and greeting Miss Carver
so soon in the morning.

"Almost costs too much to live," she sighs. Only the fireflies
outside her window hover close enough to hear. Although they
agree with her, they don't linger long, for they want a brighter
sound than her dreary complaint. They up and flee toward the
jazz echoes and the festive laughing next door where the bent
notes of a tenor saxophone glisten. Arthur Ray has found another
reason to celebrate. Louder and happier laughter lights up the
evening.

As much as Vennie wants to follow the bright cloud of night
flyers, as much as she loves Coltrane music and Dizzy Gillespie's
"A Love Supreme" and hearty partying, she is so tired it's not
long before the little flashes fade out of her sight. She falls heavily
into the night arms of sleep where the call of Coltrane's silver-
toned saxophone frees her.

Vennie's dreams are gossamer things of bygone days when she is younger and more agile and never props her feet up at the end of a day. The fireflies jitterbug low in the sky, and she chases them, tripping through the grove of blackjack trees and twilit oleander bushes. "Little green lanterns," she calls as she coaxes them into the palms of her hands.

Before the night has fled completely, she wakes up refreshed. She washes, dresses, and finishes her first cup of coffee.

Dawn finds Vennie walking down Loganberry Road. She walks until the road turns abruptly. She follows its curve to the Carver residence where she serves breakfast to Mr. and Mrs. Carver. When Mr. Carver leaves for work, Vennie cleans the kitchen and vacuums the carpets before beginning to iron.

It is ten o'clock and she hasn't stopped, yet she still has long hours ahead of her.

"Why're you walking so funny, Vennie?" Mrs. Carver asks.

"What I got is a bad case of bad feet," Vennie says as she shuffles from the ironing board to the rack to hang up another pressed dress. Then she mumbles under her breath, "People give you turpentine to drink then want to call you bitter."

"What?" Mrs. Carver says.

"I said these feet killing me." Then Vennie rambles on, "The folks next door played Aretha Franklin so loud last night my little toe twitched. Could hear rhythms vibrating through the walls. Feet wanted to move and couldn't. Aretha Franklin, the Queen of Music, was ruling the night. Feet wanted to dance!"

"Well, why didn't they?" Mrs. Carver asks.

"Corns standing up on my toes too high. Bunions under my soles too low. That's why. What I got here is joyless feet."

"Huh?" Mrs. Carver says, not really paying attention.

"Let me tell you something," Vennie begins, anger flickering in her eyes.

"What?"

"Never mind." Vennie knows she might as well be talking to the heaping piles of laundry.

Vennie slaps the iron on the board, pressing cat faces in and out of the tablecloth.

Mrs. Carver studies Vennie a moment then shakes her head like an adult dealing with a bibbed child and says, "Well, I've got to go out a while, Vennie."

"How long you be gone this time, Miss Carver?"

"Oh, I guess an hour," she answers as she preens in the mirror adjusting her hat on her head.

Vennie clamps her lips shut and keeps ironing.

Once Mrs. Carver slams the front door, Vennie starts singing as loud as she can to keep from hearing, but the loud singing doesn't do a lick of good. Vennie hears the sound of high heels tipping, and then the distinct *click-click* of the hall closet door quickly opening and closing.

Vennie sighs at the picture of a grown woman all dressed up and hiding in her own closet. She shakes her head and opens her mouth wider and sings as loud as Clara Ward singing gospel.

*"Got on my traveling shoes,"* she sings all the while slapping the iron on the clothes with a noisy force.

Mrs. Carver has been testing Vennie for a week. Just as some teachers test their students once a week, once a year Carver tests Vennie. Putting things in her way. First leaving a dollar bill between the sofa pillows, next tucking a five-dollar note under the dining room tablecloth. And finally hiding a ten-dollar bill, with dead president Hamilton grinning out at Vennie from behind a box of Aunt Jemima pancakes.

"Oh, Miss Carver," she laughs knowingly, "you got to be more careful with your moneys."

Fact is Carver and all the women like her are an aggravation:

Slyly pretending to leave the house, then hiding, secretly listening to hear if the maid jumps up to turn on the television to start watching soap operas. Peeking to see if the maid stretches out, lazily flopping her bare feet up on the Ethan Allen sofa and drinking from the bottles of aged wine kept cool and fermenting in the wine cellar.

*Got on my traveling shoes.*

Vennie is tired of smiling and ignoring these traditional insults to day women, or girls as they are so disrespectfully called. Carver has to believe Vennie is a girl—would she do this to another woman? All these thoughts scramble through Vennie's head. By the time the phone rings, she's about had enough. Her voice is becoming hoarse from hollering that song loud enough to let Carver know she is busy working just where Carver last saw her, and her arms ache from whipping that iron down with enough force to be heard all the way to the hall closet. And don't even mention the feet.

*Got on my traveling shoes.*

*Ring.* At first Vennie ignores the phone out of spite as she halfway wonders if the hall closet door will finally open.

*Got on my traveling shoes.*

*Ring.* Better take the message as usual, she thinks as she starts from behind the ironing board.

*Got on . . .*

*Ring.*

"Hello, Carver residence."

Pause.

"Miss Carver . . . She . . ."

Then some devilment sneaks its way into Vennie's aching feet, travels on up her spine, and sets up in her brain. "Just a minute."

Vennie moves fast and light as she once did when she danced at a B. B. King concert, walks as though she doesn't soak her feet in Epsom salt once a night. Makes a beeline down the hallway and right on up to the closed closet door.

"Miss Carver. Telephone."

Vennie hears a gasp, and Carver has to come on up out of the closet.

Vennie goes to the kitchen, pours herself a cup of coffee, and puts up her feet.

"Let the silly hussy fire me!"

She is too tired to care, feet propped up, sipping her coffee and mumbling, "Give you turpentine and call you bitter."

She wants to line them all up and kick the chitlins out of them. On Monday, Miss Prissy Face Clark; Tuesday, Miss Whiskey Breath Hansen; Wednesday, Miss Tight Curls Turner; and today, Miss Tippy Toe Carver.

As she sips her coffee and mumbles, she can't help but think back on her failure to find a job many years ago.

After services one Sunday, Sister Maggie Peppermill told her about a few openings. And Vennie had put her best foot forward. Clean dress, bathed, powdered, and perfumed, hair pressed and curled before appearing at that first doorstep to get her first job.

She remembers it so clearly. The look cold as a mortuary that crawled across Miss Whatever-her-name-was' expression.

The woman had opened the door, took one look at Vennie,

and sputtered, "No. I got a husband and a teenaged son. You just won't do." And slammed the door in Vennie's face.

Vennie's hope had turned to perplexity. She looked down at her clean dress, polished shoes. Buttons lopsided? No. Smudges on her shoes? No.

She walked on to the next interview and although this woman mumbled and made vague excuses as she looked Vennie up and down, the result was the same. No job.

The next Sunday right after church as the cleaning women collected on the sidewalk ready to go their separate ways, Vennie aired her complaints.

"We could've told you that," Maggie Peppermill and the women who worked every day chided her. They shook with laughter as they walked in back of Vennie.

"Look a here, at this round behind!"

"Just right for somebody's husband to slap!" Maggie Peppermill said.

These friends who boasted day jobs and who never missed a day's work chuckled deep in their throats. They walked on around in front of her and tee-heed up in her face.

"And these full glossy lips!"

"Scarlet lips, honey!"

"Scarlet lips. Uh-huh. Two ripe invitations for the husband's stolen kisses!"

They shook their heads.

Vennie in turn remembered how the successful maids looked on their way to work: baggy uniforms; laid-over shoes, clean, but ugly. So that was it. No lipstick, head rag round the head, and a sack for a dress.

"Honey," one of the successful day-workers said between giggles, "what you got to do is this, leave the polished Sunday-go-to-meeting shoes on up in the closet, learn to say 'Yes ma'am' and 'No'm' and keep your colored hips locked up in a girdle. Then on top of the girdle, corsets, and other constrictions, put yourself on a tent!"

Vennie tried the suggestions and they worked like magic. She was hired. But she could have told the Mrs. Carvers of Ponca City that their husbands had X-ray eyes, could see through sacks and bags and all on-purpose ugly disguises. Could see enough to reach over and pinch a hunk of dark meat.

"You ain't paying for that," she would sass. "Ain't nobody got enough money to pay for that!"

But her hot responses only made the men more playful, and they would decide she was trying to be cute and was giving them the colored version of catch-me-if-you-can.

"Wife cheater!" she would hurl.

"Well who else would I cheat on?" one openly lecherous employer asked. That dumbfounded her, giving her new insight into a man's way of seeing things.

Now Vennie raises the coffee cup and swallows the last sip.

She hurls the saucer at the wall, smashing it into a thousand tiny pieces. Vennie is so upset that Mrs. Carver is scared to come into her own kitchen.

"Anybody tipping around in her own house got to be off," Vennie says as loud as when she talks to a room filled with her women friends. Then she stands up, takes the saucer-less cup, washes and rinses it, and stacks it in the spotless sink.

She walks spryly back to the ironing board and, with dimpled arms folded across her chest, surveys the mountain of tablecloths, napkins, dresses, and shirts. She wonders how much laundry she has pressed without the benefit of somebody kind enough to say, "Sit down and rest your aching feet a while." Instead, these people test her intelligence and her honesty by littering the house with money, or hiding in closets to see if she is stealing time.

She looks around the kitchen at the scrubbed floor and the clear shining windows—yes she did do windows—and she snatches off her apron and goes looking for Mrs. Carver.

Vennie doesn't lower her glare, but looks Mrs. Carver directly in the eye, woman to woman, and says, "Miss Carver, here's your apron, I quit." And she walks on off the job.

Now what is she going to do? No job and needing to see a doctor about her feet.

*"Got on my traveling shoes,"* she sings.

Vennie walks down Loganberry Road, past the House of Light, and it shines like a beacon to her.

"Maybe," she says, eyeing the white and blue lightness of Abyssinia Jackson's place.

Although Zenobia's cooking tastes wonderful to Norman, she craves the spicy flavors she loves so much. One day she picks up the money that Norman has been leaving for her on the kitchen table, and ventures out to the Ponca City Grocery Store to shop for the ingredients still missing from her recipes. She walks up and down the produce section, picking up tomatoes and seeing if they are firm enough. She checks the string beans, to make sure they are not mottled with early signs of rot. Looks in the ice cream chest, selects her favorite vanilla. Then, over by the orange juice, she unexpectedly runs into a distraught Pearline, whose hang dog expression reminds Zenobia that she abandoned her several weeks earlier after promising to stand up to Isaiah.

"Zenobia," says Pearline, standing over by the milk, hurt all in her voice and on her face, "why'd you take off and leave me there for Isaiah to beat me like that?"

Zenobia leaves the frozen section and turns the aisle then pushes her cart to the section that holds the dry food. Pearline follows right behind her. Zenobia doesn't bite her tongue, she says real quick as she keeps on reaching for the grits, "Pearline, listen here, girl, long as you been knowing me you ought to've learned a little bit of sense by now. I do declare, Pearline, you ain't crazy." Then adds loud as she can, causing other shoppers to hesitate over Quaker Oats and Cheerios, "Pearline, when you see me running, you know it's time to go!"

This unplanned and unpleasant meeting in the grocery store shakes Zenobia to her core. After paying for her sage, vanilla ice cream, grits, and red curry, she hurries right back to Norman's place and stays there. Becomes a house hermit. Soon the dust and dirt disappear from the curtains and the floors, and in the kitchen every pot sits on its own bottom in its own place.

One Saturday after Zenobia waxes the living room furniture, moves the sofa and end tables to mop away the dirt underneath, Norman brings her a hot cup of coffee.

She sits down on the couch and crosses her molasses legs.

"Cream and sugar?" he asks.

"No," she says, then gives her standard reply, "I like my coffee like I like my men. Black."

P*earline* tells Abyssinia at her next appointment, "Never guess who I ran into!"

"Who's that?"

"My so-called friend!"

"Who?"

"Zenobia."

"You're upset with her?"

"She was there when Isaiah whipped me."

"I see."

"Just up, ran off, and left me there!"

"What did you expect her to do?"

"Defend me."

"Maybe she couldn't at the time."

"You think that? Then you don't know Zenobia."

"Well we're here to talk about you today."

Pearline smiles in spite of herself.

Abyssinia comments, "Your exercise program must be working. I can see some nice changes."

"Thanks. I walk my three miles a day."

"Good for you! What about the sit-ups? You do those too?"

"While I'm watching the six o'clock news."

"An easy way to remember. So how do you feel after you're finished?"

"Tired. Relaxed. Ready to get up and go. But I don't. I bathe all the sweat away and get ready for bed."

"Sleep well?"

"Like a lamb. Think the exercise helps."

Abyssinia takes out the blood pressure monitor, adjusts the strap around Pearline's upper arm, and begins squeezing the pump until she inflates it to the right pressure.

"What's it say?" Pearline asks.

"Pressure's fine."

"Better this time?"

Abyssinia nods. "Exercising can make a difference."

Abyssinia writes in the chart that Pearline's dizziness has lessened, her nervousness has diminished, her fitness level has improved, and her spirits are up.

A muted song escapes Abyssinia's lips.

"Did you say something?" Pearline asks.

"What?" Dr. Jackson hums. Then, ever so faintly, she continues to sing:

> *The buck stops here*
> *You're the one in charge*
> *You make the plan*
> *Tell any man*
> *Being alive on your own*
> *Standing alone.*

"Got more energy nowadays," Pearline says. "Feels good."

"Um-hmm," Dr. Jackson whispers softly. "Ignore all the bad stuff and keep paying attention to what feels good."

"And I been thinking, trying to put everything in perspective. I'm planting old things in a new way."

"How do you do that?"

"I take my shovel and a hairbrush, go out in the backyard by the clothesline."

"A hairbrush!?"

"Wait. I take the shovel and dig a hole. Then I lay down the shovel, and pick up the brush . . ."

"What for?" Abyssinia wonders.

"I brush the anger out of my hair and throw it down into the hole."

"That's it?"

"No."

"What do you do next?"

"I brush it off my arms and hands. I brush it off my legs and feet. I brush my entire body."

"Never heard of such a . . ."

"You mean I'm teaching the doctor something?" Pearline snorts.

"Go on . . ."

"Next? I cover up the hole."

"What do you call this?"

"An anger cemetery."

"Ha!" Abyssinia laughs.

Abyssinia sings:

> *It's time to choose*
> *You make the rules*
> *Move from the pain*
> *You hold the rein*
> *Being alive on your own*
> *Standing alone.*

After awhile Pearline continues, "I guess I been in mourning over my mess of a marriage. Marriage? What there was of it! A failure is what it was. A lot of plans and dreams that didn't happen. What I wanted so much was to have a baby. Everybody knew Isaiah was the biggest cock hound in the county. And now time's running out. The season of childbirth's almost passing me by. Babies wait for nobody."

Abyssinia nods as she adds, "Babies wait for no body."

"Now he's gone," Pearline continues, "and I'm left here without anything to show for all those years. A child . . . I wish . . . If only . . ."

"If only . . ." Abyssinia yearns.

On her way home, Pearline passes Arthur Ray Cleveland sunning himself on his break. They exchange smiles. He walks back into his carpentry shop and begins designing an oak hope chest. The rhythm of Abyssinia's song guides his movements, and it seems that his drafting pencil moves more fluidly than before.

> *Standing alone is not so bad,*
> *Giving him up's the best thought she ever had.*
> *She turned him loose, pumps her own juice,*
> *Now she's alive on her own, standing alone.*

"Gonna ask that honey for a date," he says to his workbench. "Pack a lunch. Bring her flowers. Take a lazy ride way out in the country."

That melody persists.

> *Now she's alive on her own, standing alone.*

He will bring her chocolates. Bring her to his house, where he'll set out massage oils, put on some love songs, Barry White crooning "Can't Get Enough of Your Love, Babe." Love made him think of silky, seductive things to do that he would not have thought of doing without Mother Nature touching his mind.

$P_{earline}$ keeps wiping her brow, swallowing lumps, big as hills, in her throat. She looks in her closet and chooses a strapless, sage-colored dress, patterned with green hydrangeas. She pulls a thin embroidered shawl around her shoulders, draping it gracefully over the dress. She places a wide-brimmed, fringed hat at a jaunty angle over her curly hair. Then she lowers the hat's opaque veil over her face. A trendy pair of sunshades hide her eyes. A sexy pair of high heel slippers show off her perfectly polished toes. Everything hints at the beauty that she is known to be.

She opens her front door, steps to the sidewalk, and moves agile as a dancer. She doesn't speak to anyone as she glides through the crowd of happy churchgoers chattering among themselves.

At the temple, the church begins to fill with members of the congregation who are seated by the ushers.

Pearline doesn't follow the usher's direction but seats herself in the front row. People are greeting each other, but she says nothing, just sits stoically through the preliminaries, the visitor announcements, the sick and shut in list, and the preacher's habitual "without-further-ado's," the traditional promises to move forward with the program. The impatient fidgeting of children.

When someone beckons her to the choir stand she doesn't stand up and join them.

Dr. Jackson eyes her as she opens the Testimony service. "We come to thank Him for his bountiful blessings. We come to share our sorrows in a time of need. He woke us up this morning. For that we are grateful. Can I hear an Amen."

The congregation responds, "Amen! Praise the Lord! Halle-lujah!"

Pearline watches and listens. Various men and women, some crying, some smiling, recite their troubles and woes. Pearline sits tight-mouthed.

The minister takes it upon himself to say, as he looks at Pearline, "Some of you sitting up in here won't let a Hallelujah cross your lips."

Dr. Jackson says in a soft voice, "Some prayers are whis-pered."

The minister responds with, "All right, church, without any further ados, testimony service is ended."

"Wait, wait," says Pearline as she stands up.

"You got a testimony, Sister Pearline?"

"Speak . . ." says Abyssinia Jackson.

"Saints," Pearline begins. "I'm talking to the living saints." That gets everybody quiet. They hear something strange in her voice.

"I'm here to testify about my situation."

Abyssinia stands up and peers at Pearline.

"My estranged husband, Isaiah Spencer, sneaked into my house last night and beat me so badly, I prayed for mercy. I didn't get an answer from God. And then it came to me. I realized that I had to do something. I, Pearline, have to say something."

"Well," says the congregation.

"You know it's one thing to hope the community will come to your aid. It's another thing to stand up and ask for help."

"You come to the right place, daughter," intones the minister.

"Did I? Is it the right place? I know some of you have been titillated about my problem, entertaining yourselves about all the ways Isaiah got of keeping me in line. Pretending you don't see what you're looking at. Running and telling Isaiah every time a man looks at me."

"Well . . ." says the minister uncertainly.

"You saw the marks on these hands that I covered with so much makeup, I looked in my makeup kit and every jar was empty. Couldn't squeeze a drop out of a crimpled tube!"

She holds her hands up. "How many of you seen me stumbling down the street?"

"Lord, help mercy!" somebody moans.

"You wanna see? Take a good look!"

She pulls back her veil. Worshippers in the front row study her face, mottled with marks, stark in its nakedness, with no makeup to hide the ugliness. Welts run up and down her neck where Isaiah's strong hands had strangled her within an inch of her life.

"Oh!" the congregation gasps.

But she doesn't let them off lightly. She pulls off her cloak, revealing underneath the low cut, sleeveless dress. As the material falls back, the congregation witnesses the bruises, the cuts, the angry pounding her body has taken.

"Lord, help mercy!" the church cries.

"Loose here, Satan!" the minister pronounces.

"So I'm asking you to pray for me," Pearline continues softly. "And if you see me running your way, open your doors! If you see me marked up and I tell you I fell down, don't believe a word of it. Ask me what happened until I tell you!"

Pearline turns around and stares at one wide-eyed woman, sitting with her husband's arms around her.

"And you women. You women putting up with the same treatment, I know I can't speak for you. Every situation is unique. But if you're abiding anything like what I've been going through, don't you be ashamed. You didn't do it to yourself."

She turns around and stares at a man in the next row, sitting with his head tucked down.

"And you men. You men, look at me. Look at me!" she screams.

The man lifts his head and looks.

"What did you call me? The woman with the prettiest eyes in the state of Oklahoma? Look at me! Look at me now!" she says to another man further down the aisle.

She spins around and walks out of her row and marches up and down the aisle, from the front of the church to the last pew and back again. She glares at each row of worshippers, showing two black eyes, bruised and purple.

"What do you see?"

Nobody answers.

"You see me! I am the woman with two black eyes. The two blackest eyes in the goddamned state of Oklahoma. Not a pretty sight."

"Altar call! Altar call!" says the minister. "I want every man in the building to come up here and go down in prayer."

A few men rise.

"I'm calling the guilty and the innocent! Get up! We know about some sins. But some of you hide your sins! Get up!"

All the men rise obediently.

Abyssinia Jackson beckons them to the altar. She smiles when she sees her own Carl Lee leading them, and sighs with joy when the minister says, "And I'm joining you down on my knees. Repeat after me. I vow . . ."

The men repeat, "I vow . . ."

Minister intones, "To never raise my hand . . ."

"To never raise my hand . . ."

"Against my wife, the mother of my children . . ."

"Against my wife, the mother of my children . . ."

In a faster, more powerful rhythm, the preacher says, "Or any other woman ever in my life from this day forward."

The men repeat the promise in that same faster, powerful rhythm, "Or any other woman ever in my life from this day forward!"

The minister rises and turns to Abyssinia and says, "I leave you in the hands of Dr. Abyssinia Jackson."

The choir begins to sing softly in the background as Abyssinia speaks.

"Before we say the doxology. Before we say 'without any further ados,' before we bring this service to a close, I want you to promise to do one thing. Will you do it?"

"Yes," sings the congregation.

Dr. Jackson says, "Repeat after me. I promise to go home . . ."

"I promise to go home . . ."

"And throw the words bitch, slut, heifer, hussy, and Sapphire in the garbage can. To go out in my backyard and bury that can of ugliness. And quit calling people out of their names!"

When the men in the bars look at Isaiah, he has nowhere to hide. At the Conoco Oil Company, the mark is upon him. He can no longer hide behind the notion that a man can do his wife anyway he pleases, because he thinks he owns her.

The community has spoken.

Arthur Ray, one of the astonished church listeners, sees the marred beauty of Pearline. His heart swells and he can't take his eyes off her. He takes her home, fixes her a Sunday meal, lights fragrant candles, and plays Barry White music. In the bedroom, he gets out his soothing oil, takes off her sleeveless dress, and massages her broken body from head to toe.

He brushes each blue-black curl on Pearline's head until it springs gently back in place.

She turns over on his scented sheets and reaches up her scarred arms to hold him. She guides him into the secret place that makes her a goddess. The mixed passion overwhelms them so completely that they shake with a flaming, consuming love. When the fire envelops them, the blaze lights up their entire souls.

V*ennie* Walker sits on the side of the examining table in Abyssinia's treatment room, getting her feet checked. Where does the time go, Vennie wonders as she looks at Abby, who wears no powder, no rouge, no lipstick. The kinky hair is shorn so close it shows off the haloed contour of her head. To Vennie it seems only yesterday that she, along with other Ponca women, rocked Abyssinia when she was a bench baby and molded her baby skull until it was round. And now here she is practicing medicine.

"Epsom salt," Abyssinia suggests.

"Already doing that, my sweet doctor," Vennie says.

"Propped up in the evening?"

"High as they can rise."

"Looks then like these feet need more rest."

"They just now getting that."

"What do you mean?"

"They're laid up all right."

The way Vennie says "laid up," accented just so, makes Abyssinia pause.

"Laid up? Are you working, Aunt Vennie?"

"Well, the truth is I'm laid off."

"Laid off," Abyssinia repeats.

"All right, I quit."

"Um-hmm." Abyssinia starts humming as she carefully feels each joint. "Arthritis."

"Like fire devils hacking at my bones," Vennie says. "Each morning I wake up wrestling with rheumatism and arguing with arthritis."

"You know arthritis is made worse by stress. Says right here in the Arthritis Foundation pamphlet."

"Who you telling?" Vennie accepts the booklet. "I know all about stretching."

"Stress," Abyssinia says.

"Stretching a week's worth of work into one day, now that's some stretch."

"Hmm. Vennie, there's a way we can get rid of your foot pain forever. With surgery, I can replace your damaged bones with artificial ones made of plastic."

"Plastic bones! What will our good doctor come up with next?"

"Aunt Vennie, relief is on the way."

"Surgery." A hint of worry makes her voice sag like a stocking that has lost elasticity.

"At first, the operation may cause you a bit more stress."

"Stretch? How? You gonna cut off these bones, not stretch them. And you say I'll feel better?"

"Your feet'll stop hurting," Abyssinia promises.

"Then so will my whole body," Vennie says, sighing. "When my feet hurt, I hurt all over. From the bottom of my toes to the top of my head. Talking about hurt."

"We'll schedule the surgery for next week." Then Abyssinia sets her pad down and says in a more serious tone, "Now Aunt Vennie, this is very important: You must stay off your feet for the first few weeks after surgery."

"Don't worry. These feet've had all the stretch they can

stand. Stretching out down Loganberry Road. Stretching out in the folks' kitchens. Why, I could write a book on the properties of stretching."

"I do believe you could. Staying off your feet will give you a much-needed vacation and time to think. Aunt Vennie, I always thought you had a mind could move mountains."

"Now I admit arthritis ain't touched my brain. But you can move the mountains, Dr. Jackson, I'll be satisfied with moving the feet."

"After surgery, you may do something even more extraordinary."

"Like what?"

"Move ahead with your life. What you will accomplish, Aunt Vennie, will be no small feat."

"No small feet? That's right, daughter, size nines."

Abyssinia laughs.

"Don't worry," Vennie says as Abyssinia helps her off the examination table, "these feet have stretched out for years and they're coming out of circulation for a while. The only thing stretching for now will be my body on my couch watching my soap operas and thinking. From now on until you check me in for surgery, that's where you can find me. Dr. Jackson, my feet are in your hands."

This morning, Vennie and Pearline fold sheets, one holding one end, while the other evens up the corners and keeps turning until the sheets are neat rectangles. Pearline tucks them in the linen closet.

"This is a full day's work for me," Vennie says.

"Tell me if you have any pain."

"Not a lick."

"Just as Dr. Jackson promised."

"Got me a pair of new feet!"

"They tired yet?"

"Don't want to overdo it."

"Grandma, you've done enough. Just sit."

"You got a point. Glad to help."

"Just being here is a help." Pearline takes down some blankets.

"Wish you'd at least get a couch and some furniture."

"Important thing was buying the house. I can take forever to furnish it."

"Guess you're sleeping at my place."

"No, thanks."

"Where you gonna sleep then?"

"On the floor."

"The bare floor?"

"No, not the bare floor, Grandma, a pallet on the bedroom floor." Vennie follows her to the mostly empty bedroom, sinks into the rocking chair in the corner, and watches her spread the blankets in thick layers on the hardwood.

"Looks pretty plain."

"You think so?" Pearline goes back to the linen closet and takes down a quilt and two fluffy pillows.

"There," she says as she positions them at the head of the pallet.

"This is pitiful! Wish you'd get some real furniture. Borrow some of mine. Shoot, you can have some of mine. Got more stuff than I need anyway."

"I got some furniture."

"Those four rocking chairs, two in the living room and two in the bedroom?"

"They'll do"

"A new pioneer woman. Humph!"

Pearline checks her watch. "Now it's time to go."

"Ready?" Vennie asks.

"Ready. Don't wanna be late for my appointment with Dr. Jackson." Although Pearline's job as the church secretary gets her up and going every morning, she has taken today off to ready her house and to keep her appointment.

When grandmother and granddaughter step outside the front door, they both look down the road to see if they catch sight of Isaiah's car.

"Not there again today," Pearline sighs, relieved.

"How long's it been since you last seen this fool?" Vennie asks.

"A good while. Which I hope becomes a good *long* while."

Pearline walks more sure of herself, her steps freer and less tentative. She always carries the legal restraining order in her purse.

The entire town carries the unwritten order, the community restraining order, and its force is even stronger.

Vennie suspects that Pearline's confident walk and the two restraining orders kept Isaiah at a distance.

From his car parked far down the road, Isaiah used to sit and wait. At first, Pearline would see the old Pontiac, a rusting hunk of gray metal under a tree half a mile down the road, every day. Then once a week. Then once a month. Now she can't remember when she last saw Isaiah's car. They keep a sharp eye out in case he comes back to spy on Pearline from a different angle.

"So glad you stopped being quiet about that Negro," Vennie says.

"Grandma Vennie, I don't know why it took me so long to speak up."

"Once he realized he was definitely going to jail if he touched another hair on your nappy head, he started thinking like the coward he was and decided to keep his hands in his pockets."

"I wonder," Pearline says, "what would happen if every time a colored woman opened her mouth she told the truth."

"She might say something go down in history," Vennie decides.

The two of them walk along quietly, Vennie unknowingly walking to the rhythm of the song Abyssinia was singing the day Vennie got the diagnosis about her feet.

> *You got to ask for what you want*
> *Maybe they will*
> *Maybe they won't*
> *If you don't ask for what you want*
> *Who's to say do?*
> *Who's to say don't?*
> *And if you ask for what you want*
> *Maybe they will*
> *Maybe they won't*
> *If you don't ask for what you want*
> *You'll never get just what you want.*

As the words run scrambling through Vennie's subconscious, she tries to figure out what it is she should ask for.

> *Ask for what you want*

Although Vennie is pleased and tickled about her painless feet, in the back of her mind she is counting. Her nest egg is getting smaller while her feet are getting better. Properly massaged, put up often, and coddled with rich olive and mineral oils, they feel so much better she is almost ready to dance. But she never goes that far. According to the good doctor, her feet are not yet ready for that. She still needs to stay off them as much as possible. And she doesn't want to risk a setback by going back to work and standing all day long.

"I want to dance," she murmurs.

"What?" Pearline asks.

*You got to ask for what you want*

"I want my feet to feel so much better I can dance," Vennie repeats.

"Dance?" Pearline thinks, *Arthritis and dancing?*

Vennie continues, "I want to go back to work before my nest egg's gone."

"How're you gonna go back to work and rest your feet at the same time?" Pearline asks.

Vennie knits her brow. "I don't know."

*Ask for what you want*

The melody nests in Vennie's head. Her nest egg might be going, but that song nest is growing.

They pass the Ponca City Carpentry Shop. "Hello, Arthur Ray," Pearline croons.

Arthur Ray, working outside in the open air, eyes Pearline as he rubs a glaze of varnish into the wood of the newly carved hope chest he began designing when he last saw her. Looking at her today, he hears again the inspiring melody of her song.

Arthur Ray and Pearline exchange more than friendly smiles, and the two women continue on their way.

*Ask for what you want*

Vennie keeps wondering, who could give her what she wants?

"Who can give me what I want?" Vennie repeats to herself.

"I can. I just got to ask," Vennie answers her own question.

"What?" Pearline asks, her head turned, still looking back at Arthur Ray.

"Nothing . . . and everything," Vennie says. She imagines she hears brooms sweeping and whisking the dust and cobwebs off her thoughts, making room. A clean place in her mind for the plan that is beginning to grow.

Suddenly what she has been waiting for, the design, spreads out before her. "Pearline, Pearline, I think I stumbled across me something." She starts humming and walking so fast Pearline has to just about run to keep up with her. Now the humming has grown into a full-fledged melodic repetition of Abyssinia Jackson's song.

> You got to ask for what you want
> Either they will
> Either they won't
> If you don't ask for what you want
> You'll never get just what you want.

They have come so far, Pearline can no longer see Arthur Ray. Vennie is still shaking her head back and forth, humming as they get ready to part.

When Vennie puts her hand on her gate latch, she does a little quick step, as though her feet are hearing quick music.

> You got to ask for what you want

Pearline doesn't have time to ask her grandmother to explain and still make it to Dr. Jackson's on time.

"Say hello to Abyssinia for me," Vennie says, hurry-walking up her path, not bothering to turn around, adding, "Tell her for me I got it. I got it. I got it!"

Pearline pauses, studying her Grandmother Vennie almost skipping into her own house. She wonders what Vennie means, then continues on her way to Dr. Jackson's office.

Zenobia remembers the crestfallen look on Norman's face every time he brings her a cup of steaming, freshly brewed coffee. He brings it the way she likes it, like the way she likes her men, black.

Today Norman sits on the chair, uncomfortably twiddling his thumbs and watching Zenobia sip her Maxwell House, good to the last drop. The sound of the cup clinking in its saucer from time to time is the only noise that breaks the quiet.

She swallows the last sip and says, "Remember that movie you asked me if I wanted to see?"

He replies with a smile and takes the cup and saucer away. Whistling to himself, Norman goes into the bathroom and draws his bath water. He stays splashing around a long, long time.

The movie that evening becomes their first date. It has been weeks since Zenobia has been back down Loganberry Road, and the colored side of town thinks she returned to Oklahoma City until the usher at the theater sees her that evening.

"Seen her my own self," he says to his Better Way Barbershop cronies. "Walking into the picture show dressed in a dead, White woman's clothes and hanging on to a White man's arm."

"You lying!" whoops Strong Jackson, the barber.

Well, that lets the cat out of the bag and the dog off the

leash. Zenobia Butterfield and Norman Miller. People can't get enough of talking about it. Zenobia, who likes her men black as her coffee, is living with a man white as milk.

The morning after the movie, Norman wakes up with meticulously groomed fingernails and shiny clean hair.

Zenobia wakes up in a shared bed instead of on a lonely couch.

After that night, she feels easier about going back out into the world; she can leave the house, with Norman or by herself.

She ventures out to the Ponca City Grocery Store once more, where she again sees Pearline. Zenobia remembers the hurtful words she hurled at her friend the last time she saw her at the store, words calculated to keep Pearline at a distance. She remembers the sickening shame she herself felt as a result of betraying her good friend. She ran away and left Pearline to the mercy of Isaiah's fists. And, more pitiful, with those mean words, "When you see me running you know it's time to go!" she herself had given Pearline another jolting slap in the face.

Even now, the painful memories are too much for Zenobia to handle. This time she doesn't shop, but turns right back around and leaves the store before Pearline can see her. She rushes toward home. Far down Loganberry Road, she enters the White side of town, and she slows down a bit.

Two little girls sitting on the steps of an older mansion almost stop Zenobia in her tracks when one looks up at Zenobia passing by. Then in a piping voice one says innocently to the other, "Which would you rather be, Millie, a nigger or a dog?"

Under her breath, Zenobia says, "No, don't say anything. They're just ignorant children. Keep walking."

She remembers a time when she would have called the whole family out for a showdown, but she is thinking about

Pearline so hard that all she does is mumble, "Somebody need to wring their little scrawny necks and throw them out in the snow."

She quickens her pace.

The little girls' childish, yet hurtful words stick in Zenobia's ears. Once home, the first thing she does is go into the bedroom and grab the blond woman's photo from the shelf above Norman's bed.

"Who this looking like Cinderella's stepmama?" she says, and angrily throws the picture, frame and all, into the trash.

After awhile, Zenobia says, "Probably shouldn't've done that . . . After all, that silly old witch did used to be his wife." She lets out a hearty laugh that helps relieve her tension.

She prepares dinner and makes Norman's favorite dessert, rice pudding sprinkled with brown sugar. After supper, he offers to help with the dishes, but she says, "No, I'll do them. You go rest."

Norman goes into the bedroom and soon notices the empty space where the photo of his late wife had been.

He goes back to the kitchen and asks, "What happened to the picture?"

"What picture?"

"Look, you know what picture I'm talking about."

"It broke."

"Yeah. It broke. All by itself."

Zenobia doesn't reply. She knows words alone can never explain why she trashed the dime-store portrait.

The phone wires heat up all up and down Loganberry Road. The cleaning women snuggle their receivers to their ears and listen to each other.

"Wonder what Vennie want? Now you know by the time I get home from Sunday service, cook my dinner, I don't have time to be messing 'round with going here and yonder, much as I appreciate my friends. That's why we got telephones. Be comfortable in your own house and visit . . .

"What? She is? Well if she's fixing dinner . . . All right . . . Who gonna refuse to eat at Vennie's? Who gonna refuse the way she season black-eyed peas and rice? Eat so much make the buttons pop on your Sunday suit. And don't mention the homemade rolls and gospel bird. Fry chicken so brown you want to cackle. Wonder what do she want?"

That first Sunday the called women, decked out in their Sunday-go-to-meeting hats, stoles, and glad dresses, gather in Vennie's kitchen. They make themselves comfortable around the long table extended with plywood and a pair of card tables to seat all twelve. Somewhere between passing the platter of golden brown chicken and the basket of hot rolls, Vennie says, "I been thinking . . ."

"That's what staying at home off your feet'll do for you," says one woman.

"Thinking, umm!" comments another, as she considers that sweet possibility.

"About these day jobs," Vennie says, finishing her sentence.

"You got both my ears open," another woman says.

"We got to set up a Humane Society for Day-workers."

"Humane Society? That's for dogs. Let's not get this thing mixed up now," someone says.

"Okay. All right. A union then," Vennie says.

The women prop their elbows on the crocheted tablecloth and lean their chewing chins in their palms, studying Vennie.

A union? Most of these women work for employers who hold managerial positions downtown.

"Don't you worry me," Maggie Peppermill says after she mulls over the outrageous possibility. "A union?" She thinks about her daily ritual of pouring rich cream in a tall glass and serving it to her employer at the morning table.

Before those power-driven men begin each harrowing day of business negotiations, they lose a few more gray hairs from their heads and drink an elixir of pure cream served by workers like Maggie Peppermill in hopes of soothing their ulcers.

"Another union? How they go deal with that?" Maggie Peppermill shakes her head.

"A un-ion." Another worker emphasizes each syllable.

"Give me strength." Maggie Peppermill laughs.

"A union."

Then all the astonished mouths at the table linger over the forkfuls of food before swallowing.

"Demands. A union's got to have demands."

"And grievances," somebody else says.

"Well bless my graying head," Maggie Peppermill says. "Grievances? Somebody give me strength. Grievances. Can I count? Do the birds fly south in the winter? Grievances? Don't let my mouth get started."

"Start it," Vennie says.

"First off. Don't expect me to do a week's worth of work in one day. Even a machine'll break down if you overwork it," Maggie Peppermill says.

"Coffee breaks," someone else says.

"Overtime work, time-and-a-half pay."

"No more hiding money behind the couch, under the dresser. Else what I find is mine."

"Don't you worry me!" Maggie Peppermill whoops.

"Don't want no left-over food and no stitch of hand-me-down clothes. Rather walk around naked!"

"Now that would be a sight!" Vennie concludes.

Maggie continues, "Pay me what I'm worth, I'll buy my own."

Others follow suit.

"Raises."

"Social security."

"Pensions."

"Medical plans. This work'll break you down."

"From your feet to your crown," Vennie adds.

Everybody laughs at Vennie's rhyming. She laughs too, but then stops short and says in a serious tone, "What we need is a list of employers. After dinner I want everybody writing down the employers' names."

The table gets quiet and people begin to reach for another helping of food.

"Pass me the peas."

"I'll have another one of them good rolls."

"Vennie, Vennie, this chicken, woman, so good it liable take wings and fly on up to God's own kitchen table so He can have a taste."

"Maggie, Maggie, how the chicken go fly when you done ate both wings? What about this list of employers?" Vennie asks.

Nobody says a word.

"Why don't y'all wake up. Time for cleaning women to wake up."

"We look sleep to you?"

"We already wake," another one says. "Didn't we just give you our list of grievances. We already wake!"

"Then why don't you get up out the bed, then?" Vennie says. "What about this list of employers?"

"Wait a minute now. I can't afford to be fired. Christmas right around the corner. Grandbabies to buy for," Maggie Peppermill laments.

"That's right. Christmas is coming," another housekeeper says with a concerned grimace.

"But is it coming," Vennie asks, "for your feet? For your nerves, high blood pressure, and early heart failure?"

"Why do we have to worry about that now, with Christmas at our door? That's long range," somebody says.

"Sure is," Vennie says. "I'm sitting up here watching y'all eat up my last long range pennies."

"Now, Vennie. Vennie, you know we not gon' let you starve, woman. We'll borrow some food from these kitchens we work in."

"I'm fixing sirloin for Miss Pettis," Maggie Peppermill offers.

"I'm fixing chocolate pound cake for the Ludwigs."

"Peach dumplings for . . ."

Vennie stands up from her table. "Stop it! Stop it! Don't you see? That's day to day. I'm talking about from this point forward. I'm talking about not needing to sneak food home to make up for these low wages. We got to ask for what we want. Ain't nobody never give you nothing, all of you here worked for what you got. If you worked your mind the way they work your body ain't no telling what might happen. Christmas? I don't want to hear it. When you get to work soon tomorrow morning, tie that head rag a little tighter round your brain and start thinking!"

The dinner is over in a hurry. The women leave Vennie's walking fast, more than a little ill-at-ease. Heads ringing. A persistent quivering along the silver cord tying body to soul. And even though they want to deny this disturbance, each day of piece work finds the cord quickening and trembling more. Then their eyes look different, as if they had sat around a smoky fire at Vennie's where a cinder got embedded in the corner of their eye. Each day the irritation grows just a little until they are red-eyed with outrage and blinking constantly, trying to clear their eyes and steady the trembling cord.

"What in heaven's name are we going to do?"

"Uh-oh." Mr. King, the mortuary owner, sighs when he sees a young woman glaring down at Arthur Ray's mother, who is staring into the coffin at her ex-husband.

"Every time I come in here, you sitting up with the body," the young woman, who is the young widow snipes at the older ex-wife.

Arthur Ray's mother, the elder Mrs. Cleveland, looks up from the white-velvet-lined wooden casket at the young woman dressed to kill and says in a voice soaked in contempt, "You talking to me?"

"That's right."

The elder Mrs. Cleveland props her hands on her hips and shakes her head. "Coming in here with that red dress on looking like somebody on fire."

"If I'm on fire, you must be stuck in the ashes. Dressed all in that deadly black."

"My business."

"Yours? Don't you mean my business?"

"Child, me and him had business before you were born."

"I'm the recent Mrs. Cleveland."

"I see." The elder continues to stare down the young woman with eyes that find everything wrong with what she sees.

"Man didn't want you while he was 'live," the upstart snorts.

"Say what?"

"I said he didn't want you while he was 'live, why you think he want you hanging 'round bothering him now when he's dead and gone?"

"He wanted me all right, else how could I give him a son? What you give him? A heart attack, that's what! I gave him Arthur Ray, the brightest-eyed, prettiest boy you ever seen."

"Boy?" She hadn't seen any children when she walked in.

The younger widow can't help but turn her head at that point and look at Arthur Ray, sitting in the chair alongside the coffin, observing the two women his father had married, his mother first and later this younger one. One woman is matronly and plump, the other has a waist thin as a starved waif but with the heavenly hips of a well-fed woman.

"Eyelashes up to your hairline and hemline up to your navel!" the elder fusses.

The young woman tosses the long strands of hair out of her eyes, moistens her tulip-painted lips and acknowledges thirty-three-year-old Arthur Ray Cleveland, the handsomest man in town.

"Man, oh man!" she says under her breath.

Arthur Ray's mama finishes viewing the body, holds her head up, and struts on out of King's Funeral Parlor, holding onto her son's arm as if he is a trophy, her veil quivering as she heaves and moans with a widow's pain.

The younger woman, after a few minutes of looking down at the powdery, puffy face of her deceased husband, walks out of King's Funeral Parlor, a fog of thoughts clouding her head. Her lips tug downward, distressing and wrinkling the corners of her mouth as she thinks about the other widow viewing the body for hours at a time instead of stopping in for ten minutes like somebody with some sense and leaving.

"Disrespecting me in front of the whole town!" she fusses. "Taking advantage in my time of grief. Overzealous, frog-eating woman!" Her voice toils on. "Spending entirely too much time at my Cleveland's wake."

The next day, the ritual begins anew. No sooner has the young Mrs. Cleveland come to pay her respects to the dead than she stops in her tracks.

"Old haint!" she mumbles. "Got her old gray head buried in the casket."

The elder Mrs. Cleveland's back stiffens.

"It's an outrage!" The younger woman trembles, blinded by anger.

She doesn't even see Arthur Ray sitting over to the side.

"In here again, huh, heifer?" the young woman says to the elder one.

At the sound of the word "heifer," Arthur Ray jumps up. "That's my mama, woman!" he warns.

Arthur Ray's mama takes in the sight of the younger woman.

"Yes, it's me," Arthur Ray's mother says, too sweetly. She shoots Arthur Ray a look that says, "Shut up, son, I can hold my own ground." She focuses her attention back on the casket and what she is there for. She leans over and presses her lips against the dead man's.

"What?" the young, incensed Mrs. Cleveland beeps. Then she up and tries to snatch the older one away from the casket.

"I got a right to kiss my husband good-bye if I want to," the elder sings as she snuggles up even closer to the body.

The young Mrs. Cleveland grabs the mature one's plump arm, trying to pull her away from the casket.

The senior abandons her sweet dignity and reaches up and pinches her assailant, the way old-fashioned women used to pinch their disobedient children's ear lobes, twisting the skin to make it hurt more.

A true battle breaks out.

The thin one gives the plump one a powerful shove, propelling her at last away from her perch by the casket. Now she takes up the sentry with her hands propped on her young hips as she gazes down at the late Mr. Cleveland.

Regaining her balance, the matron comes up from behind, grabs a handful of flowing hair, and yanks away her wig.

"Uh-huh!" she charges. "A made-up woman. Ha! Wake up, Cleveland!" she calls to the dead man as she twirls the wig in the air. "Wake on up!"

Then she says to the skimpy-tressed woman, "Hair no longer than a minute! I just wish he could see you now!" She looks back down at Cleveland and scolds, "Wake up, Cleveland, and see what I'm looking at!"

"Give it here!" the naked-headed, younger Mrs. Cleveland yells, as she grabs for the wig.

Her synthetically long, sparkling nails grasp the false hair too roughly and succeed only in tearing the perfect ovals from her fingertips.

The gray Mrs. Cleveland, still holding the wig up in the air with one hand, lifts her veil and peers down at the phony nails strewn like lacquered, red petals on the floor and then back up at the naked, chewed-off fingernails of her adversary, and gives a mad laugh. "Stubs! Plain stubs! You false fool! Cleveland, Cleveland, wake up!"

As the battle grows fiercer, the two women fall against a flower stand. It tips over and potted lilies of the valley sail through the air.

Arthur Ray leaps out of his seat and tries to separate the women.

The females hit each other and run. Run round and round the casket with Arthur Ray in hot pursuit.

Out of the corner of his eye, Arthur Ray sees Mr. King, the mortuary owner, dash on up to the doorway and stop dead in his tracks. He surveys the mad scene, his eyes jumping in his head, a nervous tic working at the right corner of his mouth.

"Stop it! Stop it!" Mr. King screams.

Arthur Ray is trying his best. He grabs the wigless Mrs. Cleveland. Soon as he gets one kicking woman subdued, the other starts in again.

Then Mr. King moves toward them.

As Arthur Ray looks up, he momentarily loosens his grip. The younger widow breaks loose and the fight begins again, so fierce that even Mr. King takes refuge in a corner of the room.

The women start running around the coffin again.

Then the lean Mrs. Cleveland stops, takes off a spiked-heel shoe, rears back, and aims. The shoe flies through the air, missing its gray-headed target, and shatters the angel in the stained glass window.

By this time, the whole mortuary staff has crawled up in the doorway as Mr. King yips, "Call the Law!" He hops up and down on one foot, sputtering, "I say, call the Law!"

Hit and run. Run and hit.

Nobody runs to call the law.

The floor grumbles and the coffin creaks.

The fighting becomes fiercer and fiercer. Even Arthur Ray, the son of the elder widow, can't get a grip on this female anger, unleashed like a tornado or like one of those hurricanes named after women.

The coffin rocks.

The women pay no mind as they sling insults and fists and run with Arthur Ray in pursuit.

The disturbed coffin dances.

Screeching to a halt, this time the two women clash together and bump up against the casket with great force.

Next thing they know the heavy coffin comes crashing down. As it falls, it clips Arthur Ray on the leg.

The coffin jettisons Mr. Cleveland's body and lands in splinters on the floor. The corpse's lips come open, giving the appearance of a grotesque grin smirking across his face as if he is laughing at the shenanigans of the women.

The loud shout of the wooden casket hitting the floor and ejecting the beloved Mr. Cleveland before them brings the two women up short and sends the undertaker and his men into action.

Two attendants scoop up the grinning corpse and take him on out of the room, running as if to save his life. Another grabs a broom and starts sweeping up splinters. Mr. King bends over and starts collecting the hazardous shards of stained glass.

It is awhile before anyone notices that Arthur Ray is grimacing with pain.

"What's the matter with you?" his mother asks.

"I think my leg's broke," he says. "Casket hit it."

This snaps the women out of their trance and the younger Mrs. Cleveland howls, "Somebody, somebody call the doctor!"

And that is how Abyssinia Jackson is summoned to make a house call to the mortuary.

The undertaker, attendants, and mourners sit in the chapel, meditating, heads bowed as they wait on the doctor like some people wait on the law or the minister to solve a problem, to bring understanding to ignorance, to bring reasoning to confusion.

The sound of a car motor yanks their heads up.

"Finally, she's here." Mr. King gives a relieved sigh.

Abyssinia steps into the room, surveys the chaotic scene spread out before her, and heads straight to Arthur Ray.

"Thank the Lord," Mr. King says.

"Yes," Abyssinia says as she expertly probes the leg while Arthur Ray winces. "It's broken, all right. We'll get it X-rayed, so we'll know exactly where the fracture is. What a day for this to happen," she says in a consoling voice.

"God, it hurts," Arthur Ray says, tight-mouthed with pain.

"Call the ambulance," she instructs the mortuary owner as she administers a pain killing shot to Arthur Ray. Mr. King scurries to the telephone, glad to be able to help.

"Looks like you all had a little party in here," Abyssinia adds. Even the frightened attendants give a little half-smile.

In the hospital's radiology lab, Abyssinia holds up and studies the X rays of shadow and light taken of Arthur Ray's broken leg.

"Arthur Ray," she says, as she comes back to the room where he lays stretched out on the gurney, "your leg bone's broken just about down by the ankle. We're going to set it for you. Give you a wonderful cast."

Arthur Ray nods, his pain dulled by the morphine shot Abyssinia administered back at the mortuary. Out of habit, Abyssinia holds her fingertips on his wrist and checks his pulse. Normal. She peers at his skin and notices it is a little ashen and tinged with gray.

Hospital pallor. Not the luminous brown of the Arthur Ray Cleveland she knows. Her sixth sense tells her to check beneath his eyelids. She pulls one lid up, then the other.

An echo sounds in her head, *Insides of the eyelids white as turnips.* That is her old mentor, the medicine woman, Mother Beatrice Barker's voice speaking. "Oh my God," Abyssinia winces inside.

She draws her hands away from his eyes and says, "While you're here, we'll run some blood and urine tests, give you a routine going-over, Arthur Ray. When's the last time you had a complete physical checkup?"

"Not since I was a child, Dr. Jackson. I came in here to mend my broken leg, not to discuss my health habits. Anyway, I don't have time to be lagging. The funeral."

A shudder tries to run through Abyssinia. But she turns it back before Arthur Ray notices.

"I'm sorry," she says lightly, "but you just ran into a health monitor. You know, like one of those highway patrolmen monitoring traffic. They stop you for speeding and then check your headlights."

"I really don't have time for this."

In a more serious voice, she adds, "It won't take long, and you can get on with your funeral plans."

"All right, if you promise," he says drowsily, still under the effects of the morphine.

"You don't have much choice, Arthur Ray," she says. "Like it or not, you sure can't run."

As the cast technician mixes plaster in its tub, wraps Arthur Ray's leg in gauze, and spreads the plaster around it, Abyssinia considers her injured patient. Now, out of Arthur Ray's view, she allows the shudder she has been holding back to tremble through her. Allows it to remind her of her own mortality, and of the silent agony she feels for Arthur Ray.

"Got another patient waiting back at the office," Abyssinia says to the emergency room physician on duty as she writes down the last notes on Arthur Ray's chart. "Call me when you get the results on his hematology. My receptionist will put you through even if I'm with a patient . . ."

She peeks back in the room at Arthur Ray. "See you later."

"Right," Arthur Ray says, with a drowsy wink.

*My goodness*, she says to herself, *he's almost as handsome as my Carl Lee.*

In the emergency waiting room, she informs Mrs. Cleveland, "He'll be out soon."

"What a thing to happen," his mother answers.

"On such a day," Abyssinia sympathizes.

"Will he be all right?"

"The Xray showed a definite break in the bone near the ankle," Abyssinia says.

Mrs. Cleveland still looks worried.

"Reason it took so long is he needed a cast."

"A cast. He'll be laid up then?"

"He'll be able to walk on crutches."

"Able to walk on crutches!" she says with relief.

Looking like a mother hen, as innocent and cherubic as a plump angel with wings hidden under her black dress, the elder Mrs. Cleveland thanks her, and Abyssinia leaves the woman perched on the edge of her chair, gazing hopefully toward the door through which Arthur Ray would emerge.

Immediately Abyssinia experiences a wave of conflicting feelings—her entire body breaks out in goose bumps. All around her the air thickens with premonition and sadness. At the same time, she is swept with longing as she hesitates, one hand on the exit door, recognizing in the older woman's eyes the awesome scope and commitment of unconditional, maternal love. She wonders whether she, Abyssinia Jackson-Jefferson, will ever experience that miracle of feeling, that magnificent umbilical connection that begins before the cradle and extends beyond the grave.

On her drive back to the House of Light, Abyssinia looks out at the leaves falling from the trees and fluttering along Loganberry Road, and again she breaks out in goose bumps.

Before she knows it, Abyssinia is parking her car, striding up the walk scattered with autumn leaves, and entering the House of Light.

"Janet, there'll be a call coming from the hospital about

Arthur Ray Cleveland's hematology and urinalysis tests. Put it through to me, would you, please?"

"As soon as it comes in," Janet Lacy promises.

Abyssinia picks up Pearline Spencer's waiting chart and opens the door to the examination room.

She is almost finished with Pearline when the phone rings.

"Excuse me."

She reaches for the receiver on the wall.

"Dr. Jackson," she answers.

A brief, listening silence.

"Yes . . . Yes . . . I'll be over to admit him. I'll be along shortly."

The curious Pearline can't help but wonder who Dr. Jackson is talking about admitting to Ponca Memorial Hospital.

Before turning around to finish treating Pearline, Abyssinia calls on her sources of inner strength. She can never feel blasé about any of her patients. No matter how many she has. It is with a combination of professional skill and lessons learned from Mother Barker that she evenly says, "That arm's almost perfect again, Pearline. Almost as perfect as God made it."

Pearline nods. She is feeling at least ten years younger.

"So glad I kept that first appointment," Pearline says. And Pearline is thankful that she has found a sympathetic ear in Dr. Jackson, healer, listener, to whom she has confided the source of her injuries: Isaiah.

"I wonder," Pearline ventures, "if I'll ever find happiness with a man who can put a permanent smile on my lips." What she leaves unspoken is that Arthur Ray is the only man in town who comes close.

"Happiness. That's something you can do for yourself," Abyssinia says. "Just look at you now. Looks like you're making yourself happy. When the right man comes into the picture,

you'll be doubly blessed. Until then, you're just blessed. Pearline," she says after a brief pause, "you are enough."

"Am I?"

Instead of answering, Abyssinia whisper-sings under her
breath:

> *Standing alone is not so bad*
> *Giving it up's the best thought*
> *That you ever had*
> *Turn it a loose*
> *Pump your own juice*
> *Be alive on your own*
> *Standing alone.*

"Did you say something?" Pearline asks.

"I think you're handling things in a wonderful way," Abyssinia says.

Then Abyssinia continues to sing softly as she examines Pearline's arm:

> *The buck stops here*
> *You're the one in charge*
> *You make the plan*
> *Tell any man*
> *Being alive on your own*
> *Standing alone.*

Pearline feels lightness infuse her whole being. A rising feeling sweeps through her soul.

> *It's time to choose*
> *You make the rules*

*Move from the pain*
*You hold the rein*
*Being alive on your own*
*Standing alone.*

*Is Dr. Jackson singing under her breath?* Pearline wonders. Is she hearing that melody or is she imagining she hears it?

"Say hello to your Grandma Vennie for me, will you?" Abyssinia says when she's finished with the examination.

Then Abyssinia leaves the room, her attention set on hurrying to the hospital to see about Arthur Ray Cleveland.

Abyssinia walks along the corridor from the hematology lab to the room where Arthur Ray waits to be released. Her mind sorts, adds, figures, and concentrates on the numbers of the low red-blood-cell count and the remarkably reduced platelet count. She mentally reviews the intense meeting between her and the oncologist. To be sure there is no mistake in the test results, the oncologist has taken the blood samples twice and run the test twice.

No matter how hard Abyssinia thinks about it, she can't change the diagnosis: Myelogenous leukemia, the acute stage, and the last stage.

When Abyssinia reaches Arthur Ray's hospital room, she holds the door open, quietly studying him. He is gazing out the window, his back to her.

Sitting on the edge of the gurney, he looks outside at the falling leaves, thinking how a broken leg makes moving through space so difficult. Even traveling the short distance between the gurney and the window that frames the falling leaves causes him to sweat.

His eyes, not his legs, travel the distance. He sees the chill fever of death set the clinging leaves afire. Sees autumn, stepping high through the sky, hesitate over the treetops.

Sees it linger long and scald the fragile leaves, turning the

virginal green brilliant with shades of vermilion. He is so tired
and weak, so weak that for a moment he feels weaker than air,
as if he can lean on a leaf, but that will never do for the leaves
are burning, trembling, winding out of the unencumbered sky,
down toward coldness and death.

As Abyssinia lets the door swing closed, Arthur Ray turns
around to face her. Something unspoken disturbs the fragile
doctor-patient bond.

"How're you feeling, Mr. Cleveland?"

"Call me Arthur Ray. I feel tired."

"The usual tiredness?"

"No. I feel tired, with a capital T. This is different."

"How?"

"So tired, I've got to concentrate just to lift up my head."

"I see."

"What's the matter with me?"

"I got the blood test results back."

"And . . ."

"Arthur . . . Arthur Ray . . . There's something wrong."

"What's the diagnosis?"

"Acute myelogenous. . . ."

"Acute myelogenous?" he repeats slowly. The words are so
foreign he has trouble holding them in his mind.

And then Abyssinia finishes the diagnosis by enunciating two
of the most dreaded medical syllables in human language: "Acute
myelogenous cancer."

"What?"

"Can-cer. A potent form of leukemia."

"Cancer? They made a mistake," he says, outraged, furiously
whisking invisible lint from his shirt. "I admit I've been feeling
a little under the weather lately. Aching bones. The ague. Some-

thing. The flu. You know, just a passing thing. Although it's hung on a little longer than usual, this tiredness . . ."

Then he gets up and starts moving around on the new, unfamiliar crutches, hobbling to the closet to collect his shoes. Perspiration grows cold bubbles on his forehead and breaks out under his armpits where the crutches numb muscle and skin. A single bead of sweat puddles by his ear and runs down to his chin.

"Arthur Ray," she says. "Listen to me. You have to stay here for more tests. Chemotherapy."

There is something terrible in her voice that whispers down his back, enters through the great locks of his shoulders and whistles through his heart. When she touches him, he thinks he hears humming. Her touch is a hug, and he sits back down, so heavily, on the gurney.

"After the chemotherapy, I'll be all right?"

She pauses before answering, and then shakes her head. "The chemotherapy is only palliative, Arthur Ray. Will only keep you alive a little while longer."

"A little longer? How much longer?"

She looks him directly in the eye and murmurs, "Six months to one year. One year . . . if we're lucky."

"One year?" Arthur Ray repeats softly.

"One year . . ." he says again, beyond belief.

He travels every bend and curve of his mind, down one road and then another, trying to comprehend. But still he can't understand. Tight chains wrap around his chest. His body shakes with a chill colder than winter's ice.

Then he starts laughing. Laughing so hard, he bends over in a spasm. He laughs himself into a frenzy. He laughs until the iron in his laughter beats the breath out of him. Beats the breath out of him so mercilessly that nothing is left but a gasp.

Abyssinia waits silently, helplessly. She can prolong his life for a little while, but she can't prevent his death.

She prays there will be a cure for this cancer and all cancers.

"But the funeral . . . Mama . . ." he whispers, and the incandescence is wrenched from his eye, like a light bulb yanked from its socket.

The only thing that keeps Arthur Ray from falling over is Abyssinia's gaze.

She doesn't dare blink. Steady.

"You know something, doctor, I can't stay in the hospital until after the funeral. I don't want Mama to know until way after the funeral. To know right now would kill her."

Abyssinia understands. She remembers the look on Mrs. Cleveland's face. That vulnerable expression, unprotected, as she sits out in the lobby. She knows Arthur Ray's mother is still waiting, perched on the edge of her emergency room seat.

"Isn't the funeral tomorrow?" Abyssinia asks.

"Tomorrow," he says, still in a daze.

"All right. The day after the funeral we'll check you into hospital for chemotherapy."

Arthur Ray's voice comes to her from as far away as an echo from the cemetery or from as nearby as the falling leaves outside the hospital window. And the tiredness he has been holding back for so many months scrapes over his body, paring it into a stooped and ash-gray sculpture.

He says, "I know, I'll tell her I have to go out of town on carpentry business, some big Oklahoma City order I have to fill. Yes," he says, "I'll make up something. Something she'll have to believe. Anything to explain my absence."

After Abyssinia leaves, Arthur Ray hobbles off with his mother toward the taxi stand.

As the cab pulls away, Arthur Ray squeezes his mother close

to him. He begins to talk with lightning speed. He is trying not
to think, throwing words out to hide his stormy thoughts.

He speaks of his sixth Christmas when his father gave him
a chunk of wood, a pocketknife, and a small saw.

His mother strokes his hands. And he thinks of his father's
hands.

"Daddy's hands," Arthur Ray says, "seemed so big to me
then." Under the watch of his father's close eye, Arthur Ray
learned to whittle that year, the year the muscles in his young
hands had gained enough dexterity to make small, precise movements.

"You made your first piece of furni . . ."

He cuts off her response, talking so fast he is near about
gasping.

"Oh, that table. That table. That little table. The crooked
top. The four bowlegged legs. It wobbled when I sat at it to
draw and design my simple furniture ideas, and then I built a
play chest for my toys."

"Your father . . ." His mother tries to interject.

Arthur Ray cuts her off again. "Every birthday and Christmas
from then on, I got a chunk of wood." By the time Arthur Ray
was a teenager he had built a bedroom set for his parents.

"Son, one of the best gifts . . ." His mother tries to continue.

Arthur Ray hurries on, "I was never sure the dresser drawers
would open right."

"Made us proud," his mother says. "Not opening right? Did
and didn't. Proud."

"Proud? You kept that to yourself. At least at the time I
thought you did. Anyway, there were times when I wanted to
rebel against your curfews and rules and do-this and don't-do-
thats."

"Every parent's job is sometimes hard. One day you'll know

what I'm talking about when you've got your own little Arthur Rays running around."

"Mama, who would have me?"

"Oh, I've seen how the women look at you."

He smiles as he thinks about Pearline and the Sunday after church. In a strange moment of excitement in which sweet memory shuts out the unpleasant truth of his meeting with Dr. Jackson, he opens his mouth to tell his mother his feelings about Pearline, but he stops mid-voice.

Years ago Pearline had broken his heart by marrying Isaiah, but it was Arthur Ray's own fault. He had never told Pearline how he felt, content to stare at her from a distance. After all, the woman was no mind reader. But he is going to have a second chance. She is divorcing Isaiah and, when the divorce is final, he will win her hand. *This time*, he thinks, *I won't let her get away.*

A shadow falls across his face. Out of the corner of his eye, he glimpses his double tragedy through the taxi window.

His mother pats his arm.

"Who knows how long the season of love lasts," Arthur Ray says with a sigh.

"Well, your daddy and I didn't make it all the way, son, but we had some very good years and you were our greatest blessing."

"Forty *very* good years," Arthur Ray says wistfully.

The cab reaches the carpentry shop and they get out. "These crutches make my arms ache. Think I'll design a pair that's a little more comfortable."

He mops the sweat from his brow as they reach the front door, "Rest yourself, Mama. Tomorrow's the day."

R*oosevelt* Tate plays "The Chariot Is Coming," pumping the sad and lively Steven Roberts song throughout the sanctuary on the day of the funeral. Arthur Ray and his mother, dressed in respectful black, sit in the first row. Other Ponca friends fill the church. The minister gives a solemn welcome, then hands the service over to Abyssinia Jackson.

"Death where is your sting? Grave where is your victory?" she begins. "A special angel appeared to me last night as I prayed beside my bed.

"And this is the message she brought. 'There will be many miracles of science!'

"Somebody in this very room will live to a hundred and ten."

"Touch the scientists, touch their mighty minds, oh Lord!" Vennie Walker moans.

"A team of geniuses," continues Abyssinia, "a chosen team will discover a cure, not only to cancer, but to death and pestilence, will find the answer to turn back a host of devastating diseases."

"Prophesy!" somebody calls.

"The word 'genius' means gift. To be a genius is to be blessed by gift. It might look, to the average person, that this team of geniuses will come across the cure by accident. But there

are no accidents. Their minds will be guided by a compassionate
God!

"The hundred and ten years that the angel heralded did not
apply to our Deacon Cleveland," she intones. "We don't know
the day or hour, for when God calls us, we have to go, even in
the face of miracles."

"*Um-hmmm,*" the choir sings mournfully.

She promises, "He's gone up yonder and he's busy receiving
his just reward: Eternal peace and rest!"

"*Um-hmmm,*" the choir hums.

The heaviness of this loss makes Arthur Ray tired, so tired.
And he longs for those lighter memories, appropriate swaddling
to clothe the meaning of the man who did so much more with
his life than lie in a casket with his arms folded across his chest.

The memories fail him not. Arthur Ray blocks out the honey
words of Dr. Jackson and hears the distinct voice of his father.
His thoughts sail back in time to another Christmas.

*He is five and his father young and strong and searching for the way
to be a good parent.*

*Arthur Ray drowses in front of the fireplace. The Christmas tree,
decorated with real oranges and apples for ornaments and peppermint
canes instead of lights, is part of the drowsing as are the carolers out
in the snow singing "Jingle Bells."*

*"Sandman's got this one," his father says, lifting him up. Arthur
Ray lays lax and trusting in his father, Cleveland's, arms as he is
taken to the narrow bed and slipped between thick quilts.*

*Later, his mother comes in and kisses him gently on the brow. She
sniffles and a tear falls onto his cheek.*

*Drowsily, he wipes it away. He turns, snuggling deeper into the
warm quilts. He drifts into visions of toy soldiers and electric trains
and building blocks and puzzles and a fire-red wagon. He knows he*

won't get all he hopes for. He has not been that good. He is still wetting the bed.

On this Christmas Eve night, he is so excited he wakes up every now and then and wonders if morning has come. His dreams start out like the night dreams of any five-year-old. He plays tag, slipping behind dogwood and cypress trees.

Along toward the last hour of night he smells the aged ham his father brought in from the smoke shed. Its aroma drifts thickly from the kitchen oven and on up under the door of his room, tantalizing the air with the smell of cloves and honey. Arthur Ray unglues his eyes.

That's when he hears a shotgun go off.

He sits straight up and bolts out of bed. He hears someone running from the kitchen and the sound of the front door opening.

When Arthur Ray opens his bedroom door, he sees his father and mother looking out into the snow.

The snow flies in the front room like feathers from a white hen getting her neck wrung. The gust of air discovers his wet pajamas and chastises him with cold.

When his parents hear him coming, they slam the front door, standing guard against his opening it, the yawning white gusts of snow trapped inside.

"What happened?" he asks.

"Somebody just shot Santa Claus," his father says.

"Santa Claus? Shot?"

"They took him away in an ambulance," his father volunteers.

Bewildered and outraged, Arthur Ray cries his heart out for the Santa Claus shot by robbers, cries until his bright eyes turn red for the missed gifts that Santa was bringing to his house.

His mother serves warm milk with his breakfast.

Everything is all mixed up in his mind:

The waffles and Alaga syrup and the heated smell of pee seeping *through his size-five pajamas. His mother's assurance that Santa Claus was recuperating in Ponca Memorial Hospital. His father's promise that from now on Santa would get to their house safe and sound. Even if it means his father himself has to stand guard on Loganberry Road on Christmas Eve night.*

*After breakfast, Arthur Ray looks out the window at the other children playing in the snow with their new toy sleds and shiny balls and green-helmeted soldiers lined up in cold trenches. Evidently, Santa Claus had made it to his friends' houses before being waylaid and shot.*

*The one saving grace is that his mother is so upset about what happened to Santa that she doesn't scold him about peeing in the bed.*

The opalescent appearance of his father's new casket brings Arthur Ray out of his reverie. This new casket is not wood but is pearly in texture and tone. The champagne-colored satin cushions his father's sculptured face. This stillness in a man once so vital brings fresh pain and fatigue to Arthur Ray.

His mother sobs low and quiet beside him. Farther down the row the younger widow holds her head high while tears streak mascara in a deliberate path down her face, creating scarifications he could carve in his spare time. Time? Spare time?

His stare catches the young Mrs. Cleveland's eyes as she looks up, but then he looks away.

Dr. Jackson ends her sermon with a poem:

When the chilly eyes of Death catch you in their glare
And cry water cold enough to ice the blood
Just when you think Death's forgotten and left you warming
    there
The water turns into a flood.
Remember this: Beside the cold angel another burns bright

Takes hold of the soul, flies the spirit through the night,
Beyond the sky and into the light.

Now comes the singing. Pearline Spencer stands up in the
choir loft and joins Abyssinia Jackson.
Abyssinia sings,

> *Angel tipping in the room*
> *Sat right down*
> *Angel come a stealing in the room*
> *Sat right down*

Pearline sings backup,

> *Getting ready to fly*
> *The spirit to the throne*
> *Getting ready to carry him home*

Abyssinia sings,

> *To God.*

Now the people, row by row, are all lining up to view the
body for the last time. The mourners in the back of the church
file down first. Then the congregation in the penultimate row
follows.
Abyssinia sings,

> *Next time he stops by here*
> *May be coming for the brother,*
> *Mother, daughter, sister, or son*

*Only God knows who'll be the one*
*When*

Pearline joins her,

*Angel whispers in the room*
*Sat right down*
*Angel comes a swooping in the room*
*Sat right down*
*Getting ready to fly*
*The spirit to the throne*
*Getting ready to carry you home*

Abyssinia sings alone,

*To God.*

Now the ritual reaches the front row of family. It is not unusual for families to take up one whole side of the church, but the Cleveland family occupies only three seats on the front pew. Arthur Ray hobbles on his crutches, his widowed mother beside him, the younger Mrs. Cleveland closely behind.

With one black-gloved hand, his mother signals for him to go first and there, in front of the coffin, Arthur Ray looks down at the remains of his father, thinking of the truth about the Christmas secret they had never voiced man to man. Long ago he realized that in order to save face in front of his son on the Christmas that Arthur Ray was five, his poor, broke father was shooting only at snow that holy morning so long ago. In fact, when Arthur Ray was six years old, his father had granted safe passage to Santa, just as he had promised.

Abyssinia sings,

*One wing got your crown*

Pearline echoes,

*Sat right down*

Abyssinia:

*One wing got your long white gown*

Pearline:

*Sat right down*

As the two widows faint in unison, Abyssinia and Pearline croon:

*Getting ready to fly*
*The spirit to the throne*
*Getting ready to carry you home*

Abyssinia ends the song:

*To God.*

After Arthur Ray and the ushers restore the shaken widows to consciousness and they are back in their front row seats, Arthur Ray looks up into the choir stand and catches the compassionate gaze of Pearline Spencer.

With the slightest twinkling inflection, her eyes promise if he'll catch the meat, she'll fix it. Together they'll candy sweet potatoes on Thanksgiving Day. She promises Christmas Eve by the fireside, babies snuggling warm in their beds, and Santa Claus dancing through the snow past bullets and phantom burglars to deliver the carved, sculptured store-bought and home-crafted gifts. Together they will turn all their children's dreams bright on Christmas mornings.

"Oh, my God," Arthur Ray moans inside, "I'm the only one. The last one of my line."

He bows his head to the absent family in the empty seats surrounding him in mute and innocent mockery. And he bows too to hide the dying light in his incandescent eyes.

As promised, Maggie Peppermill stops by early from work to visit Vennie.

"Wasn't that funeral something?"

"Missionary Cleveland and that other woman . . ."

"You mean the new wife," said Vennie.

"Uh-hm, the new wife. Falling out like that."

"Funerals are always interesting around here. And they always make me hungry. Enough food afterward to feed a whole town!"

"Well you won't be hungry today. Didn't I tell you I was gonna bring you some steak?"

"Maggie Peppermill, you're a friend in deed." Vennie takes the food out of the paper bag and turns on the oven to heat it. "Sit down and rest those tired toes."

*Briing!* the phone rings. Vennie answers.

"Hello . . . Yes, this is LaVinia Walker.

"Yes, that's right, that's what I owe . . .

"I been paying a little on it. I know I promised to pay . . .

"What? If you had me in Texas I'd pay?

"I said I don't have it yet.

"Sir?

"Yes, sir. Come right on."

Vennie hangs up the phone, forehead wrinkled.

"Who was that?" Maggie Peppermill asks.

"The bill collector."

"Bill collector?"

"Calling about my hospital bill."

"What the hospital doing?"

"Wasn't the hospital. They don't do their own collecting. They hire somebody to do it. Maggie, do you know what he said? He said if he had me in Texas he bound I'd pay."

"In Texas? This is Oklahoma. What he mean?"

"Oh, Maggie, stop, don't you remember how they used to beat the colored folks up in Texas when they late paying their bills?"

"I kind of recall hearing . . ."

"Anyway, he said he's coming by to discuss it."

"Well, let him come on. I ain't leaving from this spot. In Texas?"

Maggie Peppermill is beside herself and beside Vennie. She is there when the doorbell rings and the transplanted Texan comes to the door.

"Vennie Walker?"

"That's me. Come on in."

He steps inside, a wrinkled-necked, scrunched-up man. "Now, you people have a bad habit . . ."

Maggie Peppermill is bolting the door. Setting chairs in front of it.

The Texan doesn't notice, he just continues talking in an accusatory manner.

"Now you people have to learn to be responsible . . ." Finally, he hears the loud clap of the bolt. His mouth flaps open. He doesn't see anything in the house anybody would want to lock and bolt doors to protect. "What . . . ?"

Next thing he knows, Vennie picks up her broom and starts

cleaning house, sweeping the man all on his head, in his eyes, his nose. Maggie Peppermill is standing guard with a shovel. Every time he tries to advance on Vennie, Maggie Peppermill raises that shovel. When Vennie gets through with him, his face looks like a razor-toed raccoon had clawed it all up, down, and crossways.

He tries to bust out the door, but it is bolted and guarded by Maggie. Finally, Vennie says, "Maggie, I'm getting tired. You can let him out now."

Vennie and Maggie stand looking out the front room window watching the Texan race to his car, watching as steadily as housewives sending their husbands off to work. At the sound of his tires screeching down Loganberry Road, the two women sag. They are so tired they sit down and fold their arms across their chests and stare at the door. Pretty soon Maggie Peppermill gets up and leaves.

Now this incident of the bill collector threatening Vennie is a prise on the cleaning women's understanding. If this could happen to Vennie, the same thing could happen to them. Surgery has taken her last dime. The hospital board has hired the bill collector. At one time, some of the board members had employed four of the eleven cleaning women Vennie invited to her house to discuss day work during that first Sunday dinner.

The Sunday after the bill collector incident, the same called women return to Vennie's. And they sustain their sister with pots of Sunday meals. Lima beans and baked breast of lamb. They bring hush puppies, and ground-nut stew made of chicken sautéed and stewed in bell peppers, onions, red peppers, and ground peanuts.

The following Sunday, they bring catfish jambalaya and okra gumbo with corn served over rice.

As has become their habit, the women come directly from

church with Abyssinia's Sunday singing still in their minds. They come faltering, with their litany of employer abuses. They come stumbling, trying to decide how to improve their working conditions. They come until they can stare at Vennie Walker without blinking back tears at the possibility of ending up penniless, worn down and worn out, broken and broke. They have come to understand that when you are bound by rags, tears only soak and tighten the bonds that strap you down.

They carve away their objections to the possibilities of a union, the way Abyssinia Jackson took her surgeon knife and carved away the unwanted arthritic bones in Vennie's toes and crooked feet.

They can see straight now.

"When are you gonna call these employers?" Maggie Peppermill asks.

"I think on Monday," Vennie says.

"Well, I'm ready. I stored up enough food to last my family a month."

"Me too."

"Got me a pig in the pen and ten chickens in the coop."

"Enough money to pay the gas and lights and telephone for two months."

"No new Sunday-go-to-meeting clothes. Don't need them right now."

"My grandkids may just have to think about what Christmas truly means this time."

"I'm proud of you all," Vennie says. "And I'm more sure now than ever that we must fix this mess."

"Who you calling first, Vennie? Which one? Carver?"

"I thought about it," Vennie says. "Maybe not Carver. That hussy's the worst crosspatch in the batch. No, I think my Friday woman will do."

"Celestine Hutton? You can't mean Celestine Hutton!"

"It ain't right!" one worker strenuously objects.

"You can't do that to Hutton," another worker complains.

Maggie Peppermill adds, "She called me after you didn't come back to work, worried sick about you, wondering if she'd done something wrong. She said she tried to talk to you, but you didn't want to be bothered. When she asked me if you were all right, I told her about your feet."

"I know Hutton's the nicest employer in town. Going to her house is almost like working in your own. She treats you like a person," Vennie says with an agreeing nod.

"She got a good attitude. Why should she suffer with the likes of Carver?"

"Because," Vennie says, "Hutton come the closest to giving us what we want. She's the one, all right. Yes. She's gonna have to convince the rest. And believe me, that ain't gonna be easy."

Maggie Peppermill chuckles. "Carver's been screeching like some stuck pig ever since you left her. What did you do to her to make her hate you so? The woman's walking around looking like she lost something and don't know where to start searching to find it."

Vennie looks down at her plate, hiding the shadows in her eyes. She says, "I pulled the covers off her. The truth'll make you see the strangest things."

What had Dr. Jackson asked that day at the hospital, "Can you pull the covers off anybody without revealing some of yourself?"

The women nod, not quite understanding what Dr. Jackson meant by revealing yourself, but they figure it must be all right.

*You got to ask for what you want!*

echoes in Vennie's mind.

•   •   •

This Monday morning, the day-women meet in front of Hutton's house. Dressed in pleated cranberry and leaf-green uniforms with narrow-cuffed sleeves. Their appealing attire does not deny their bodies, but dignifies their figures. No tents, hats the colors of their uniforms, all of one accord in their appearance and in their minds.

Vennie, who can see Hutton at her window looking out with sad, panic-stricken eyes, walks up the steps and is welcomed by an avalanche of fussing as Hutton opens the front door.

"Why me?" Hutton cries as Vennie enters the house. "What've I done to deserve this? I don't deserve to be picketed. I'm the nicest employer in this whole town. Do I call you out of your name? No. I'm the one calling you Mrs. Walker. I'm the one sitting down with you for coffee. I'm the one paying the highest wages in this old town. I don't deserve to be picketed. I'm the one . . ."

"Hush," Vennie says kindly.

Hutton continues in a keen voice, "I'm the one sent you flowers in the hospital. I'm the one . . ."

The telephone has been ringing for several minutes.

"You better get your phone," Vennie says as she turns to observe the picketers parading outside.

"Excuse me," Hutton says, picking up the receiver. Her swollen eyes run watery, puffed up, rimmed with red.

"Yes?" Hutton asks.

"It's Carver," she whispers as she holds her hand over the receiver. She bows her head, then listens to the irritated caller whose indignation crackles through the wires, so that even Vennie hears the outrage.

Hutton answers, "I don't know. They just swooped down like some bats out of hell."

The cry in Hutton's voice almost unnerves Vennie. "More like bats out of heaven," she shouts, then watches the faithful eleven parading outside, honoring the commitment they have made. Vennie stands firm, steadfast.

Maggie Peppermill's placard reads, WHAT I FIND IS MINE.

Another reads, COFFEE BREAKS.

And Vennie reads aloud the women's demands:

INSURANCE

VACATION PAY

I DON'T NEED YOUR HUSBAND, another poster reads. Vennie repeats the message loud enough to blot out Hutton's telephone tantrum. " 'I don't want your man, I want my money.' Now ain't that the truth!" Vennie hoots at another sign's message.

"What is it, Vennie? What do you all want?" Hutton asks after hanging up the phone.

"Look and see for yourself. Those are some of the things we want."

"But what can I do?" Hutton asks as she joins Vennie to stare out at the parading women.

Vennie answers, "You can start by telling all those women calling you on the phone that they get no cleaning women this week. Get none until we get these demands met. When they ready to talk, I'm ready to discuss it. Until then, we gonna be outside your house every day from nine to five."

Having delivered her message, Vennie goes out and joins the women, leading them in the song, "Got on My Traveling Shoes."

The gospel sound of the women almost drives the neighborhood up the wall. Every time one of the women employers wants to call the police, Hutton says no.

When the employers gather at Hutton's house, they call Vennie out of her name.

"Instigator!"

"Damn holdover from the time when Black women chased lynch mobs and cut Black men down from the hanging trees."

"Troublemaker."

"Worst worker in the lot."

"Now, I know that's not true," Hutton says.

"Just look at them," one employer says. "Henchwomen. Clumping down the grass and trampling the begonias. Hutton, I don't know why you think you have to stand up for the likes of them. Now look at that sign, one of them wants to be called *Miss* Peppermill."

"Why not ask Vennie in. Let's talk to her," one of the employers says. "Maybe we can just buy her off and the others will get back in line."

"Good idea! Yeah."

"Yes, a bribe. Let's do it."

"Call Vennie in. At least let's give it a try," one of the others agrees.

Hutton responds, "I say no. As Vennie would say, 'it ain't right.' "

"Well, who's running this show? Them or us? Let's vote on it!"

"You want to vote?" Carver huffs. "Well, here's my vote. I vote to not give Vennie or any of them one red cent more!"

"I agree," another employer grumbles. "Vennie shouldn't be rewarded for causing this mess!"

"Well, I think we ought to try talking to her," another employer says.

"Me too," another agrees.

Someone finally says, "Okay then, let's vote on it."

The vote is forty-six to nineteen in favor of calling Vennie in and trying to buy her off. Of the nineteen, some, like Carver, don't want to give Vennie anything; others agree with Hutton that a bribe is not the right thing to do.

It is with great trepidation that Hutton stands on the steps and calls, "Vennie!"

"Yes," Vennie answers.

"We'd like to see if you'll accept what we've come up with," Hutton says, a nervous tremor in her voice.

Vennie holds up crossed fingers as a sign of hope to her group of cranberry-uniformed soldiers. She walks up the steps ready to address the women in Hutton's house.

But once inside, Vennie's smile soon turns to outraged disbelief. "What! You want me to do what?" she rants.

Her loud lamentation reaches outside and the cleaning women start lining up, feet pointed toward the house.

"Uh-oh," Carver says as she looks out the window at the women. "Now what?"

The cleaning women leave their songs on the sidewalk and start marching up the walkway.

"Uh-the-hell-Oh!" Carver says.

The dark Sisters push their way into the living room. They stand around the walls and glare. "What is it, Vennie?"

"They say they want to pay me double what I been getting. Give me a month's vacation a year. Three coffee breaks . . ."

The day women start cheering. Victory so soon.

Vennie raises one hand to silence them. "But," she continues, ". . . that's only if I tell you to call the strike off and go on back to work. Nothing in it for you. Same old wages. Same old conditions."

Maggie Peppermill props her hands on her hips. "Who said that? Who said it?" Her rising voice sounds like somebody dangerous, ready to strike.

"I think," says Hutton, "that we owe Vennie and all these women an apology."

"Yeah," the day women answer as one voice.

A few of the employers look shame-faced, but most just look disappointed their ploy didn't work.

"We've had enough excitement for one day," Hutton says. "Why not do this in an organized manner and meet every day until we reach a fair agreement?"

"Organized, um-hmm even the union can understand that," Vennie says.

Peppermill, along with the rest of the eleven, chorus, "Um-hmm!"

Beginning the next morning, the cleaning women take up their daily sentry. Each workday, instead of going to their employers' houses, the day women meet, march, and sing outside Hutton's home. Inside the house, along about nine A.M., the employers gather. They stay until late afternoon.

Now and then between choruses of "Got on My Traveling Shoes," the striking women hear loud shrieks and arguments coming from inside the house. Other times it is so quiet they wonder if the women inside have stopped talking and are staring at their parading backs.

Finally, one afternoon along about four o'clock, a couple of weeks after the vigil began, Hutton sticks her head out the front door and announces, "Ready, Vennie."

"Come on, women."

The twelve march up the steps singing. Inside, the two factions eye each other warily.

"We've studied your demands, and after much deliberation," Hutton says, "here's what we propose: A twenty-percent increase in wages. Two weeks' paid vacation per year. Fifteen-minute coffee breaks, one in the morning, one in the afternoon. One hour for lunch. Disability, pension, and hospitalization benefits."

Some of the employers' faces still flush red from arguing and they grumble at the announcement of each concession as though they are being stolen from.

Vennie looks back at her group to read their faces.

"We'll let you know."

Vennie and the colored women gather in a corner of the room to discuss the proposal.

"Sounds right," Vennie says.

The group is satisfied with the proposal, but they keep their voices low.

After a few minutes, Vennie speaks in her most powerful voice. "We believe your offer is fair. But please understand that if we accept it, we cannot turn back."

Carver swallows hard and winces.

Vennie looks at Carver and remembers what Abyssinia Jackson told her: "You can't pull the covers off anybody without revealing some of yourself." She realizes just as she is a negative of Carver, so too Carver is a negative of her. One reflecting light. The other absorbing it.

Vennie hopes that one day the negative will develop into a black and white photograph, an artistic balance of both colors.

The room is filled with women frowning, smiling, pouting, grinning, and gritting their teeth, staring silently at one another.

Are they reaching to soften, to shade the grays between them into the subtle artistry of good conscience? Are they fugitives from stagnant old photographs, groping for new movement, new light?

Vennie and Carver stare at each other under their eyelashes, glimmers of compassion leaping and fighting for the light between them.

Then Vennie turns around to acknowledge the eleven domestics standing behind her. She studies this band of going-on-anyhow women, their glowing faces registering their victory. They dared take the first step, they had asked for, and gotten, what they wanted. Saying with their eyes that they knew the message of the music long before Abyssinia ever sang it.

As they walk down the steps singing "Got on My Traveling Shoes," the lyrics live anew, and Vennie steps spry, as spry as she once did on Saturday nights.

She is light on her feet.

When Vennie leads the parade of women the last few steps down Loganberry Road before reaching her own gate, her toes itch. And she . . . she feels . . . she feels like dancing.

One chilly Sunday morning, Zenobia turns the radio on to the colored station that plays gospel.

Shirley Caesar is singing full throttle "You Must Be Born Again":

> *You got to be*
> *You must be born again!*

Then segues into "Yes, Lord, Yes":

> *When your spirit speaks to me*
> *With my whole heart I'll agree*
> *And my answer will be Yes, Lord, Yes*

She is so engrossed in the compelling rhythms, she pays no attention to Norman as the music of the gospel stars Shirley Caesar, James Cleveland, and the Jackson Southernaires tear through the house in one blessed hour of undiluted gospel.

Norman sits in the living room, feeling left out, his dog, Fetch, watching him while he watches Zenobia.

Norman wants to experience what she is feeling when she pats her feet uncontrollably to the driving beat of the gospel sound.

And his yearning grows.

After several Sundays of radio gospel, he can no longer contain his desire to understand. "Zenobia, when are you going to take me to church to hear some live gospel?" he asks with Fetch wagging his tail at Norman's feet.

"Oh, Norman, I don't know," she says, uncertain as to how he would fit in at the church.

She glances over at him sitting in his chair and she is torn. She doesn't want to leave him, not even on Sunday. The radio is her compromise. She wants to sit in a church house full of her own kind, appreciate the music and not have to explain it like you would translate a language for a foreigner. Be too busy beating the tambourine to interpret. She prefers her gospel music undisturbed and undiluted.

Every Sunday he presses her about it, this time right after the radio program plays Aretha Franklin singing "Amazing Grace" as the closing number.

"Zenobia, when will you take me to your church?"

"Maybe soon."

He goes to the local library to look for some books on Black gospel music, but is surprised to find there aren't any that tell him what he needs to know. Plenty, though, on spirituals.

"What's the difference between gospel and spirituals, Zenobia?"

Zenobia flinches.

"Does the gospel go like this?" he asks, and he starts singing, strained and off-key, "*Go down, Moses, way down in Egypt's land, tell ol' Pharaoh,*" and she wants to hit him. His singing voice is as irritating to her as fingernails scraping across a chalkboard.

"No, that ain't it," she says, exasperated.

The next Sunday, right after Clara Ward rounds out the gospel radio program, he tries again.

"Does the gospel go like this?" he asks, and he starts singing. With one foot hopping up and down on the bottom rung of his stool, trying to keep time, his drawling voice whines, *"Take me to the water, take me to the water, take me to the water, to be baptized."*

This time, even Fetch can't take it. He throws his head back and starts howling. Zenobia has to glue herself to her chair to keep from jumping up and whaling on Norman's head. She has to remind herself that Norman fixed her breakfast and served it in bed on her birthday. That he rubs her feet whenever she asks. That he massages her back just the way she likes it when they lay down at night.

But the way he messes with the music, how can she explain? "No. That ain't it," she says weakly.

Before they know it, winter glazes the wind yellow and sheets every surface with ice. The roads must be negotiated with care, for the treachery of ice can be devastating. It is even too cold to walk to the store. A few minutes exposed to the sub-zero temperatures can result in frostbite and even death.

"Hope there's snow tomorrow," Zenobia says as they exchange gifts on Christmas Eve. A red wool scarf and a new set of stainless steel and copper pots and pans for her. A blue plaid flannel shirt and a pair of new snow chains for his truck.

As they lay in bed that night, they bask in the closeness, snuggle in the warmth of quilts, and savor the mesmerizing sound of seasoned wood popping and crackling in the open fireplace.

They spy the fire's glow from the bed when they look into the living room.

In their hurry to turn in that night, they leave the Christmas tree lights blazing. Surrounded by colors and warmth, Zenobia feels more secure than ever, feels generous.

"Let's go to church tomorrow," she says. "Wanna hear some real good gospel music?"

"Gospel?" Norman asks. Dare he hope?

Early Christmas morning, Zenobia pops the turkey in the oven. Then, as she lays out her wardrobe, she tries to prepare Norman for his first visit to her church.

She says, "The people dress up as a sign of respect. They're not showing off. They consider it a low insult to God and to everybody who has to look at them to be setting up in the church house dressed in rags. If that's all they've got, then fine, nobody says a word. But if they've got better, they wear better."

Norman smothers a chuckle. "Poor as they are, come on. I don't believe it. I don't believe a bit of it." He sits on the edge of the bed like a judge, with his dog Fetch grinning up at him as he watches Zenobia fit his dead wife's hat with a pheasant feather sticking out of it on her coppery head.

He continues, "If they really carry on as my friends say . . ."

"What do your friends say?"

"Oh, that Black people reach way back in their closets and find the most striking costumes they can put their hands on."

"Well," Zenobia says, "look at it this way. Maybe they also just like to look good and have a good time."

"In a dance hall maybe. But in a church?"

"Some people have a costume for everything," Zenobia says. She turns and adjusts the hat until it fits at just the right angle.

"I don't know," Norman says. "If they carry on as my friends claim, what they buy uptown in the Ponca City Department Store won't do. The costumes won't be enough for what they have to do in them. I want to know what's really behind this gospel music."

They leave out the door in a hurry to jump in the truck so they can be at the service before it gets started.

As the truck bumps and jostles along, Norman says, "I hear the service starts out real slow, and then it gets real lively."

"What's that mean?" Zenobia asks.

"It means, I think, that colored people don't warm up, they just turn the record over."

"So?"

"So I want to be there when they turn the record over."

"There's a name for that," she says.

"What?"

"It's called shouting."

As rain sings against the windshield, the truck fairly flies over the road. Only Norman's new snow chains save them from sliding into a ditch.

They enter the church in a rush.

Everywhere Norman looks, he sees ebony and brown bodies, in all shades, glistening in cloth colors and patterns that nobody he knows would wear to a church service.

In the solemn church of his youth, the worshippers wore black as though in perpetual mourning. He looks at Zenobia, wearing the brightest thing she could find in the closet. He decides if you are black maybe you don't have to wear the color.

*Maybe I'll soon find out all I want to know about gospel,* Norman thinks wistfully as he looks around at the congregation.

He sees the members dressed in their finest, from the men's highly polished shoes to the women's gay assortment of fur, flower, and feather hats. Zenobia's pheasant feather hat that once belonged to Norman's late wife towers above the other headpieces.

The Christmas worshippers shrug off their heavy winter coats. Ushers robed in splendid white uniforms with bottles of smelling salts tucked in their pockets stand by the altar. Deacons strut and patrol the aisles in three-piece charcoal suits and raisin-red ties. People sit squeezed in the pews, shoulder to shoulder.

Pearline, sitting up in the choir, takes in the sight of Zenobia with Norman. She hunches up to the singer next to her and whispers, "Now ain't that pitiful." She puts her hand to her chin and studies her used-to-be friend.

When the last worshipper tips in with one finger held in the air, the gathering has assembled completely, and they begin to sing an old-time congregational number. Slow. But already Norman feels the tension. The curtain on this great drama of gospel is about to rise, and his Zenobia of the pheasant feather hat has brought him here to share this fabulous experience. The singing starts a cappella:

> *It's a highway to heaven*
> *None can walk up there*
> *But the pure in heart*
> *It's a highway to heaven*
> *I'm walking up the king's highway . . .*

The head musician bounces up to the organ. Adds a new dimension to the song:

> *It's a highway to heaven*
> *None can walk up there*
> *But the pure in heart . . .*

The organist plays with the most expansive, friendly smile Norman has ever seen.

"Who's that?" Norman whispers.

"Roosevelt Tate, the choir director."

Roosevelt is short, as though his height is compressed in order to keep his considerable musical talents in a tight space. He swoops down and tickles the keys on the Hammond organ just as the minister approaches the pulpit to welcome the guests.

"Before we ask all visitors to speak, we'd like to welcome back Sister Zenobia Butterfield. Brother Roosevelt Tate, would you do us the honors by singing the Welcome Song?"

Roosevelt begins,

> *You ain't never been welcome,*

The choir answers, except for Pearline,

> *'Til you've . . . been welcomed by God.*

Roosevelt Tate sings,

> *You walk in a place, you're no longer alone.*
> *No strangers*
> *You're safe back home. Now look all around you.*
> *You'll see He's there*
> *Waiting to welcome you*
> *To show how He cares*
> *Because you ain't never been welcome*

Roosevelt Tate's fingers tremble with precision as he intones,

> *'Til you . . . been welcomed by God.*
> *'Til you've . . . been welcomed by God.*

Even though it is cold outside, Zenobia feels the warmth

from springtime stir her soul and warm her blood. She feels at home among friends.

"Will all visitors please rise?" the pastor announces after the singers sit back down in the choir stand.

Norman is one of several newcomers who stand up from the pews. He nervously runs his fingers through his thinning straight hair and waits his turn.

"Your name?" the minister asks when he reaches Norman's row.

"Norman Miller, visiting with Zenobia Butterfield."

"Praise the Lord," the preacher exclaims and the congregation, remembering the gossip they have heard, smiles behind Bibles and tambourines.

Norman sits back down feeling like a fifth wheel, feeling like a stranger. For the first time in his life, he is in the minority. A surge of stage fright overcomes him as he looks around at the sea of dark faces glancing at him. As though to protect himself from searching eyes, he folds his arms in front of him.

He watches Zenobia to see what will happen next. Everybody, it seems, knows the order of service but him.

The preacher speaks a while, misquoting the Bible as Norman knows it: Jesus has wooly black hair and thick lips. "Who else," the preacher asks, "gets turned away more often than a dark child?"

"Amen," the congregation cries.

Then the order of service changes.

When a singer stands up in the choir loft, Norman studies her black cashmere hair, the golden dress with a high collar. She whispers in a musical voice,

> Some sacred child,
> Stopped in the world a while

*One cold and chilly*
*Crystal morning,*

The church, as one body, sings out,

*What did He give*
*That we might live?*

The singer answers,

*He gave mercy,*

The church sings,

*So deep,*

The singer,

*He gave grace,*

The church,

*So sweet,*

"*He gave,*" then she sings long and low, "*charity.*"
The church fairly shouts,

*He gave it all to you and me!*

And the choir members whip the tambourines with a dedicated delight.

*He gave mercy (So deep)*
*He gave grace (So sweet)*
*He gave charity*
*He gave it all to you and me!*

Norman is amazed. This is like no Christmas carol he has ever heard before. The singer's voice dips and flies.

*Who is she?* Every time she opens her mouth, light bounces.

"Dr. Abyssinia Jackson," Zenobia whispers as though reading his mind.

He stares, mouth open. The singer's message is so woven with enchantment and power that the notes of her voice touch him, ease their way inside his mind, and play upon his emotions like Roosevelt Tate plays upon that organ.

*Dr. Jackson*, thinks Norman, *isn't she the one Zenobia makes all those appointments with to see about dizziness and high blood pressure and never keeps?*

*Mercy (So deep)*
*Grace (So sweet)*
*Charity*
*All for you and me!*

The tambourines jangle off the hips of the women. The drummer continues driving the rhythm as though a great fire shut up in his bones hesitates, then springs down through his powerful hands to his wooden drumsticks.

All around Norman sound bounces off the church house walls, and the light from the spectacle of people keeps up with the music. Although it is cold outside, inside the church the temperature has zoomed to one hundred degrees.

Suddenly, his own Zenobia startles him. Something he can't

see shakes her like a loose rag, and she is tumbling down the aisles of ecstasy, her feet spinning under her, the hat almost swallowing her eyes as it jiggles on her head.

An unchained reaction. Some draw up their shoulders, while others tattoo the floor with high heels. Heads weave back and forth. Arms box with invisible worries. In this corner. That corner. In front of him. Behind him. They swoon and dance until sometimes their sleek shoes fly right off their feet, and their glorious feathered, flowered, and fur hats slide off their heads.

One woman speaks in an unknown tongue, and the power of the secret language flies her spirit up to God with such speed and her body down to the thrashing floor with such force only the usher's smelling salts can bring her back around.

Norman wishes he could join them, but he doesn't yet know how to physically express that infectious joy.

He is mesmerized by the circus of jubilation exploding around him. What had Zenobia called it? Shouting. People who through the week stand in the unemployment lines, in other people's kitchens, in the social security offices, on the construction crews, in barbershops, in classrooms and courthouses, all are being released because of the doctor up there singing in the choir. All. Let go from poverty, arthritis, prejudice, rheumatism, lower backache, and high blood pressure. Why, Zenobia is moving as if she never had a dizzy spell in her life.

Exalting the name of Jesus, people cry out their hallelujahs. Norman's head aches from the building pressure, needing release, needing to understand. *What does it all mean?*

All around him, the congregation lift their voices and arms to heaven. Then some Abyssinia note straight out of paradise propels him up from his perch on the edge of his seat, ungluing him from the pew.

He claps so loud, he claps the dancing Zenobia on out of

the aisle and back into their pew. But Zenobia, shaking beside him, is still lost in the music. She is so into the shout that she takes no notice of him.

Abyssinia Jackson sits down, her carol ended. Yet the drummer drums on. Roosevelt Tate coaxes musical thunder, slow and growling, from the organ, and the people are satisfied to do what they have come to do; be released without bond.

After a little while, Dr. Jackson, still aglow from singing the first Christmas song, stands up in the choir loft to sing again. The congregation waves her on with their outstretched hands looking like so many gold, tan, and dark brown flags.

*If anybody knows the mystery of gospel, she does*, thinks Norman. That doctor there with the passionate gospel voice, unparalleled and undiluted. That singer in her golden dress, with the collar loose, that lithe figure, that hand extended toward Heaven as she hits a low note.

After what seems like a long and exalting time, the service comes to an end. Zenobia stands up to take part in the benediction and Norman follows her lead. They use no clocks; he is the only one who doesn't know the order of service. He does, however, recognize the benediction as the minister intones,

> "May the good Lord bless thee and keep thee
> While we're absent one from another
> May His face smile down upon thee
> And give thee peace
> Until we meet again
> Amen."

After the doxology, which signals the end of the service, the congregation stands, turns to each other, and says, "God bless you."

Dr. Abyssinia Jackson, who sang such stirring and hushing Christmas carols, is shaking hands with worshippers. Norman will shake her hand too, he thinks, and then he will ask her where this gospel comes from.

He walks with Zenobia down the aisle toward Dr. Jackson, radiant in her smile and her golden dress.

"Zenobia," Dr. Jackson says, "we miss your voice in the choir. Look to see you soon. By the way, I expect you to keep that next appointment."

Before Zenobia can answer, Norman interrupts, "Hello, my name is Norman . . ."

"Mr. Miller, a pleasure to have you with us this Christmas morning. Do come again."

Norman says, "I wonder if I might ask you about gospel . . ."

"You're welcome," Dr. Jackson gently interrupts before Norman can finish his sentence. "And Merry Christmas to you. Merry Christmas," she says, and turns to the next well-wisher.

Norman stands there for a long moment tangled up in his question, watching Dr. Jackson greet the many church members.

After awhile, he feels Zenobia touching his arm.

With knitted brow, he wonders what these people know that he doesn't. These people who sometimes leave S's off words and add them where they don't belong, who wear bright colors to worship, who go tumbling down the church aisles of ecstasy, or who get the facts of the Bible mixed up.

Self-consciously, Norman looks around and realizes that everyone, and no one, is paying any special attention to him.

"Come on, Zenobia," he says as if he is talking to his dog, Fetch.

"Who you talking to?" she asks looking around.

Norman and Zenobia leave the church, the two of them

leaning into the driving rain. They climb into the pickup and he drives silently along the icy-wet slick road.

"There's a snow flake," she says. The first white feathers of snow sift down out of the clouds and tremble to rest briefly on the windshield. "Good thing you got a new set of snow chains. Gonna have us a white Christmas after all!"

Norman doesn't answer. Something is still bothering him. He realizes he experienced something special happening inside that church, and he wants to put that experience in a place in his mind where he can study it, examine it, understand it. But how? He doesn't realize that so much of understanding gospel is in the feeling. And he has felt it, but he doesn't know that he knows what he knows.

"Did you hear me?" Zenobia asks.

He still doesn't answer. Why should he answer, when he doesn't get any answers?

His lips, clamped tight together like a vise, remind Zenobia of his dog, Fetch.

She starts laughing. The gales of laughter start in her toes, burst out through her fingers and her chest, wiggle behind her eyes, and make her feel almost like good gospel music does on Sunday mornings.

"Christ," he finally says in a frustrated voice when her giggles careen out of control.

Eventually, her giggles turn to intermittent snickers. They stop completely when she looks out and sees the flying snow whipping against the windshield.

*Was it snowing this hard when Christ was born?* Zenobia wonders as her mood turns more somber.

Now the snow is falling so heavily she can barely see out the window. This snow rages as it whips through the air, and she becomes worried and a little scared.

She gets quiet enough to match Norman's stillness.

Thank God they are turning into the driveway. Home, safe and sound.

Fetch doesn't run out to greet them. They left him in the house, where Norman had given him the command to stay.

The front window shines, sparking with color from the Christmas lights.

Norman steps down and slams the truck door shut behind him. He walks on ahead of Zenobia.

She takes her time getting down into the snow.

She hears the front door of the house slam closed.

*He's keeping out the cold,* she thinks.

Cold snowflakes drip off the pheasant feather onto her face, causing her to shiver. *Warm soon.* She reaches the front door.

Anticipating the warmth and aroma of the house, she slips a gloved hand over the doorknob and turns. Nothing happens. Door's stuck. She pushes harder. The door doesn't budge. He probably accidentally turned the lock.

"Norman!" she calls, but the sound of the rising wind muffles her voice. Even to her own ears she sounds far, far away.

*He's in there sitting up on his stool.*

She starts around to the back. The cold wind howls and coughs the snow out of the sky faster and faster. Out of the corner of her eye she sees the Christmas tree lights blinking off and on. Then even the lights are snow-blind.

She doesn't know she spends five minutes getting around to the back of the house. The wind wails and the snow falls faster, blizzarding around her, and the temperature dips to forty-five degrees below zero. She feels no panic. She feels no pain. The numbing cold sends a hospitable heat coursing through her veins. Lit up like a bright Christmas tree, warm bulbs in her fingers, in her toes, in her hair under the pheasant hat.

Wonderful and warm as she feels when she hums along with a good gospel song.

She reaches the back door, turns the knob. Nothing. Through the window she can see Norman sitting on his stool close enough to heed her, for she can hear the dog whining low. Norman is looking right at her, and the dog is looking at him. She tries the door again, but it won't budge. "Locked" echoes in her brain.

That's when her knees buckle and she starts sliding off the icy porch.

*On purpose. He did it on purpose!*

Left her out in the snow to . . .

As she slides, she thinks about the shovel propped up next to the front door. Could pick it up, bust the window open. Be inside by now. Be in the middle of fighting, in the middle of raking him with the shovel the way she rakes hot coals in the fireplace.

"Straw-haired, dead-eyed dirty man with a raggedy dog! Dog sitting looking at him!"

She lets loose a terrible rage.

"You pitiful White men ain't nothing but niggers in the woodpile! And you White women! Faded Aunt Jemimas! Black men: shameless hussies. Broomstick witches!"

She is so drowsy from the bitter cold that she sounds drunk.

"Oh hell, I'm free!"

And she is sliding free. Free to tell the truth to nobody but herself.

"Forget 'em! Forget 'em all!"

The words of the playful little white girl tumble through her mind, like music in a dangerous movie, and she voices it:

"Which would you rather be, Millie, a nigger or a dog?"

She slides laughing the way only Zenobia can. She lands in

the delicious warmth of the featherbed snow, away from the back door. Nothing to worry about anymore. She is with Pearline climbing pecan trees in fall, running home runs in spring, eating sausage biscuits in summer, and, best of all, returning the supportive hugs of Black women. Hugs that warm her through and through with a single touch in winter. The icy arms of the snow thaw and become the warm, tender, binding arms of the dark women of mercy. Of the sisters. True friends. Somebodies. Somebodies who answer when you call.

Too many precious minutes pass before Norman moves from his stool after he hears, "Open the door," the plea sounding like a dog begging in the snow.

The clock has moved what, five minutes? Ten? Fifteen?

*Some sacred child stopped in the world awhile,*

He smells all the wonderful aromas of Christmas desserts. The sweet potato pies. Pound cake. Apple cobbler.

On the shelf, Norman spies Dr. Jackson's name on several cards. Zenobia placed them there and neglected to keep the appointments dated from as far back as a few months. Zenobia. Way back in his head, Norman hears Abyssinia's song,

*One cold and chilly crystal morning,*

He hears those lyrics just as clear and distinct as if he still sits transfixed in the church house while colorfully clad worshippers and the pheasant-hatted Zenobia spin around him in the shouting dance.

*Snow dressed the holy ground . . .*

*Snow,* he thinks as he quickly picks up one of the appointment cards with the address of the House of Light on it. Appointment date December 8, and here it is Christmas, two and a half weeks later.

*Snow dressed the holy ground . . .*

That one lilting line stays with him, lingers in his mind, touches the back of his throat, and unclogs his ears. Through the passionate notes he can hear the snow falling, falling. Something white and delicate laying itself open to molasses scalding the snow.

"Fetch, would you shut up?" Norman hollers.

He walks over and tries to silence the whining dog, who is looking out into the backyard and pawing so desperately at the window he leaves claw streaks, like skid marks, on the glass.

"Fetch, let me get you some food."

Even the mention of food doesn't quiet him.

The pungent aroma of celery and sage cornbread stuffing for the turkey drifts from a slow oven set to bake way before Zenobia put on her pheasant hat and they started out for church. Norman's eyes sweep the kitchen and linger on the spice cabinet chock full of cinnamon, nutmeg, filé, dill weed, and cayenne pepper.

Something Zenobia said about the spice rack sends Norman racing for the back door, "Salt and pepper looking like two orphans sitting up in your spice box."

*Snow dressed the holy ground.*

He unlocks the bolt, grabs the knob, and flings the back door open.

*Snow . . .*

Outside Fetch races ahead.

*. . . dressed . . .*

The cold air bursts like fire into Norman's lungs as he runs
to where Fetch has found her.

*. . . the holy ground . . .*

Norman picks up Zenobia's unconscious body. Her pheasant
hat falls to the side and lies on the ground looking like a bird
trapped in the snow in the dead of winter. As he carries her to
the truck, he thinks he can hear the song beckoning him.

*Mercy (so deep)*

And the snow is deep.

The truck looks like a phantom, it is so covered with snow.
The wind ghosts all around the windshield, the tires. Norman
lays Zenobia on the passenger's side and holds her with one hand
as he carefully backs the pickup through the snow out of the
isolated driveway.

The Fetch dog whines softly near the truck door.

"Get in the house, dog!" he yells from the truck window.
"You want to freeze to death?!"

The yelping dog high-tails it, loping around to the back
door. Can't stand to be yelled at. Might as well've hit him with
a brick.

As Norman speeds down Loganberry Road, it seems that the
carol swells imperceptibly until it nests in his head.

*Grace (so sweet).*


Zenobia begins falling off the seat. He can't hold her up and drive too, because the driving conditions are so treacherous. She slides on down to the floor.


Charity


The light from the pickup falls on the snow and shivers.


*All for you and me*


He hopes against hope that Dr. Jackson can save Zenobia. Sweet Zenobia, who makes the bed rock on Saturday mornings, who makes the oven talk on Christmas day.

In his panic, he sees the snow ghost illuminating the way and guiding the truck down Loganberry Road.

"She's all I got and that's a lot," he says, pushing the gas pedal almost to the floorboard.

The truck whistles with dangerous speed and at last skids to a stop in front of the house twinkling with the glow from a Christmas tree visible through the downstairs window.

At the front door, decorated with an evergreen wreath, he leans on the emergency bell.

"Dr. Jackson," he gasps.

When Carl Lee opens the door, he sees Norman holding Zenobia in his arms.

Norman yelps, "I swear I didn't hit her. Didn't touch a hair on her head."

•   •   •

*Charity!*

"Oh my God! Abyssinia! Come quick!" Carl Lee's voice reaches way back in the residential part of the House of Light and Abyssinia sprints to the medical wing.

She looks down on the almost-frozen Zenobia Butterfield. "Take her to the treatment room!"

The storm gathers full power. The wind whistles the snow against the windowpane and the blizzard rages, whipping the electrical wires back and forth against the trees.

Above the treatment table, the lights tremble and snatch at the dark.

"Hook up the machines," Abyssinia says.

Swiftly Carl Lee hooks up the power to the oxygen and heart machines. The equipment starts, stutters, and then suddenly stops.

Abyssinia looks up at the dead spot where the overhanging lamp should be alive.

"Oh, God, why now?" Abyssinia whispers.

"I'll get the candles," Carl Lee says.

"Hurry!"

"Got 'em." Carl Lee places two candles near the table.

"I need more light!"

With her bare fists, Abyssinia starts pounding Zenobia's chest.

Carl Lee finds more candles, lights them, and places them along the windowsill. He stands behind Abyssinia as she works, then he kneels down and prays.

Abyssinia continues working in the dark, pounding at Zenobia's chest, just over the heart. Perspiration pours down her face.

Abyssinia starts to sing the song she sang just that morning in church.

"*Some sacred child stopped in the world awhile,*" a cappella and deep.

Abyssinia's hands become numb from the cold and the constant pounding. She pounds harder.

". . . *One cold and chilly crystal morning,*" Carl Lee sings.

She drums so intently on Zenobia's chest that she moves into a trance of healing, oblivious to everything and everyone except Zenobia.

> *Snow dressed the holy ground*
> *In that most holy town,*

Carl Lee's bass voice continues.

Abby thinks she feels a heartbeat, but she's not sure, so she keeps drumming.

> *. . . where the holy child was borning.*

Has Zenobia's chest swelled, or is Abyssinia just wishing it has?

> *Came to save, came and gave, all we need this Christmas morning.*

"Is that a heartbeat? We need you Zenobia."

Abyssinia stops and leans her head over Zenobia's chest, listens, then softly sings, "*Mercy.*"

"*So deep,*" sings Carl Lee.

And Zenobia moans.

Abyssinia insists, *"Grace."*

Carl Lee, *"So sweet."*

Suddenly, the electricity comes back on and it is as though six angels holding candles stand around the treatment table.

Zenobia's eyes flutter open on the singing light.

*"Charity!"* Abyssinia's voice colors, dips, and sighs, then soars and flies so softly it is almost muted.

Light floods the room. Abyssinia grasps Carl Lee's hand and they look at each other.

A glow wraps Zenobia's body in an envelope of light. It spreads upward and a halo surrounds her head.

Abyssinia leans forward, wraps her arms around Zenobia's shoulders, and softly says, "You are our gift. Reborn this Christmas Day. A light in a storm, striding into the afternoon of your life."

Norman stands poised on the edge of himself. Face to face with an undiluted element of strangeness.

"Let's keep her warm," Abyssinia says to Carl Lee and Norman.

Abyssinia begins rubbing Zenobia's legs and feet to keep the blood flowing. Carl Lee rubs Zenobia's left arm and hand.

Wanting to help, Norman touches Zenobia's other arm too unsurely.

The snowy forty-five-below-zero look in Zenobia's eyes kicks him clear across the room.

"Zenobia?" Norman calls.

"Get away . . ." Zenobia murmurs.

"Please, Zenobia."

"Get away."

"Zenobia, I just want to say . . ."

"Get away," Zenobia chants weakly.

"Please," whispers Norman.

"Save your strength," Abyssinia says to Zenobia.

Zenobia lifts her head slightly from the table and looks Norman in the eye.

"Get away. You're standing in my light."

Norman slinks away from the House of Light, his head hanging down, looking like his dog, Fetch.

Abyssinia picks up the telephone and calls Pearline from the House of Light. "Pearline, there's somebody here I need you to talk to."

"Who, Dr. Jackson?"

"Zenobia."

Quiet lasts for a while on the other end.

"Pearline?"

"What's this about, Dr. Jackson?"

"It's an emergency."

"Emergency?"

"Zenobia almost died."

"Died?"

"And she needs a safe place to stay for a while."

"Zenobia needs me?"

" 'Fraid so."

"I got to see this. I'll be right on!"

"Curiosity will kick-start an awkward situation every time," Abyssinia says to Carl Lee.

"So she's coming?"

"Yes."

When Pearline takes Zenobia home, it is her time to stand up and be a good friend.

"When I came to visit you from Oklahoma City, I was running from some horrible man!" Zenobia explains.

"Who?"

"Nightclub owner."

"What did he do?"

"Just acted stupid. Didn't want me to leave. So I knocked him out."

"Good for you."

"I needed a time of respite. R and R. Rest and recreation. So I came to you, my best friend."

"You needed space. And you came to me to get it?"

"Sanctuary."

"Well I'll be."

"Even so-called strong women need a shoulder from time to time. I ain't made of steel. Contrary to what most folks think."

"Dr. Jackson said you almost died."

"Another fool tried to kill me."

"The one with you in church?"

"The very same."

"I'll be damned!"

"What did you do to him?"

"At the time? Nothing. I was out like a light. He made sure I couldn't help myself."

"When you get better, we're gonna find him and kick Mr. Little Dick's little white ass all over Ponca City. The nerve!"

"Got nerve all right. Trying to make up to me right after he messed up!"

"Where'll we find him?"

"Oh, forget his simple ass. I need to rest. I have already shut him out of my mind."

The way she says "I have shut him out of my mind," Pearline knows that this fool will not be given a second chance. Not at least by Zenobia. Isn't gonna be no Isaiah-scenario, no woman tail whipping, female badgering from day to day. Not even from hour to hour. Zenobia is short-suffering.

"Good!" Pearline says after she digests all this. "I'll cook something real special." And she goes into the kitchen and starts rattling the pots and pans.

I*saiah* sits on the edge of his bed with his head in his hands.

"Oh, Pearline," he moans.

"Why did you leave me? Why did you do this to me?"

In his mind, the trouble started when she reached twenty-three.

"Don't you want a baby?" she had asked.

"A baby?" he said. "Why, I think the two of us just doing fine."

Every month she asked, and every month he said no.

The ghost of his father rears up in his mind and scrambles his brain cells. No, he doesn't want a son. A daughter either, for that matter. He doesn't want his wife fondling over anybody except him, even if his own blood does run in the child's veins.

Then Pearline stopped asking, and that's when Isaiah's suspicions cropped up. Full-grown, ugly, giant monsters.

"She went and asked somebody else about having a baby." Even as he mumbled, he tried to convince himself this lie was the truth.

His fears escalated into jealous rages. He used the tricks as old as time that jealous mates often employed: suspicion, surveillance, accusation, and absurd shenanigans.

"Ain't no man getting away with sticking his finger in my

eye." Before he left to go to his job at Conoco, he took the time to sweep around the house with a broom to catch the footprints of sexual predators.

"No, you can't come over here. I'll see you at the bar," he told his men friends on the telephone. Might be looking at Pearline!

Once he turned his heat off in the winter so Pearline couldn't take a warm bath and beautify her body. Irrational. Ignorant. At cross-purposes with happiness.

Isaiah spent more and more time away from Pearline, scandalizing the barbershop gossip committee with back-road women who wanted to see if he was really as big as he seemed, who swooned as they felt his muscles and flashed their eyes at his big feet and his height.

Pearline believed she was at fault, that she had failed, that somehow she was the cause of his abusive verbal behavior and his wanton acts of adultery.

When Pearline was completely beaten down emotionally, Isaiah started whipping her physically.

Something strange happened to Isaiah when he hit Pearline and she cried. He remembered his own beatings.

When he knocked Pearline around, his own eyes reflected the same vacuous, stony expression of his father's face. This trick of memory was an outrage that only infuriated him more. Half of him wanted to quit hitting her; the other half wanted to continue bruising her until no other man would look at her and feel the warm blood rush through his loins.

After Isaiah finished pounding Pearline, his head would ache.

The snapping pains crushed him down. Finally pulling him to the ground when Pearline filed for divorce. Pulled by the restraining orders of the court and the community.

Despite his actions to the contrary, Isaiah thinks that he really loves Pearline. He didn't want their marriage to end. He wanted the marriage to get better. He wants to get better. But he doesn't know how to rid himself of his violent ways.

He hoped the divorce wouldn't go through, hoped that Pearline would change her mind, that somehow he would win her again and make things right between them.

But the divorce did go through. And as the agonizing headaches once again torment him, he desperately wants to strangle Pearline. To keep himself from running out and choking her, he slams the bolt to his bedroom door from the inside. He stomps around the room, eyes glazed, punching the walls, pounding the top of his dresser. "Goddamn it!" he curses. "Damn it to hell!"

Beside Isaiah's bed sits a small nightstand, upon which rests a reading lamp, an alarm clock, and the Bible that holds their wedding date and other family history.

He kicks the nightstand, sending the lamp smashing to the hardwood floor. The clock rattles to a corner of the room. The Bible drops at Isaiah's feet, its pages flying open.

Isaiah becomes lightheaded, his mind swimming furiously, fighting to remain afloat in a river raging with currents of conflicting emotions. *Kill her! No, don't kill her . . . Kill her! No!* The voices taunt him. On the last "Kill her!" Isaiah drops to his knees at the edge of the bed. For several minutes he remains on the floor, hands resting on his knees, eyes closed, head bowed, gasping.

When his breathing begins to return to normal, he opens his eyes, tilts his head up slightly, and looks around at the havoc he has wreaked. "God help me!" he moans.

As he prepares to pick up the pieces of the shattered lamp, his gaze falls upon the Bible resting open at his feet. He lifts the book from the floor and stands up to set it back on the nightstand. As he places the Bible on the little table and begins to move away, he glances at its open pages: Exodus. The chapter of Exodus. The twentieth chapter of Exodus. His gaze falls to the thirteenth verse: "Thou shalt not kill."

The words cause Isaiah to pause as he teeters. Out of the whirlwind, the words are delivered to him.

The headaches, even fiercer than before, have again ravaged him with their unbearable intensity. He had succumbed to their wishes in the past, he had done their ugly bidding, but he knows they have succeeded only in mocking the power of his own will. He is determined not to obey their evil demands any longer. He is determined not to become his father.

This time, this battle, he has not gone out and killed Pearline. He has summoned the strength to fight back the demons. But, as strong as Isaiah is, this is one war he knows he can't win alone. He needs the help of another kind of strength.

Something tells him to make an appointment with Dr. Abyssinia Jackson.

At the kitchen table, Abyssinia hands Carl Lee the sports section of the newspaper.

"What's to become of this team?" Carl Lee asks.

"Sometimes they win. Sometimes they lose." Abyssinia shrugs.

"Even champions . . ."

". . . have bad days," Abyssinia finishes.

"I'm looking forward to my own little champ," says Carl Lee.

"Me too."

"Thank goodness for modern medicine."

"Sometimes medicine has no answers."

Carl Lee puts the paper down.

It has been a good while since Abyssinia started taking fertility pills.

"Don't think they're going to work," she says.

"Well, we have other options."

"I know."

"Adoption."

"You're right. Plenty babies need homes."

"Plenty babies need good parents."

"And we'd make good parents."

"Yes, we would," Carl Lee says. "Boy or girl?"

"A boy for you?" Abby asks.

"A girl for you," Carl Lee concedes.

"Or both," they say in unison.

"It's decided then?"

She nods.

"When do we call the agency?"

"Could we wait a few days? Something at work's got me worried."

"Even with kids there'll be something at work . . ."

"This is different."

"Want to talk about it?"

"Isaiah."

"Isaiah?"

"The man made an appointment."

"You know I'm Pearline's lawyer and I'm handling her divorce, so I know a little of the problem," he says with sympathy.

"You might have heard about the problem, but I'm the one who saw it," Abyssinia says.

"Full of the devil all right," Carl Lee says, remembering Pearline's complaints.

"Full? That man's brimming over with demons!" Abyssinia says. "The very thought of treating the man guilty of beating up one of my patients . . . It's as though I'd be getting him well the better to abuse Pearline."

"Want me to stop by?"

"No. I can handle him. I'm not afraid. I'm just trying to figure out how to separate the patient from the man. All those years I spent in medical school, were they just so I could end up attending wife beaters?"

"Now, Abyssinia," Carl Lee says. "If I recall correctly, when you were an intern specializing in broken bones, you treated a few men whose wives had fought back. It's just that you didn't know those people the way you know the folks here in Ponca."

"That's not the point, and you know it. Women fighting back? Why that's nothing compared to the damage violent men do to their wives and women friends!"

"You're right," he answers softly.

Abyssinia pauses and remembers. "And I recall you defended one of those women who fought back."

"The mistreatment of women always horrifies me too," Carl Lee says.

"Glad you're not that kind of man."

"There but for the grace of God . . ."

"Don't start! You had a choice and you decided to be a good man."

"Remember when I was public defender and I had to represent men I knew were guilty? Some of them were murderers. Every time I read the charges or saw the prosecutor's bloody evidence, it turned my stomach."

"But imagine how the victim felt."

"Now, that's the bitter pill," Carl Lee says. "Bound by our professions to swallow it."

"Even when it gags us?" Abyssinia wonders aloud.

She is seeing the purple bruises on Pearline, the mangled arm, the black and swollen eye, the strangle marks on the neck.

"I suppose I could refer him across town . . ."

"I suppose . . ." Carl Lee says.

"How can I treat him without remembering, without re-membering . . ."

That night Abyssinia dreams about Isaiah.

*Why should I heal a wife beater*, she wonders.

*You took an oath*, a faint voice replies.

"If I treat him, I bound you I won't sing."

*You took the oath.*

"The way he beat up Pearline, I just don't . . ."

*Gonna let his evil touch you, are you? You the one supposed to do the touching.*

*Wait*, Abyssinia's inner voice says.

*Evil. I can see it hanging 'round your throat trying to jump inside.*

"I didn't start the evil."

*You took the oath.*

"Make him stronger to prey on the weak?" Abyssinia huffs.

*The oath.*

Then the voice changes. "Abyssinia," it calls.

"Mother Beatrice?" she whispers, remembering her mentor's voice from the past.

"Here's his song." Mother Beatrice Barker begins singing the healing words for Isaiah.

"I'm the one supposed to call up his song."

"You need help on this one. Trust me."

"I don't intend to do this," Abyssinia says.

Mother Beatrice Barker keeps talking as though she doesn't hear a thing Abyssinia says. "The song is a secret, the only one who knows the words is you. After you sing it to him, he will forget the lyrics."

"And the tune? Usually they can remember the tune."

"In Isaiah's case, he will forget the tune as well."

"I've never done it that way before. And, anyway, you made mistakes when . . ."

"So you haven't forgotten that once . . ."

"Healing Lily's husband when . . ."

"You haven't forgotten! You haven't forgiven!"

"I see Lily!"

"I had no choice."

"Well, I do!"

"Yes, you do."

"Now I'm the composer and the lyricist! Don't tell me what to sing for the likes of Isaiah!"

"His is a special case. To understand the man you must understand the child inside."

"I understand this: I'm not singing for the likes of him!"

"Sing so he'll forget the words and the tune, Abby."

"I won't. I won't. I won't!" But all the time Abyssinia is saying "I won't," Mother Barker goes back to singing the strange, cruel, beautiful song.

After Mother Barker is certain that Abyssinia knows every word, every turn of the melody, she stops and says, "Sometimes the healing's for the ones the healed will have to someday touch.

"Many's the time when light thrown on ugliness guides us through," Mother Beatrice counsels. Then reciting a lesson she had taught Abyssinia long ago, she adds, "What I said to you as a child, I say to you as a woman, 'Abby, there is no greater joy on earth than the joy of healing'. I don't know about that hippo oath you took . . ."

"Hippocratic oath, Mother Barker."

". . . But let me remind you of the oath you took with me." Mother Barker begins another song that Abby used to sing when she was a young apprentice root worker. In her distant, yet still audible voice, Mother Barker makes the song more distressed, snagging the ragged notes on the words of commitment:

> *When darkness spreads giant hands*
> *Shutting out the sun everywhere*
> *Blotting despair*
> *Horizons of fireflies*
> *Mount the air*
> *Night lanterns of care*
> *Gilding the House of Light*
> *And if you can be healed*
> *I will be here*
> *Morning, noon, and night*
> *A beacon waiting*
> *In the healing House of Light*
>
> *Come on in the house*
> *In the House of Light*
> *Find yourself a healing room*
> *In the House of Light*
> *You will find me waiting there.*

"That is the promise, my Abby, my dear Dr. Abyssinia Jackson, that is the oath you made which shall not be broken!"

"I can't!" Abby objects. "Let me explain . . ."

But the ghost of Mother Barker is already gone.

Abyssinia wakes restless. Restless because sleep had been hard, her argument with Mother Barker taxing.

"I'm an educated doctor now," she whispers. "I can't . . . What am I gonna do? Go around healing the devil?! The man's got to show me something first!"

She throws off the covers, leaps out of bed, and proceeds to pace the floor. "I won't! I won't!"

Something snatches at her mind and she can't remember one musical phrase that Mother Barker had sung.

"The song! Oh, my God, what was it? How did it go? Where?"

"Where what?" Carl Lee asks. He hands Abby her morning cup of broomweed tea.

"I was just thinking about Mother Barker. Can't think about going to church without thinking about her." Abyssinia stirs a generous spoonful of honey into her cup, and then takes a sip.

"Seeing her in church every Sunday made us think everything was gonna be all right."

Carl Lee nods. "Same with you, folks say."

"Maybe I see more than even Mother Barker saw."

"What do you mean?"

"Wonder what she saw when she looked out over the congregation."

"What do you see?"

"All stripes of sinners: Nodding addicts. Pimps and prostitutes
in Sunday-go-to-meeting suits. Red-eyed stumbling drunks, bodies tilted forward, feet running unbraked down the church aisles
as they lurch into the sanctuary. Mean-spirited folks all hunched
down in the pews, demons rubbing shoulders with the living
saints. And wife beaters with manicured hands.

"And now I got to deal with Isaiah. A woman torturer!"

In the medical wing, Abyssinia stitches up Maggie Peppermill's
grandson. Dressed in cut-off jeans, he anxiously swings his legs
back and forth as he tries to sit up bravely on the examination
table.

"How'd you get here?" she asks.

"Grandma brought me."

"Nurse said you fell off your bike."

He nods, turning his head away, a little scared of the blood.

"We can fix this up in no time," she assures him.

He doesn't wince, but sits tight-mouthed against the pain.

"Hey, I was spinning circles!" he boasts.

"First time riding?"

"Uh-huh."

"What color's your bike?" His detailed answer, which includes stripes, handle bars, and wheels, takes his mind off the
procedure. She works quickly before the numbness from the
nurse's shot wears off. When she finishes, he heads for the door,
grinning at his stitches.

"How many stitches you say I got?"

"Fifteen."

"Wait 'til I tell!"

"Now that was why I became a doctor," she murmurs as the patched up youth bops down the hall to join his grandmother.

Abyssinia glances at the framed Hippocratic oath on the wall. *Mother Barker,* she thinks with a smile. Still she can't remember the Isaiah song. "Not that I'd sing it anyway," she mumbles.

Maggie Peppermill is next in line.

"Brave grandboy you got there!"

"He's so brave he liked to scared me to death, spinning on that bike. I can see now why God lets young people have the babies. Just don't have the energy or the nerves when you get this age."

"Your thyroid problems exacerbate the tiredness."

"Whatever you say."

Abyssinia prescribes thyroid tablets for the senior woman's deficient hormones.

"You get old, your body's just like some old car. Soon as you fix one thing, something else breaking down," bemoans Maggie, shaking her graying head. "First you fixed my broken hip. Now you treating my hormones. What you call it again?"

"Hypothyroidism," Abyssinia says.

"Go on with you," she says, delighted at Abyssinia's precise enunciation of the name for her ailment.

When she says good-bye to Maggie Peppermill, Abyssinia still can't remember Isaiah's song.

The song she won't sing.

Then Isaiah is waiting. In the treatment room already. And still no song. She checks his chart. Weight: two hundred and forty pounds. Height: six feet four. Reason for visit: headaches.

"Good afternoon, Mr. Spencer."

As he acknowledges her greeting, she looks him over and makes a cursory medical assessment of his general physical condition. Then on the examination table she checks his reflexes, his eyes, his pulse, and his lungs. No broken bones or visible injuries.

"Would you describe the headaches?" she asks.

"Damn headaches," he grimaces. "Been hacking at me like hatchets."

"How long do they last?"

"Hours. Sometimes all day. They go 'way for a while then come back like an unwanted visitor you send off, then he returns, lifts up your door knocker rapping harder than before."

"Must be pretty ugly?"

"Debilitating."

Debilitating enough to keep him away from Pearline? *Good*, she thinks.

"I see. Where're you from?" she asks.

He tells her, but he thinks no one who lives here on safer ground, on dry red clay dirt higher up the hill, can imagine the muddy Bottoms.

"You ever had a nickname as a child?" she asks.

"Nickname?"

"Or any other name besides Isaiah?"

"I had me another name once. A childhood name. A river name. Cat Fish."

Why waste a magic song with hypnotic, healing words, whatever they are, on the likes of Isaiah? She definitely won't be singing today!

Abyssinia studies Isaiah's chart a while, and then says, "Well, I think we'll start out with a series of CAT scans and blood tests. Then maybe a therapist."

"What kind of therapist?"

"A psychotherapist. A psychiatrist. An expert in mind healing.

There's so much we don't know about the human brain." She hands him the therapist's card.

"So I got some screws loose, Dr. Jackson?"

"I'm not saying that."

"A nut case," Isaiah decides.

"It's just that optimum health more often than not requires working with both the body and the mind."

"Well," Isaiah says, "I don't care what you say. I refuse to see this head doctor."

"The cause of the headaches may be just physical. We'll see what the lab tests and the X rays reveal."

"Guess he thinks he's a mind mechanic!" The card shakes between his nervous fingers.

"One way of putting it."

"So I'm an insane asylum case. A nut."

"Don't worry about what it's called," she says.

"A disgrace."

She doesn't answer.

"Hopeless."

"And you do want the headaches, whatever's causing them, to stop," Abyssinia says.

"That's true," Isaiah said, "but I don't have to go to a psychiatrist to get aspirins."

"And you don't have to come to me for them either," Abyssinia agrees. "But something must be wrong to bring you here."

"Okay," says Isaiah. "You're the doctor."

Isaiah takes the hospital lab test sheets that Abyssinia offers. He reluctantly tucks them and the therapist's card in his pocket.

"Nothing worth attaining is ever easy. This may take a lot of work, a lot of change, Isaiah."

"I'm used to work," Isaiah declares. "Change? I don't know."

•　•　•

"So, you saw your lab test," the therapist, a squeezed-together man in a tight, neutral brown suit, says, as he looks down at his notes.

Isaiah thinks that the therapist, Dr. Jones, kind of blends in with the furniture. *So this is who is going to be tinkering with my mind.*

"Yeah. No sign of brain disease," Isaiah offers.

"And nothing else that might be causing the headaches," Dr. Jones continues.

"That's why I'm here now. Headaches."

"That's part of it."

"Guess you think I'm off my rocker too."

"Who's that talking? You or Dr. Jackson?"

"Me," he admits.

"Why do you think you're here?"

"The devil sent me."

Dr. Jones leans back in his chair and says, "Now don't go back four hundred years and start talking about demons, when sometimes people just need a little medicine."

"Well what's the matter with me then."

"Might be a chemical imbalance."

"Chemical imbalance?"

"Something organically wrong, a chemical imbalance mixed in with all else that might be messing up your mind."

"So there is something else."

"We'll see."

The next week he has another appointment with Dr. Jackson.

"How's your head?" Abyssinia asks.

"A little . . . much better in the morning."

"And are you seeing the therapist?"

"Dr. Jones? Yeah, he listens right good. And I think I can trust him."

"How's that?"

"Something about him. I like the way he talks."

"What do you mean?" she asks.

"Said I might have to be looking up in his face for years. When I said, 'huh?' he said, 'Mind healing can take up all your life. Unless you just wanna let Dr. Jackson lay her holy hands on your head.' "

"What did you say?"

"I said, 'Thick as my head is, she'd have to lay her hands on it longer than all the time in eternity.' "

Abyssinia joins Isaiah in laughing. "Sometimes the truth's funny, even when it hurts."

"That psychiatrist is funny all right, but he thinks there's no such thing as demons."

"Evil does exist, but please do what Dr. Jones prescribes, even if it does take years."

"I will," Isaiah says.

"I'd like to ask you about your diet. Just routine questions. What do you eat?"

He rattles off a list of foods. Restaurant food now, vastly different from the wholesome pots of fish and freshly picked vegetables Pearline used to fix. Since he doesn't have Pearline anymore, he has no home cooking. To Dr. Jackson's question he recites foods heavy in fatty gravies, white starches, and tooth-decaying sweets.

"Let's see, Mr. Spencer, if a change in eating habits helps to make a difference."

She prescribes a list of foods, taking into account his tremendous size and the strenuous work he performs at the oil refinery.

She replaces the white sugar with fresh fruits. She takes away the breakfast of cinnamon rolls and bacon slices, fried potatoes, ham steaks, and coffee. She substitutes baked potatoes with just a small pat of butter, whole wheat bread, a drink blending orange juice, bananas, brewer's yeast, and low-fat milk. She tells him how to prepare fish broiled in lemon juice. And other meats baked until most of their fat is rendered away and left in the bottom of the pan instead of in the bottom of his stomach.

"You didn't mention whether you drink alcohol."

He says, "I drink me some Jack Daniel's sometimes."

"Oh, whiskey."

"Just a little," he fibs.

"You know, I can look at you and tell that like many of us, like many folks in the world, you don't do so well on alcohol. It can be like poison to our systems and to our minds. If I were you, I'd stop drinking and see if that helps."

"You mean I might be allergic to alcohol?" Isaiah asks.

"That's certainly one way of putting it. Please make an appointment for your next visit with Miss Lacy."

On the next visit, Abyssinia continues to question Isaiah.

"Now you say your headaches go away in the morning. Tell me, what do you eat in the morning, and what do you eat the rest of the day?"

He tells her.

He starts off making food changes slowly. Breakfast. Less appetizing, he thinks as he eats the bowls of oatmeal and drinks whole quarts of orange juice.

He feels good until about noon.

He explains all this to Abyssinia at the next appointment.

"Head doesn't hurt until afternoon? Okay, Mr. Spencer,

you'll have to cut out the fried fish lunch, the sweet potato pies, and the red soda water."

Isaiah looks as if she has taken away his last joy.

"Do you want to get rid of the headaches or not?"

"I do."

She wishes he won't follow directions. She wants him to stay disabled, so disabled he can't hurt Pearline.

Working on the diet and following Dr. Jackson's directions keeps him busy, so busy he doesn't have time for such devilment.

He is teaching himself to cook. For lunch he packs the left-over stew made from catfish, carrots, celery, yams, and cabbage seasoned with onions, garlic, and lemon. He remembers that Dr. Jackson said, "Use just a pinch of salt, substitute lemon if you want more flavor."

The next week he reports back. "Head don't ache 'til evening."

"And how's the therapy coming?"

"Good. Got me a little medicine I have to take just before I turn in at night."

"What do you do in the evening?"

"Go home, cook my dinner, then go sit in the bar."

"Are you still drinking?" she asks.

"No. I just like to sit around with the folks."

"Inhaling all that smoke?" Dr. Jackson asks.

He raises one big hand, "Now I don't smoke, so you can't tell me to stop smoking."

"You don't have to smoke to inhale smoke," she says. "If you're in a room where people are smoking, you're breathing more potent tobacco vapors than the ones doing the puffing. Whenever you see smoke, run as if your life depends on it."

"Now I can't even socialize like I want to," he grumbles.

"Do you want to get rid of that headache or don't you?"

"If brain surgery could take away part of how I am . . ." he says.

"What do you mean?"

"If necessary, I'd consent to an operation with a butcher knife if it helped me be a better man."

She stares at him.

"Pear . . . Pearline," he stutters.

"You want her out of your head?"

"Not what I mean."

"What?" Abyssinia asks.

"I hurt her. I need all the help I can get. I don't want to hurt her or anybody else ever again."

"Pearline," she murmurs. Time has come. The wait is over.

"Mother Barker, you often told me I have good instincts and to, 'Always listen to your right mind,' " Abyssinia whispers.

*"This is the day I've been waiting for, Abyssinia. You have gone past my old ways and put them together with new ones. You have surpassed me, Dr. Jackson. Congratulations!"*

Bidden and unbidden, the memory of lyrics streams from her heart and slips into her mouth. The secret words to the Isaiah song purr like a tiger in her throat. The disquieting chorus rumbles thick in its authority.

What were Mother Barker's parting words? "Abby, you sing this song, you'll be dangerous to the devil!"

The capsule of music unfolds in all its undiluted strength. Defining. Insisting. Enabling.

But she only sings half of it. Abyssinia studies Isaiah. She knows something else, more than her mentor had foreseen. In his case, there has to be a test. Will he pass?

Isaiah stays out of bars, sitting alone in the evening reading his Bible and gardening books. He cooks the vegetables he has stored away in his winter shed. His urge to hurt Pearline subsides along with the headaches. He winces when he tells his therapist that when he beat her, nothing could stop him until he was finished, satisfied, exhausted. And as big as he is, it takes a lot to exhaust him. The thought of the monster he had been sickens him. Waves of nausea engulf him.

Alone with his thoughts, Isaiah whispers softly to himself, "What's life without a woman? She is life." And he thinks more about Pearline.

And now he has lost that part of life forever.

*To bed*, he thinks after taking his medication.

He dreams of Abyssinia Jackson's warning that his healing would take work and time. How much work, how much time, not even the psychotherapist or Dr. Jackson could say for certain. He isn't sure how he can get to that healthy place.

His greatest fear is that the sickness will return. According to the statistics, the violent meanness often ricochets, bouncing back worse than before. The rescission rate is indisputably high.

He wakes up in a cold sweat.

"Christ!" he mumbles, sitting straight up in bed. "Must be something else I can do."

He dresses, and then makes an emergency appointment to see the therapist.

"I've got to see them," he gasps as he paces up and down the office.

"See who?" the therapist asks.

"My parents. It's been thirteen years. And now, I think I'm ready."

Turning right, he walks the path that leads to the Bottoms. He travels half a mile from Loganberry Road, hurrying past the river waters slapping the shores, on the brink of crawling up and swamping the fields where the root women harvest their herbs and teas.

As Isaiah starts down the dirt path that leads him to his old home, storm clouds gather.

He rounds a curve just as the sky turns a troubling shade of gray.

Clouds thicken. He walks on until he reaches the part of the river where his folks live. A huge turtle pokes along the edge of the shallow part. Birds twitter and chirrup as they fly in and out of the tree branches bordering the twisting river. The dark clouds bring an early dusk to the afternoon.

For a moment, Isaiah stands in place, shoes miry with the red clay mud. He takes in the shadowed sight of huts, shanties, and boats tied loosely to tree trunks. The boats rock with the gathering breeze. Signs of a coming storm.

Now the sky blackens.

He spots his father fishing at the deep end of the river.

Lightning cracks the sky wide open. Thunder runs rumbling toward him, then stops.

Isaiah feels again the muddy pain.

•   •   •

*"Cat Fish," the diners say referring to Isaiah's spirit name, "just loves catfish." They sit around his thatched pallet watching him eat, holding their round bowls of food, murmuring in soft voices, whistling to cool the hot fish stew jumping in their mouths like hot-legged frogs.*

*Isaiah's father, a man with a potbellied waist, with waddling legs like two turtles', yanks open the door and rants, "Why, I need to beat your behind again. Sittin' up in here suckin' on your mama's titty and having these women waiting on you!"*

*His father drags him away from the shanty, Isaiah's mother in tow.*

*"Mama!" Isaiah cries.*

*The cooking women run after them, shouting, "Stop! Stop! Stop it!"*

*"Mama!"*

*Isaiah's own mother seems not to hear his pitiful cries for mercy. It is as though for the duration of the beatings she turns deaf as stone.*

*His father beats him until he is too tired to lift the tree branch he uses for a whip.*

*Afterward, his mother bathes him in blue feather tincture and then lets the warm sun finish healing his wounds.*

*Never once does she lift her voice at either of them, at Isaiah or at his father.*

This dark day, Isaiah's mother steps out of her shanty. She straightens, holding one hand over her eyes, peering at the familiar figure. She gasps with surprise as she recognizes her son.

"Cat Fish! Cat Fish!" she shouts, glad to see him.

He waves back.

As Isaiah starts walking toward her, his anger intensifies and blinds him until rage zigzags behind his eyelids.

Lightning crisscrosses the sky.

Isaiah's father is older now and hard-of-hearing. He doesn't hear his wife welcoming their son or see his son striding toward them. He is bent over pulling up a chain of fish from the river. When he looks up and sees that a tall, muscular man who looks like an adult Isaiah is standing near him, close enough to walk over and hurt him, he loses his footing.

He screams as he falls headfirst into the waters. He flails and shouts helplessly, fear tightening his throat.

Isaiah stands stiff as stone as he watches his father, who can't swim, thrashing around, trying to tread water.

When the neighbors hear the yelling, they come running. Ready to jump in and rescue their drowning neighbor. Isaiah's presence stops them in their muddy tracks. They watch Cat Fish, and they recall his father's abuse. They wonder if he will let the old man drown.

Thunder roars.

Another crack of lightning zaps through the clouds.

The wind howls.

Isaiah stands paralyzed in his tracks.

"Let the deep take him," he mutters. "He deserves it."

A crying wind sweeps the river. His father bounces around like a water-sopped log. The water heaves and churns violently.

"Save him," another voice implores above the raging wind.

"Let the devil have his way," Isaiah mumbles.

He turns and starts walking back in the direction he came.

Thick drops of rain pelt him. Deafening thunderclaps echo.

"River's rising!" he warns over his shoulders.

"No," the neighbors chatter instead of running for shelter.

A tornado twists inside Isaiah's mind.

"No!" his mother calls.

"Help!" howl the people.

"I will not help this child beater!" he says through clenched teeth.

Sopping wet from the rainstorm, he reaches the clearing and can see the road winding away from the river, can see the red brick pavement that will lead him away from this damned and dangerous place.

"Damn bucket headed bastard!" he rants.

Rain streaks hate on the red earth and he walks on.

The pounding in his ears roars louder and louder. Sounds like Satan laughing.

The longer he walks, the louder the thunder.

Sounds like God talking.

Lightning reaches a crooked arm out of the sky and cracks the tree just in front of him.

He jumps to the side just in time.

Feels the force as the flaming tree falls, coming within an inch of flattening him.

The burning tree hits the ground and dents the soggy earth.

The shattered splinters burst into smoking torches.

He falls to his knees.

The scorched smell of lightning burns thought from his mind.

Saved!

From the sixth chapter of Ephesians new words take the place of fury, reminding him, "Honour thy father and mother; which is the first commandment with promise; that it may be well with thee, and thou mayest live long on the earth."

The verse is very clear. It does not say, "Honour thy father and mother if they treat you well." The verse teaches, "Honour thy father and mother," without reservations.

But the reservations are real. They intrude. They come up through memory. How can he forgive when the perpetrators have not apologized and asked to be forgiven?

*"Forgive us our debts as we forgive our debtors . . ."*

Will they ask his forgiveness?

He wants to go back as a child and cuss out grown folks, old folks. Anybody who saw violence against the child that he was and didn't stop it.

It isn't too late to call them all a sack of motherfuckers.

Isaiah turns back around, and from this distance, he sees his mother who can't swim stepping into the river. "No!" he yells.

She is intent on saving his father.

"No!"

He starts running and she keeps walking.

She will surely drown.

The water is almost up to her knees.

He gathers speed. The lightning crackles all around him. Thunder groans.

On he runs.

The water reaches her knees. Then she steps down into a deep crevice and suddenly the grabbing water is up to her chin.

He dives in and lifts her out of the whirling hole, then sets her on the bank.

Now he swims toward his father, a bobbing figure thrashing and flailing. An eddy spins and grabs at leaves and branches.

The tumbling water catches Isaiah's frantic father and pulls him toward a churning current.

"Not going to make it," Isaiah decides.

The current is too strong, even for his trained muscles.

A tree lining the shore plummets and is swiftly pulled and swallowed up by the roiling river.

Isaiah strokes his way through the turbulence.

Soon he is within reach.

*Drowning trying to save a fool.*

Isaiah approaches his father from behind.

"I ain't gonna die with him!"

His father can't hear him, but soon the old man makes out his son's face. His father's fright, driven by guilt, heightens. He gulps and inhales the rancid water. The first signs of drowning.

The vortex increases its tug.

Isaiah argues with himself even as the whirlpool sucks at him.

"Old stubborn bastard!" With all his might, he delivers a powerful punch to his father's head. With the third punch, the old man goes limp.

Isaiah reaches underneath his father's right armpit, then across his chest, and upward toward his left shoulder.

He leans back until his father is on his right hip.

With both hands beneath his father's armpits Isaiah treads water backward until his father, whose head is now above the surface, floats parallel with the ripples, with his legs in front of him, and therefore more buoyant.

At last they are free of the powerful undercurrent. Soon Isaiah feels the backward momentum he wants. Then, with his one arm wrapped around his father's gray and heaving chest, Isaiah holds him and succeeds in keeping his father's weight on his hip. With his left arm and left leg available for the kicking, Isaiah scissor-kicks his way to the shore.

He brings his father over to the bank where his mother stands frozen in horror. "You killed him!"

Shocked onlookers squat on the ground, staring at Isaiah, waiting for him to tell them why he brought the body back.

Then Isaiah begins pressing the swallowed water from his father's lungs.

"Oh!" everyone gasps.

The old man was not dead yet?

He pukes up rivers of debris and liquid. But the old man is

already knocking at death's door. Still, Isaiah does everything he knows, works on and on to save him.

He is losing the battle. The river is exacting its due.

Isaiah's father heaves again. Exhausted and near death, he whispers, "Cat Fish, son, stop."

With his last remnant of strength, he pulls Isaiah closer until father and son are face to face.

His father rasps, "You're . . . you're a good . . . a good . . . man. You're a good man!"

Isaiah cries, "Why? Why do you tell me this now?"

All the while, lightning and thunder keep talking.

"I'm sorry," his father says. "I'm sorry. Forgive . . . me."

Between tears Isaiah sputters, "Daddy, for all the beatings you gave me, I release myself from this pain. I forgive you."

His father gives a long sigh followed by a death rattle. And his contorted face relaxes.

Isaiah holds him close. "I loved you so," he confesses. "I loved you so!"

His father's friends unwrap the weeping Isaiah's arms from around his deceased father.

"He wasn't trying to kill him, he knocked him out to bring him to shore," a trembling moonshine drinker says.

"Oh, he was trying to hurt him all right," his father's fishing crony insists.

But nobody knows for sure but Isaiah.

Isaiah calls a funeral ceremony, the Bottom's version of a wake. The mourners bring herbs, fish, and plants to the bank and place these gifts on the float. They help Isaiah lift his father aboard.

Isaiah bows his head and says these parting words:

"Father! You who gave me life, you have saved my future

by regretting all the pain you cost me. I believe I will be a better man from this point forward. Perhaps you learned your cruelty from the cruelty of your father. I did not know your own childhood burdens. I wish you could have made peace with them as I am making peace with mine. Peace be with you in all the dark and light places you find in the hereafter."

After the ceremony, Isaiah follows his mother into their little shanty. When he looks around at the places where he used to be a child, he falls apart, weak again. "Why?" he raves. "Why did you let him beat me like that?" The familiar newspaper-covering on the walls doesn't answer him, though it waves back and forth until he is dizzy. He looks helplessly at the stove where so many delicious meals have been cooked, the mat where the women sat and soothed him after his beatings. "God, why?" he moans.

Now his mother cooks for him again. She lavishes him with all the unperiled attention he yearned for as a child.

The women bring more goodies.

He thanks them and fills his stomach with wild greens, cooked with tomatoes and green onions. He eats the meal, which includes free-range chickens, until he is near bursting. The women bring fish prepared ten different ways.

"I wish it had always been like this," he tells his mother.

"Often it was," his mother answers.

Her answer makes him stop.

"You're right. But the beatings . . . they messed up even the good times."

"Son, please forgive me," his mother begs.

"Would you all leave?" he asks his neighbors.

They clear the place for him to be alone with his mother.

Only then does he stand up to face her.

Isaiah says, "Just give me one good reason why!"

"I can't."

"You can't!"

He breaks apart right before her eyes.

She rocks him in her arms. Mothers him.

The next morning he says, "For being there when he beat me and not stopping him, I release this pain."

"I couldn't help you."

"You mean you didn't help me. You let him run me away."

She cries and shakes with grief.

"I should've took you and run away before it got so bad."

"But you stayed."

She has no more answers. Grief stricken and frightened, she trembles. "He . . . We . . . I . . . was wrong. Please forgive me."

Isaiah feels a new compassion; he hugs her and says, "Mama, I forgive you."

The neighbors who are eavesdropping just outside let out a collective sigh of relief.

Isaiah sticks his head out the door. "And what do you say?" he challenges them.

"Forgive us," they ask.

"For knowing and doing nothing, I forgive you all," he says to the neighbors, who now bow their heads.

After a sumptuous meal, he bids them good-bye. He waves to his mother as he starts trekking toward the muddy path leading back to Loganberry Road.

At Pearline's house Vennie sits sipping a cup of tea that Pearline prepared. "Wait," says Zenobia, who stirs a spoon of brown honey into the golden brew.

"So glad you're feeling better, Zenobia," Vennie says.

"Yes. Thank you, Aunt Vennie."

"Pearline told me what happened. You still taking your walks?"

"Uh-hm. And I'm hankering to do some fishing."

"You're in luck," Vennie says. "Farmer's Almanac says tomorrow's a fine day for the fish gods. Who's that dog barking and keeping up such a racket?"

"Oh that's Fetch. He's out in the backyard. Norman's dog."

"What you say?"

"The dog ran away from home to visit Zenobia right after Norman acted a fool," Pearline says.

"Never heard tell of such a thing. What kind of dog is this?"

"A mutt. A hound dog."

"Not one of the brightest breeds then."

"In this case the dog has more sense than the man," Pearline says defending Zenobia.

"Hope I catch enough fish for all three of us," Zenobia says. "Plus one for the dog."

"I hope so too. We're on a budget. And Grandma, she's been feeding that dog our leftovers," Pearline complains.

Vennie sits open-mouthed.

"This is the first time I ever saw you speechless, Grandma. I do believe the cat's got your tongue!"

Vennie frowns. "Not the cat. The dog!"

Pearline and Zenobia hurry to refill Vennie's cup. They want to keep her talking.

"What's his name again?"

"Fetch," Pearline says.

"What does the Bible say about dogs?" Vennie wonders.

"Oh, stop, Grandma," Pearline says as she suppresses a giggle.

•   •   •

Early the next morning, Zenobia, her fishing pole on her shoulder, a straw hat on her head, and baggy pants with checkered cotton shirt on her tall frame, walks along the road toward the river, swinging a bucket and fussing at Norman's dog, Fetch.

Zenobia asks, "Why do you want to go fishing with me, Fetch? Wanna see if the fish god's gonna appear?"

Fetch yips, his short quick legs keeping time with Zenobia's long-legged strides.

After awhile of walking and not talking, Zenobia says, "Fetch, my nose tells me this is the place. The fish god is out today! Just like Aunt Vennie said. Can't you just smell the fried perch sprinkled with hot sauce?"

Zenobia relaxes near the high cattails and water reeds on a grassy mound by the river, dozing off and on, talking now and then to Fetch, and coming awake when the fish nibble her line. "Look at the size of this rascal!" she shouts as she reels in a huge catfish.

The sun rides the sky, watching as she pulls in more shiny fish, cuts off their heads, unhooks them, tosses them in her pail, threads live worms for new bait, then sends the line snapping out over the water and down into the slow flowing current again.

She naps again and jerks awake in time to reel in another one.

Fetch seems to count the fish as he looks in the bucket, barking every time a new one comes flying out of the water, cursing the rejecting air, and flashing to its death under Zenobia's quick knife.

"So you liked that meat loaf I fixed you, did you?" Zenobia says to Fetch. "Never thought I'd be treating a dog with such respect."

Zenobia has bought a puce colored plate for Fetch's food at

the supermarket and an aluminum bowl for his water, exclusively for his use when he comes visiting, barking, and jumping around her door, glad to see her. "Pretty dishes for a good dog," she adds in the way people talk dog-talk, with a hint of baby-talk in the mix. The thought of which makes her add, "Now don't you go thinking I'm like those other people who confuse the kingdoms. Thinking dogs are children. I don't do that stuff. You're a dog, and I respect you like a dog."

Fetch barks a friendly answer.

"Three catfishes and two perch have jumped into our bucket off our line, Fetch. One for me, one for Pearline, one for Grandma Vennie, one for Aunt Maggie, and one for you. A fine fish fry. Not a minnow in the bunch. Why, just one of these whoppers can feed a whole family. Should we try for more?"

But Fetch is not answering. His ears perk up. He rises from his kneeling position and the hair on his back stands up like tall weeds.

"What's wrong with you, Fet . . . ?"

Fetch barks so ferociously and so unexpectedly, that Zenobia jumps. A rat the size of a young dog leaps onto her pants, yellow teeth bared, bent on sinking his fangs into her thigh.

Zenobia screams as her pole goes flying, "Holy shit!"

Fetch leaps at the rat, knocking it from its grip on Zenobia's pants and knocking her down. The rat jumps off and she jumps back and grabs her fishing pole.

She beats at the rat with the pole, missing and whipping up furious clouds of dust.

But Fetch claims the battle as his own. He tears into his adversary, wrestling, biting, and snarling. The rat tries to escape, but Fetch blocks his exit. All the while the rat gives shrill beeps, pawing at the air, baring huge, yellow teeth. Fetch's growls and the rat's shrill cries seem to go on forever.

Still Fetch fights on.

Zenobia sits down on a stump at a distance, her fishing pole ready in case the rat runs her way, but she doesn't have to use it. Fetch has the rat cornered just this side of a high rock.

He knocks the rat around some more until the red earth powders the vermin's slick hairs. A murderous snarl stays in Fetch's throat.

Where's the gentle Fetch? Zenobia wonders.

Even as the rat in the last throes of death recovers and rears his head and hisses meanly, Fetch attacks again and twists the rat's body until it is bleeding rust and fur. The rat is far-gone and still Fetch whips the limp body this way and that until the rat lays stiff and motionless, eyes staring and gelid.

When Fetch is certain the rat is finished, he gives a satisfied bark, looks at Zenobia, and whines.

"All right, Fetch. Guess in this situation you're the boss. I'm following your lead."

She tags along behind the dog, her bucket of fish in one hand, the splintered and beat-up fishing pole bobbing over her shoulder. She figures, "Rabid rats just like mean people. Downright malicious! You're going along minding your business and they're hiding under the bushes looking out at you, watching you catching your fish or catching your breath or talking to yourself, then jump out the bushes and gnaw at you. Fetch, sometimes dogs got more sense than humans. You smelled that rat before I did. You know something, Fetch, you're welcome to come visiting anytime you like. Yipping or whining. Barking or snarling. Fetch, honey, your plate will always be fixed!"

Zenobia is standing on the porch with Fetch at her side when she hears Pearline coming home.

"Any luck?"

"Lots."

Pearline stops in her tracks when she sees Fetch. "Why, he's all shiny and clean."

"Had to give him a bath. He had a hard day."

"I see he helped you clean the fish."

"Don't be sarcastic, Pearline. He's not a lazy dog."

Pearline whistles as she picks up one prize catch. "A blue ribbon swimmer if I ever saw one."

"The fish god was generous today!"

"Gonna start heating up the skillet right now!"

"Course we wouldn't have a fish fry if it hadn't been for Fetch."

"Huh?"

"Fetch killed a rat. Teeth like yellow razors!"

"What?"

"Jumped on me."

"How big?"

"Looked like a possum!"

"Rabid! And he didn't get a chance to bite you?" Pearline's quick eyes check for the tiniest bruises.

"No way. Fetch was on him before he could get a good chunk out of me. Anyway, Fetch already had his shots."

"That's my boy," says Pearline. "Guess this dog's not worthless after all." Stooping down she tickles Fetch behind the ears. "Rat-killing son of a bitch!"

When she says "son of a bitch," Zenobia whoops with laughter, because a female dog in anybody's dictionary is defined as a bitch.

"What's so funny?"

"What you said."

"This definitely calls for a celebration, Zenobia. Feel like hitting a few licks?"

"A special command performance for Fetch. Hot dog!"

"Guess this here's the stage." Zenobia runs into the house and brings her guitar out to the front porch. Propping one foot up on the railing she sings.

> 'Tis the old ship of Zion
> 'Tis the old ship of Zion
> 'Tis the old ship of Zion
> Get on board,

Pearline ad-libs,

> If you want to see Jesus,

Then the two harmonize,

> Get on board.

Fetch lays down between them on the porch and listens to the near musical perfection, an interesting blend of contemporary Black gospel and a little bit of Rosetta Tharp influence with flashing twists and scintillating turns of country music color and shading.

Fetch thumps his tail between the singers' pauses and the guitar licks.

His applause, when the last verse fades, is the waving of his tail back and forth as he looks from one glad singer to the other.

They tune up for another song, when the phone rings. "That must be grandma. Said she'd call me to see how the fishing went."

"How's she doing?" Zenobia asks when Pearline comes back from answering the phone.

"Sounded happy today."

"Why?"

"First, she's glad you caught some fresh fish. Can't wait to get over here and wrap her lips around a catfish sandwich. And, oh, I almost forgot, Widower Parsons visited her this morning. She says it does her heart good just to see him smile toothless when she pecks him on his bald head."

A few months later, on her way to church, Zenobia notices a red envelope dangling from Fetch's collar. Next to Zenobia in the choir loft, Pearline studies the Church Bulletin. Two events headline the newsletter: Arthur Ray Cleveland's death and a short entry about Norman Miller.

Zenobia opens her purse and reaches for the red envelope. She takes out the crinkled letter and reads it.

*Zenobia, I can't believe I've lost you. The light has left my spirit. I don't know which way to turn. So much to ponder. I'm leasing my place. I'm leaving Ponca. When I get myself together, I'll return a better man. And, God willing, I'll woo you until you let me back into your heart again.*

*Love,*
*Norman*

After the Norman Miller announcement, Abyssinia Jackson says a special prayer.

"God, we know you don't make a difference among people. And we're hoping you'll take this offering from Norman Miller as one indication of his need to do right, to repent, to cleanse his spirit for his continued journey through life. Mr. Miller has left money for the church, money he set aside from the leasing of his property. We have created a special fund for his generosity, a gift he specified to be dedicated to spreading gospel music all over the world."

And the church says Amen.

"Choir, I guess you'll be doing some traveling," Abyssinia continues. "I hereby name his charitable organization 'The Norman Miller Gospel Foundation.'" Then she sings, *"Is It Well With Your Soul?"*

> *Is it well with your soul?*
> *Are you free and made whole*
> *It is well*
> *I thank God it's well with your soul.*

Pearline leans over and whispers, "Was it really little?"

"I never said that."

"Well, was it?"

Zenobia gives a secret smile. "Not really," she answers and tucks Norman's note back in her purse.

Then words are ringing out about Arthur Ray.

"Arthur Ray Cleveland has passed over. Cancer."

"A true child of God." Tambourines jangle in a show of respect.

Pearline knows that now with Arthur Ray gone, she really has to rely on the goodwill of the community even more.

In the testimony service, she announces to the congregation that she is pregnant.

"Amen," the church says. Everybody knows, without saying, that it is Arthur Ray's baby. A love child. A child whose natural father had been well loved and respected.

Missionary Cleveland, after Arthur Ray's passing, grieved.

"Honey my face dropped so far, you could mop your floor with it!" This morning she whips up a holy dance, even without benefit of Roosevelt Tate's organ.

She is overjoyed with the prospect of a grandchild. Arthur Ray's child. Her and Cleveland's grandchild.

This baby will make Vennie Walker a great grandmother, but Vennie lets Missionary Cleveland claim the day. After all, she needs something to lift her long face.

Later on the church steps, Isaiah says, "Well, I guess it's gonna be a boy, you're carrying it high." Keeps repeating it to anybody who will listen.

Abyssinia searches Isaiah's face for a flicker of resentment. She doesn't find any. She sees concern and a willingness to help.

"Be sure to make another appointment for next week," Abyssinia reminds her.

"Got the book right here," Janet Lacy says, and pulls out a pen. "We'll squeeze you in."

Zenobia and Isaiah nod, quiet for a moment, living witnesses to the healing powers of Dr. Jackson.

"Dr. Jackson will handle the delivery just perfect," Missionary Cleveland adds.

"A grandbaby!" She hugs Pearline, then rushes down the church steps shouting, "Hallelujah!" on out into the middle of the churchyard. "If idle hands are the devil's workshop, what are busy hands? The Lord's workshop that's what! They'll be holding, they'll be rocking Arthur Ray's child!"

"Missionary Cleveland," Pearline says. "Bring the Lord's workshop by my house anytime!"

Twins, a boy and a girl. This morning Pearline goes to her checkup appointment with Dr. Jackson and leaves the babies with Zenobia and Grandma Vennie.

"Got to meet Widower Parsons at the house, otherwise I'd stay longer," Vennie says as she hands the boy twin to Zenobia, who is already holding the girl.

She studies Zenobia, her guitar case propped against the wall behind her, sitting in that rocking chair with a baby in the crook of each arm.

"Now there's a photo opportunity if I ever saw one!"

"Uh-hum," grins Zenobia. "Queen Zenobia with her two royal offspring!"

"The turns life takes," Vennie says, thinking of her date with Deacon Parsons. "New babies. New life. Leaving something new to go meet something old. The Widower."

"Don't worry, Aunt Vennie. I can handle it. Anyway, Pearline'll be back soon."

"Course that Pearline needs all the help she can get," Vennie adds on her way out the door. "Twins! A woman's just one big titty. First comes the man then here come the babies!"

Zenobia sings a soft lullaby to the twins and they soon fall asleep. She tiptoes into Pearline's bedroom and places them in the middle of the crib. She stands there for a moment appreciating the peaceful countenances of these new earth angels.

Back in the front room Zenobia strums softly on her guitar.

*I'm not far, my love, I'm just a hug away.*

She is so lost in her music that she doesn't notice Pearline is late until she hears the babies squirming awake.

She removes the guitar straps from around her neck. Feeling very motherly, she hurries to soothe the fussing babies.

Her touch is not magical. The babies' crying becomes more intense. Their piercing wails leap higher, shriller.

Zenobia walks the floor from one end of the house to the other, jiggling the two infants, one on each hip as she sings,

*I'm not far, my love, I'm just a hug away.*

But the hungry babies, though well hugged, cry fiercely.

"A woman's just one big titty," Zenobia repeats. "I'd give anything to have a milk-congested titty right now. No make that two.

"Now where's that Pearline? Probably taking her time along the way home.

"Shh!" Zenobia says, and she starts humming.

*Anyway, Pearline can't be far.*

But the squalling continues, changes keys, and turns the infants' faces purple.

"Lungs! You babies got some powerful pipes," she says, loud enough to penetrate the screams.

They holler so pitifully that Zenobia feels like crying herself.

She unbuttons her blouse and sticks a plump breast in each baby's mouth.

At first, they close their tear-blurred eyes and suck, humming thankfully, content at last.

Then, when they realize that this is not it, this is not the fluffy breast of their mother, this is not the taste of her sweet milk but of air, their eyes fly open and the humming turns to a steady slow fussing, grumbling almost like old folks.

Suddenly their lusty complaints break out afresh and Zenobia wants to go run and hide her head under the bed and cover her ears.

Their piercing suffering assaults her nerves further. Accosts her tranquility.

"Oh, my sweet little angel babies, I'm trying and your mother will be home soon, I promise."

But they do not hush.

Her whispers make them holler even louder.

So loud that perspiration streaks down the sides of her cheeks while she walks the floor, pacing with her two charges.

Seeing her woebegone face reflected in the mirror, Zenobia starts laughing, "That's right, you two must be two true colored babies. If it hurts, make a racket!"

Their stomachs ache for milk.

Zenobia's ears ache from hearing the babies' howling.

"Hey! What's going on?" Isaiah bellows from the front porch.

"Oh, you've brought Pearline!" Zenobia fairly flies to the front door, the howling babies in her arms.

"Pearline! Pearline! Pear . . ."

Isaiah is alone.

"Oh," Zenobia says, her voice sagging, "I thought Pearline was with you."

"No. I came to see her and the twins. She's not here?"

"No. Went to the doctor. Come on in."

Isaiah pushes the screen ajar and steps inside the house.

He says, "Thought she'd be back by now. I knew about her checkup with Dr. Jackson. My goodness these babies sound hungry."

"You're telling me," Zenobia yells, trying to be heard above the racket.

He yearns to satisfy the babies' hunger. "Mind if I help?"

"*Help!*" Zenobia sings, a pitiful effort at humor.

The complaints of the children push Isaiah into the kitchen, where he takes down a box of oatmeal. He finds pots and pans in the bottom of the cabinet, pours in the meal, adds water, and boils the mixture atop the stove into a gruel that resembles the couscous of the river recipe his mother used to make. He stirs sweet applesauce into the oatmeal, then adds sweet milk.

"This might not fool them into thinking it's Pearline's milk," Isaiah says to Zenobia as he brings the bowl of baby food into the living room, "but I hope it'll be a satisfying substitute."

Zenobia sits down in the rocking chair with the twins, while Isaiah squats in front of them with the bowl of cereal. He spoons the unfamiliar thick porridge into their mouths. The babies wrap their lips around the spoon, smack their lips, and for a moment are startled quiet at the strange texture.

They don't know whether to laugh or cry.

Soon they start humming and swallowing, enjoying the oatmeal.

The dark velvet eyes of the babies look into the deep brown eyes of Isaiah.

Mama's face? No. No.

They tune up, but instead of crying, they gurgle. The infants coo.

"Hey!" Pearline yells as the screen bangs shut behind her. "Why's it so quiet? Babies sleep?"

" 'Fraid not," Zenobia says, in a chastising voice.

"Oh." Pearline sees Isaiah and Zenobia feeding the babies.

"What took you so long?" Zenobia and Isaiah look at her blouse stuck to her heavy breasts, dripping mother's milk.

"I misjudged the time. And Missionary Cleveland and I went shopping for baby clothes."

"Baby clothes?"

"Grandma Cleveland takes her grandmothering seriously. She brought swatches of material into the sewing store to match the colors she wanted, then proceeded to choose yards and yards of cotton. She explained to the clerk, 'Got little pajamas to make, and I can't find what's in my head in the department stores!' "

"Sounds like her all right," says Zenobia.

"When my breasts started leaking milk, Grandma Cleveland stopped in her tracks, gathered up her purchases and said, 'Child, your titties must be throbbing. The babies heads bobbing trying to find your nipples. Better get you home in a hurry!' "

"It's about time!" Zenobia fusses.

"Where's Grandma Vennie?" Pearline asks as she sits down to nurse.

"She had a date." Zenobia and Isaiah hand the babies over to Pearline.

"Oh, so you held down the fort all by yourself?"

" 'Course she didn't do it all by herself," Isaiah speaks up quietly.

For a moment, everyone in the room hushes, remembering that responsibility was not something any one of them could shrug from their shoulders like a dress or throw away like a worn-out pair of shoes.

What had Abyssinia said? Accepting responsibility is one of the first steps in nourishing love in the world. In the universe. Every single day it takes spine to answer. And anyhow, Pearline, Isaiah, and Zenobia think as they look at the babies and listen to their satisfied coos, the future is crying for attention right up in their faces.

Zenobia hurries out of the room to prepare dinner. Gospel star Shirley Caesar is preaching "His Blood" on the kitchen radio and sending cancer and kidney disease back to the pit, praying, *"It's some mother's child. Some father's boy."* Zenobia hums along as she pulls out a big iron pot and starts candying yams, a side dish for her perfect fried chicken.

*"If we go to Him and be sincere His blood will restore your soul."*

In the living room, Isaiah says, "Pearline . . . Wanted . . ."

"Huh?"

". . . to see if you need me . . ."

He hesitates, not typical of his charging ahead, wanting-to-control-everything self.

"Need you?"

". . . for anything."

"No," she answers softly. "We're okay."

He stands without moving to leave, so she asks, "What is it?"

"What do you think about my working with the young people?"

"These babies?"

"Not exactly what I mean."

"Then what?"

"Older."

"You mean teach Sunday school?"

"That too, but I mostly mean working with the young men who aren't coming to Sunday school. See if I can help."

"Why, Isaiah, that's a fine idea."

He is certain he hears a little light in her voice. She no longer seems afraid of him, and this makes him even more assured that what he wants to do with the young men is a good thing.

"Better get going. See what I can do today.

"See you later, alligators," he says to the babies. He wiggles their baby toes. They bubble over with glee as he tickles the bottoms of their feet.

On one of the rocking chairs, he leaves a recent magazine article on African Americans, hoping she will read it later when the babies are sleeping.

"Call me if you need anything. Anything at all."

He walks down Loganberry Road thinking about Pearline, the new babies, and the magazine article.

Isaiah feels he has just left the most beautiful version of the Madonna that he has ever seen: Pearline, in her rocking chair with two twinkle-eyed babies. He hadn't had the good sense to give the children to her himself. Anyway, he thinks, he would have been a terrible parent if he and Pearline had given birth to them when she was twenty-three and he much younger than now. "Shoot," he admits, "I would've been a terrible father just several months ago."

And yes, he still loves her.

As long as she lets him, he will be there for her and the children.

What he feels is so encompassing, so far-reaching, that he wants to show it by honoring all young folks.

The magazine he left with Pearline states that the per capita income of African Americans is thousands of dollars below that of White Americans. And the employment rate among Black teenagers is staggeringly low.

He thinks about the devastating effect of this data.

All teens, regardless of color, look at the same TV commercials advertising the cornucopia of plenty—compact discs, boom boxes, VCRs, diamonds, gold, cars, mansions, designer clothes.

Some of the Black teens, obviously more constrained economically and educationally, turn to crime.

Some are able to get jobs or are part of the thriving Black middle class, financially secure, and well educated. Usually armed with allowances, they walk into stores and buy what they want. When they graduate from high school, they have going-away-to-college parties, with bands and family and friends cheering them on.

He is also aware that a few of the middle-class Black teens disregard the advice and wisdom of their parents and, pressured by their nimble-minded peers, turn to crime.

Isaiah hears a high laugh followed by a "Gimme five!" He looks across the street to see a group of young men high-signing, signifying, and talking loud. He easily picks out the leader, Jericho, tall and exuding power, flexing his biceps. Jericho adjusts his Ray Bans as he peers down on his homeboys, his posse.

Jericho stands in place, talking authoritatively as he towers above the other young men surrounding him, "Everybody here up to snuff!"

Isaiah is impressed by Jericho's voice, a bass sound so deep he could sing the bottom out of a note.

He admires the unity he senses among these young men. The trust. Their rhythmic manner of speaking. The way they use their hands. Their attitude. He wants to get their respectful attention, but at the same time he knows he'll have to earn it.

"Hey, fellows, anybody here know Mama Vennie Walker?"

The handsome young brothers immediately stop talking, but they mad-dog him. Look at him like he just dropped down out of the sky from the moon.

"Headz up! The man want somebody to wreckanize him," says a short brother whose mouth has been running rampant ever since Isaiah studied the group before crossing the street.

"Anything the matter with Mama Vennie?" Jericho asks in a serious tone.

"No, Mama Vennie's fine. I'm starting a group for young men up at her church, and thought you might want to be part of it."

"She tell you to say that?" Jericho asks in a challenging voice.

Isaiah wants to answer yes, but he knows he'd be lying. Anyway, he realizes from the quick flicker of Jericho's penetrating eyes, and the alert way he listens to every nuance of the words Isaiah speaks, that he'd know right away too.

He isn't about to make the mistake of thinking the brothers are anything but the smart, living-on-the-edge—no, *break-dancing-on-the-edge*—full of deriding laughter young men that they are.

"No," Isaiah answers simply. "She didn't tell me to say that."

"Who you, old man, to come jumping all up in *my* face?" asks Jericho.

The mouth-almighty short one snaps, "Garbage. Gonna try to stop us from ganging up on the bad boys down the way?" Then Isaiah remembers Jericho's main man's name, Muscle. Muscle Adams. Muscle descends from the Blacks who intermarried with the Cherokee Nation.

While Jericho, with a cast in his right eye, is the tallest of the crew, Muscle, the shortest, is known for his legendary ruthlessness, and, Isaiah notices, Muscle is well-armed. Isaiah realizes he has stumbled upon a fight in the planning stages. He spies the cache of bricks, knives, and chains.

He senses that at any moment these young men could and would turn their venom against the gang down the way, and anybody else who got in their path.

So much passes before Isaiah's eyes. A generation armed with attitude and abilities. Thirsting for guidance and not getting any, they have found their own way. That alone is something to be celebrated. What they found has a beat, has a color, has a world following. As far away as China, young people are listening to the latest hip-hop albums. In every nation, young admirers tend dreadlocks and wear their caps shifted to the side just like Jericho and Muscle.

When you talk with Jericho's people, you have to come correct.

"We ain't no krumb snatchas, just sittin' on the curb waitin' for your ol' lame advice!" Muscle sneers.

Isaiah realizes he is dealing with mental students, young geniuses dealing daily in deep thought. Raw talent. And he wonders about what he can do, even as a jacked-up car makes doughnuts in the street, catching rubber and sending up sparks as it skids in circles in the intersection.

If life is a series of choices made at crossroads in his own youth, for these youngsters, life is a maze of speedy racetracks. Which exit will they take?

The derisive laughter of the young men echoes behind the freestyling music blasting from a boom box.

The hardcore rhymes of DMX slap Isaiah between the eyes with their in-your-face directness. For a moment, he wishes his own youth had been washed in such revolutionary rhythms. Would he have been saved?

Above the lyrics, he hears Muscle claim, "There is no God!" in a rock beat so perfect, he has to question his own spiritual journey.

Isaiah reflects on his recent quest for God. His search led him to the early and existing African religions. To Buddhism, Islam, Shinto, Christianity, then to Judaism, meditation, and prayer.

Does it matter what faith is called as long as it is life affirming?

Then he realizes the God these young men denigrate is a God who they think has failed them.

Deny me, I deny you. Pure and simple.

*The older generation*, Isaiah thinks, no, he personalizes it, *my generation too has been hampered in trying to make a way in this hostile land.* The ones he calls his people are still spinning from physical, mental, and spiritual attacks dating back hundreds of years. No, not just four hundred years ago. Dating back to yesterday when another Black youth was found shot in the back by somebody who said he looked like a crook.

*Have we neglected, forgotten, or been too overwhelmed ourselves to try to understand this younger generation? Have we turned away from all such as these who have been entrusted to us?*

"Ol' folks need to get up to snuff!" Muscle blurts.

"You're right," Isaiah answers.

"Um-hmm!" they all respond in one voice.

Isaiah remembers how much it hurts to hear some of these same ol' folks Muscle refers to declare, "These young folks just ain't no good."

Parents, leaders, elders find facile reasons to be blameless, to feel they are better than their own offspring, that they are apart and different.

Even as the older people unwittingly betray this generation's trust, exasperation in the senior voices betray their instincts that something is very wrong. And all the while, the number of suicides, which used to be unheard of among Black youth, catapult.

"Why don't you try church?" Isaiah asks, knowing that the question is just a quick entry to open a way for the group to respond, even if it means opening himself up to ridicule.

"God *been* buried!" Muscle retorts.

"Not all churches are bad," Isaiah continues.

"Ain' never done nothing for me!" Muscle growls.

Isaiah makes another appointment with Dr. Jackson. When she examines him, she shakes her head.

"Why's your pressure up? Taking your medication?"

"Yeah."

"Something making it shoot up like this?"

"How do you say it? Stress?"

"Stress."

"Just became aware of some things."

"Oh?"

He tells her about meeting with the tough young men.

"How can they, so young, so inexperienced, know that the very ones who murder religion also supply the spirit-numbing drugs?"

Isaiah continues, "All the while these evil folks line their purses with the gold they steal from the ignorant, untaught children who stole it from their mothers who never had much in the first place."

Abyssinia nods. "It's easier to be ignorant in the short run, but never in the long run. For the long run we need our wisdom teachers."

"Thank goodness for the likes of Mama Vennie Walker."

"She's paying a steep price."

He knows that some of the younger mothers, tired lines around their puffy eyes, scrub floors in other kitchens, look after other people's children so their own can eat. But while they are busy working, their own untended children keep booming, "God is dead! Buried. Never been and never will be on your side!"

"Mama Vennie? Paying a steep price? What do you mean?"

"With her health. Overworked all her life. Raised a son then lost him to the war."

"Mama Vennie in bad health? Can't tell it by looking at her."

"Silent killers rage among us. That's why checkups are so important."

"I know women in general are unappreciated. And I was one of the ones doing the unappreciating. Then tried to blame it on my folks."

"It's an old, tired line, and often true. Children resent their parents for their mistakes. Yet, many of these resourceful women, like Mama Vennie, still find joy, smile, play patty-cake with the children, defend their offspring. And carry invisible First Aid kits on their backs to heal their families and communities."

"And like Mama Vennie, they still keep stepping," Isaiah says.

"We have so much to do," says Abyssinia, looking off and looking inward.

"Take a nation to work this mess out!" Isaiah blurts.

"I'm holding meetings up at the church every Wednesday, seven o'clock. I'd like to talk with you," Isaiah begins when he sees the young men again. "I'm thinking of a program where men shoot pictures instead of guns."

The rest of the group, leaning against a wall that glows with bold graffiti, glare at Isaiah with frozen expressions.

"Pathetic!" Muscle spits. "Cameras for guns?!"

"Wanna talk with somebody?" Jericho asks. "Man, who you think you is? Somebody's daddy? Daddy hell! I ain' never seen the monster! If my daddy did show up, I'd kick his behind for running off and leaving me and my mama. You wanna take his place? Keep it up, hear? We'll show you what we do to daddies."

Isaiah, confronted with this undiluted male hurt, almost turns around. But he doesn't. He recognizes himself in their unforgiving faces. He shivers from the cold, congealed pain.

"I hear you," Isaiah answers matter-of-factly. "For a long time I wanted to smoke my daddy."

"Say what?" Jericho asks, the eye with the cast suddenly changing.

"I said, for a long time I wanted to kill my daddy! I inherited his meanness. Man was so mean, brushed his teeth with razor blades."

"Mean!" Muscle says.

"When he hawked, he spit bullets!" Isaiah says.

"Talkin' 'bout mean!" Muscle says.

"Razor-blade mean!" Jericho says.

"Spittin'-bullets mean!" The gang members chant.

"Talkin'-mean!" Jericho says.

"Walkin'-mean!" Muscle rhymes, with just a touch of appreciation and a teeny bit of respect. As is his habit when he is tickled, he says, "Humph! Humph! Humph?"

When the banter subsides, Isaiah continues in a more sober vein, "I hurt inside just thinking about how mean and abusive he could be and it made me hurt somebody I should've been loving and I just don't need that kind of hurt anymore. I wanted to talk to other young men like you who might want to see what's happening for us down the highway. So I started these sessions up at the church house. Wednesday nights, seven o'clock. Stop on by if you feel like it. I'll be there. Same as I've been there night after night after night. I'll be there. I'll be waiting."

All the time Isaiah is talking in his serious tone, the young men stand speechless.

"Man got a mental problem," Jericho decides when Isaiah is finished. "Sitting up in a empty church house waiting for folks who ain't coming."

"Must be crazy," Muscle says to Jericho. "But did you get a load of what he said about Papa? Daddy was bad! Almost bad as me. Humph! Say what?!"

"If you wanna come, I'll be in the church every Wednesday night, 'round seven," Isaiah tells the group again.

The young men hear him, but they fold their arms across their chests, soldier style, and don't reply.

"Beats jail," Isaiah says as he moves to leave.

He turns around and walks away. Their proud laughter rings out all up and down the road.

"Hey, ol' man," Muscle hollers after Isaiah's retreating back, "I got me some boon buddies just waitin' for me in the joint. I like my Dogz better'n I like you. Hell, I don't even know you!"

"Got that right!" another young man says.

"Dig, man, you know he can't be for real, talking about using baseball bats for hitting home runs and a damn gun for a plowshare!"

Jericho studies his shoes while his men listen to Muscle put his take on things. They listen to Muscle, but it is the cast in Jericho's eye that they carefully watch.

"Hey, going to jail's like going to camp," Muscle shouts. "Get to be with my click! My folks! Locked down with them's better'n being locked up in a church house listening to squares like you. Jail ain't nothing but another name for homey camp!"

The raucous, hand-slapping laughter nips at Isaiah's heels. He hears the squawking all the way home.

When Isaiah turns on the television, he happens upon a talk show. Before he can turn to the news, a colored man says, "They're just no good, these bad children." The black-suited, shiny-shoed Black man, all propped up on television pontificates, "These Black kids? See how they steal even from their own overworked Mamas. Lock their tails up. Get rid of them!"

Isaiah jumps up and glares at the screen. He wants to go through the set and kick the man up and down the packed-with-people studio audience. He wants to snatch a knot in his butt so tight, it would take ten teams of horses to untie it. And the audience! "Damn monkeys!" Isaiah complains, "They so dumb they don't even know their own emotions. Only applaud when the flashing lights prompt them to."

Mighty mouth continues belittling the Black youngsters, "On top of that, they messy. Littering up the school grounds. Won't even pick up after their selves."

This man belongs to a breed that doesn't know that over in the White schools, the kids are just as careless. Even more so. Many of their parents are not domestics. Only difference is they have an army of janitors to clean the yard. The teachers don't usually berate the students. They realize that their primary job is teaching children how to think. The administration hires janitors to pick up after the "smart" kids.

"Damn!" says Isaiah. "I got to go see the doctor again." His blood pressure veers out of control. He can always tell. His vision blurs.

Before he can click off the set, the swaying, woozy image of the Black betrayer leans back and continues pontificating.

"I started a program where those bad kids had to pick up trash a whole hour after school!"

The applauding audience swims before Isaiah's eyes.

What the audience doesn't know is that those students are picking up leaky condoms, grimy litter swarming with bacteria, trash ridden with rat droppings, and used hypodermic needles stained with blood. All of this without benefit of surgical gloves, but with their bare hands.

At the more well-to-do schools, the administration hires an army of trained janitors who wear protective clothing.

Inching up on some more ignorance, the idiot continues, "I'm pushing the program where they plan to plant chemicals under young Black girls arms as a form of birth control. Take 'em right out of class and imbed the implants! Talk about efficient! Good program!"

"No, it's not!" Isaiah protests. He doesn't know the scientific answers, but his instincts tell him something is out of kilter.

He convinces Janet Lacy to squeeze him in for an appointment. "Can you be here in fifteen minutes?" she asks.

*I need some exercise anyway*, he thinks. He runs to see Dr. Jackson. His legs remember the days when he could outrun a jackrabbit.

Abyssinia listens, and then looks far off. "It's going to get worse," she says. "Those unsuspecting girls will have keloids, long fat scars all up and down their forearms. Some of them won't have a period for years! Who knows what else these drugs will do to their bodies? I wonder if anybody's studied the long-term risks?"

Isaiah sputters, "How come the drug companies going into the Black neighborhoods using our children as guinea pigs? Bet they don't take that stuff to the kids in their own households!"

"I've heard whispers."

"What?"

"Doctors have been told they will be paid for every child they put in that program. So much for the Hippocratic Oath!"

"Rumors?"

"I wish."

"And the mamas are too uneducated, too tired to understand their children being sold into another kind of slavery. What's happening?"

"Take it easy. Remember your high blood pressure, Isaiah."

"That's right." He takes a deep breath. "I wanna live long enough to help do something about this."

"You're a good man, Isaiah."

"I sure needed to hear that today! Think I'll go to college. Get better educated."

"You've got a great mind. A great mind in a good man is a wonderful thing."

"Then I'll be going."

"You must remember, Isaiah, there will always be followers.

There will always be leaders. What we have to do is choose our leadership carefully. Leaders have to look out for all our best interests."

Head down, Isaiah silently ponders all he has heard. Then he looks up and says, "Who would've thought I'd be listening to a woman and following her advice?"

"Who?"

"Not me! Not me!"

When Isaiah gets home and turns on the TV set again, that same fool is on every channel, spewing ignorance, "Why, some of these Black kids so dumb they can't even find Africa on the map! Think Rosa Parks is a flower garden. Think the Klan's a new hip-hop group. They don't know who Martin Luther King was. Why, I heard one of them say, Martha Lucy King."

Bristling, Isaiah clicks off the set. "Then we haven't done our job," he grunts. "And you don't understand," he cries, now talking to a blank television screen. "Damn it! We haven't taught them! And they have so much further to go than King, who knew it even before they killed him!"

Isaiah sits in the dark and mulls over what Abyssinia Jackson said.

When Isaiah goes to church the next Sunday, Vennie Walker, heavily bandaged and limping, testifies about getting mugged after her purse was snatched.

"*Strapping* young man grabbed me right outside the sanctuary! Knocked me down, broke my arm when he snatched my purse. Then kicked me in the head."

"Lord, help mercy!" the congregation gasps.

"Musta been on one," somebody moans.

"Had to been," somebody else agrees.

"God's got to raise up some men to help guide these kids," Vennie continues.

"You said it, Mother," a young woman chimes in.

"Some of 'em forgot what the insides of a church house looks like," somebody else responds.

"I want the whole church to go on a three-day fast!"

"Amen!" they call. The fast has begun.

"Don't let them tear down the churches," Vennie pleads, tears snagging at her words. "If they destroy the churches there'll be nothing to help protect these children from evil. All people, in every country in the world, have their criminal citizens. And all people on Mother Earth believe in some higher power. There'd be a whole lot more wickedness if we didn't have the law. Evil would have a hard row to hoe if more folks believed in God."

"Got to have God!"

"Demons prowling the earth!" shouts the church, a cadenced call and response.

"KNOCK the devil out!"

"Knock the devil OUT!"

"Knock the DEVIL out!"

"I was the one got knocked out," Vennie Walker says, in a heaving, worn-down voice. "But I want these kids protected!

"The police upholds the law for the government, the worship of God keeps us from doing wrong when we need to do right. And when the police come, they're not thinking about helping our children," she bleats weakly.

"Can't anybody help these young men?" Mama Vennie begs the church as tears mottle her face. She can stand up to other people's abuse, but it is hard to stand up to abuse from her own kind, young or old.

"Oh, Spirit! Save us," Vennie cries as she buckles and falls to her knees.

Nobody answers this time. They are so overwhelmed, so paralyzed with disbelief and outrage that in a place where call and response is the norm, they hear the call, but the response is missing.

Abyssinia Jackson slips down from the choir stand, gently wraps her shawl around Vennie Walker's shaking shoulders, and whispers comforting words in the elder's ear.

The mugging of Vennie Walker spurs Isaiah to go out and meet the tough young men yet again.

"Somebody mugged Mother Vennie Walker the other night," he begins.

"Say what?"

"Somebody mugged Mama Walker."

"Mama Walker?"

"When?"

"Where?"

"Who did it?"

"Thursday night, on her way to missionary service up at the church. Don't know who did it."

"What happened?"

"Caught her right outside the church house door. She always gets there first," he tells his listeners, some of whom have been fed butter cookies and homemade vanilla ice cream by Vennie Walker when they were young toddlers.

"Mama Vennie Walker? Who you say did it?" Jericho repeats. He remembers the cool ice cream dripping off the cone and onto his fists. Relief from the heat wave had sent rivulets of sweat down his five-year-old face. The noonday sun parched his throat. When the precious cone fell on the ground, Mama Walker, looking at the specks of grime like dirty ants on the cream, had said, "That's all right, Child, you can have some more."

"Mama Walker was like my own mama," Jericho says in an irate voice.

He squeaks his words the way he hasn't done since he was a young kid. Now, this memory of Mama Walker's affection leaves him raving, squeaking, and ranting, "We'll kick his can! Let me at him!"

Muscle uncrosses his arms; tight bands of outrage squeeze his chest. He scowls, ready for battle.

"No," Isaiah says. "We can't do anything 'til we see what Mama Walker wants. She's already figured out who she wants you to beat up."

"So you do know who did it."

"I didn't say that."

"Then who she talking about us hurtin'?" Muscle asks, ready to do damage.

"Who?" Jericho repeats.

"Come on up to the Wednesday night meeting," Isaiah says to the throng. The still livid young men grimace menacingly. They stare at him as he walks away.

"I wonder what Mama Walker's got in mind," Jericho says as he adjusts his Ray Bans.

"I think I know who hurt Mama Walker," Muscle says. "Last week we beat them punks down! Cleaned their clocks! Since they couldn't whip us, they come over here messing with Mama Walker!"

"Yeah! Yeah! Yeah!" the group chants.

"Pathetic bustas! Let's go fix 'em! This time they won't be able to trip their slouchy butts over here and hurt nobody! A defenseless, helpless, old woman! When we get through, they won't even have legs!" Muscle rants.

"Mama Walker. Man!" Jericho says. He takes off his glasses and rubs invisible dust from the lens with a soft handkerchief. "We'll take care of it," he decides, the cast in his eye still, then

stormy. The gang members quiet their mumbling when they see
the color change in his eye and hear the turf protecting call-to-
arms in his voice.

Isaiah knows that to get to any young man in these parts all
you have to do is talk about his mama. Mama Walker represents
everybody's mama in the gang.

"Said these Wednesday night sessions up at the church are
for *men* only." Jericho enhances Isaiah's invitation. "No boys allowed. *Men!*"

"Wonder what Mama Walker wants. Wonder what this old
man's up to?"

"Did he say Wednesday?" Jericho asks.

"Seven o'clock," Muscle answers.

Jericho nods and repeats, *"Men* only!"

Isaiah faces the Wednesday night altar, gazing at a dove in flight in the stained glass window on the far wall behind the podium. He meditates on the etched beauty of the sublime bird tipping wings across the blue and green spangled sky. Light refracts each section of the peace mosaic. Bits of sky and wing kept in place by dark, raised strips of lead. His eyes rest on the congregational pews, with their bow-shaped backs. The minister's oak podium. The choir music stands covered with white linen dust protectors, embroidered with the church initials by the members of the missionary board. Roosevelt Tate's ebony organ, shining.

Roosevelt Tate, the choir director, has promised he'll help Isaiah with the young men. And so has Dr. Jackson, who composed a special song just for the new group.

Isaiah glances down at his wristwatch. It glows 7:05. As time inches ahead and nobody comes, he whispers, "Can't believe I'm sitting here all by my lonesome with only meditation, prayer, and hope for company. Again." Then he reflects on what he's just thought and his heart skips with gratitude. Meditation, prayer, hope.

Almost in response to this last reflection, he hears the church door open. Sounds like a gate. He thinks, *When the devil builds a fence, don't just complain about the fence, get up and look for the gate.*

Whoever has entered moves quietly. It isn't Mama Vennie Walker, for the minute she enters the sanctuary, she kneels down in the first pew she comes to and prays before coming forward. Footsteps don't hesitate, not even for a moment and certainly not long enough for Mama Walker to pray a fervent prayer. It isn't Roosevelt, the choir director, for he always greets everyone with bubbling-over affection in a baritone heard from the podium to the church steps. It can't be the young men, Isaiah decides, for he hasn't heard any loud signifying approaching the church. No loud braggadocio.

When he turns to look, he can't believe his eyes.

The young men have eased into the middle pews.

He beckons them to sit nearer.

They move closer. Watching. Wondering.

He quickly assesses the group, but Jericho Hayes, their leader, and his main man, Muscle Adams, are not among them. Was there a breach in the group? Is Jericho going his own way and taking Muscle with him?

He looks at the men as they reseat themselves, but they don't give him a clue.

The clock keeps ticking.

Ten minutes and he'll have to start without the young leadership he needs.

Then the church doors swing open again. Another gate opening or another gate clanging shut? Is somebody coming to tell him Jericho and Muscle have gone to battle with the gang up the way? And lost?

Is somebody coming to tell the church to prepare for the next funeral?

Isaiah sighs with relief. Jericho and Muscle. The two men escort Vennie Walker, right arm in a sling, bandages covering her hands.

She is walking slower than anybody remembers, even after her foot surgery. Jericho and Muscle escort her down the aisle and up to her special seat, across from the offering table.

When she is settled as comfortably as they can make her, Jericho places her cane beside her. Then he and Muscle move to the pew with the rest of their group.

Isaiah's heart expands. "Good evening, young men."

"Evening," they respond.

"I'm sorry we had to gather on such a solemn occasion," continues Isaiah, "yet I'm mighty glad to see you. To begin, I want Vennie Walker herself to speak and tell you about what she wants you to do. Mother Walker . . ."

Vennie struggles to get up from her chair.

When Isaiah moves to help her, she feebly waves him away. "I can do it," she says.

At the same time, all Jericho's men jump half out of their seats, ready to come to her aid, but when she chooses to help herself, the young men's eyes smart, and they sink back in their pew.

After she is as straight as she can stand, Vennie Walker, leaning on her cane, positions herself before them and looks up and down the rows, focusing on each face one by one. She remembers this one crying at the drop of a hat, at the slightest teasing from his playmates. She remembers that one bullying everybody with his loud taunts. She remembers Jericho and his sticky ice cream cone. In a worried voice, she begins, "We got us a battle to fight."

Jericho's men, ready to defend her, grunt their agreement.

"Now, I want you to know right off," Vennie Walker continues, "the young man who mugged me wasn't from 'round here. And anyway, I was in such 'scruciating pain I wouldn't remember his face if the police showed it to me. But I remember each of your faces from way back. And it wasn't nair one of you."

"Knew he wasn't from 'round here," Muscle sputters.

"Hush. Listen," Jericho says.

"In a way, the main thing is this," Mother Walker says with a wave of her sling-supported arm. "I know who told him to do it."

"Who? Who ordered it? What's his name?" the young men grumble.

Mama Vennie Walker holds up her hand. "Wait. This here's kind of complicated. But as Brother Isaiah told you, there's a part in it for you young men. What I want you to do," she begins, and the young men, elbows on their knees, fists on their chins, hunch forward at full attention. "I want you to knock the devil out. I want you to kick Satan from one end of this town to the other."

Finally they hear language they understand. Action.

"But the devil?" Jericho grunts to himself. Who is she talking about? He needs the person's name.

Mama Walker holds up one bandaged hand. "Now Brother Isaiah has been made a deacon in this church. And I'm asking you to sit there and give him a listen. The brother's come a long way in his own battles with the devil, and I think he can explain in vivid detail just how I want you to whip Satan's rump. I believe Brother Isaiah is true to his Biblical name, for in the Bible it was the prophet Isaiah who said, 'Here am I, Lord, send me.' Will you give Brother Isaiah a few minutes to map out the way we gonna do the devil in?"

"Yes, ma'am." Jericho nods. The cast in his eye waits in shadow.

Brother Isaiah has never stood before an audience and spoken before. He is going to have to depend on God. But he knows that God is looking and listening. Didn't God speak to him from the Bible when he was at his most murderous? The sudden appearance of the Exodus verse, "Thou shalt not kill," when he was dangerously close to strangling Pearline reminds him of the mysterious workings of God's hand. The ten commandments. He has already accepted the call to handle this situation.

"My Bible tells me," Isaiah begins, "that 'faith is the substance of things hoped for, the evidence of things not seen.' In other words, men, we'd better start believing what we don't yet see. Faith is one part of the ammunition we need to fight the good fight in the name of our personal God, in the name of our mother, Vennie Walker, and in the names of all our mothers.

"Faith and mercy." His voice washes over them, smooth and rough.

"Have mercy on ourselves so we can believe we have the power to stop this ride toward madness and begin cruising toward gladness. In order to stop anything, a jalopy, a Mustang, a BMW, a Cadillac, a Benz, you got to know when to turn the key off and stop the wheels a-spinning."

"Deliver us from evil," Vennie Walker chants in an encouraging voice.

The young men don't say anything, they sit unmoving, in steely anticipation, waiting for Isaiah to give Satan a name, a face. To direct them to one of the gang members across the way.

"Make it plain," Roosevelt Tate, the director of the choir says. He enters with a sheaf of sheet music and sits down at the organ.

Isaiah continues, "I know some mother tonight is down on bended knee praying for a wayward son, crouched over his steering wheel, speeding down the streets of destruction. I know—" He pauses, catches his breath, and lets out a rhythmic hum. "—I know some grandmother is walking the floor wondering what her grandson is doing out on the street. She sees him busy wheeling 'round the back alleys headed for the devil side of town and the wrong side of life. I can see her head hanging low, wondering when he'll come ease the key in the lock, so she can stop worrying and close her sleepy eyes and rest easy. Many's the time she wonders if God's busy somewhere else and paying no attention to her no how. Many's the time she wonders if old Satan's got his pedal on the metal."

The young men are squirming in their seats. This means Isaiah is touching a nerve.

"He be comin' real with it," Muscle murmurs.

Isaiah can see that Jericho is not ready yet to get totally involved in the church. He has more he wants to say, but Jericho's mind isn't on church, it's on finding out the culprit's name, the flesh and blood devil who attacked Mama Walker.

"Can you come back next week?" Isaiah asks, his question directed at the crowd of young men, but specifically at Jericho.

Jericho nods. He needs time to think about what he's heard so far. He promises to come back the next week, for he just has to get the name of the punk who did this to Vennie Walker.

The next week Isaiah picks up where he left off.

He can see that Jericho might be ready to receive the rest of his words.

"I tell you right now," Isaiah begins, after the prayers and preliminaries are over, "many a mother, aunt, grandmother is watering her couch with tears, so many tears that her floor's flooded, flooded so high she's swimming in sorrow. Just because some young person's riding toward hell in a hurry."

"Um-hm!" Jericho says with a nod, his elbows on his knees, his balled-up fists on his chin. "Hell in a hurry." He likes the sound of it, and the whole crew of young men stop squirming in their seats, relax, and lean back.

"Hell in a hurry!" the young men respond in unison.

"I ain't feeling nobody else!" Jericho says, going with Isaiah's flow.

"And that old devil," Isaiah continues, "don't you know, that old devil, all dressed up in his itchy red suit, is oiling the spokes. Satan's greasing the bearings. Lucifer's standing at the toll booth saying take that steep highway going down, don't you see yonder's the easy way. And he's saying, see here, young man, you don't even have to steer. Listen, says Satan, I'll give you a quick push and you can just coast your way on down, don't you see?"

"Don't you see?" Roosevelt Tate, the choir director, chants.

"All these drugs, all these street gangs, can't you see they're just a different version of a Benz bound for hell? Look at the newspapers, listen to the radio, can't turn on your TV without seeing somebody young, somebody gifted, somebody beautiful heading down the highway to hell!"

"Headed down the highway to hell," the young men respond.

"We got all kinds of hell. You name it, we got it. Young Black men are being destroyed by the system! You know what I'm talking about. Many of you've been there. Guards making young men kill each other. Watching it for sport. Police egging young men on to battle their young brothers and standing back laughing, their own babies safe somewhere in secured neighborhoods."

"Ain' nobody care!" Mama Walker bawls.

Muscle squirms, scrunches down lower in his seat. Isaiah's analysis is too close for his own personal comfort.

"Part of your job will be to dry some mother's weeping eyes," Isaiah says. "Lift up her bruised spirit. And yet, the first part of your job is to listen to what's right for you and save YOURSELF!

"Save yourself, then save somebody else.

"Your battle is to stop that downhill skid. This Wednesday, this perfect night that God sent. Pull up, pull up, pull up, I say. Pull up a new gospel brake."

"Pull up a new gospel brake," Mother Walker says with a flourishing wave of her handkerchief.

"And if the brake gives out and stops working, plant your feet on the ground and drag Satan's old forked tail to a halt."

Muscle's head is spinning. He gags. His memory betrays him, letting in stuff he'd just as soon forget.

"Turn off the road to the cemetery," Isaiah says. "Bypass the mortuary. I promise you, you'll see a change. Satan won't like it. And the minute Lucifer, old Beelzebub, sees what's going on, devil'll come showing his ugly face, wrinkled as a new tire, come poking his pitchfork in your Firestone wheels, trying to mess up what's going on."

"Umph," Muscle mutters in a troubled voice, still remembering what he hates to remember, the first time he was thrown in jail. The irony is that he wasn't doing anything illegal, just walking down the street with the typical young Black man's swagger. His Black, male, bopping walk drew the ire and the baton of a "can't step no-how, no-way, got-no-rhythm" cop.

"Who can touch a black-as-tar, handsome, muscular brother?" Jericho had asked, knowing how the mix of hate and, yes, sexual jealousy for his kind uglies up the whole wide world.

Worse punishment than the baton lay in store for Muscle. His manhood had been further assaulted once he got trapped behind bars.

Raped and left for dead.

His boon buddy found him, stinking in his own excrement and wallowing in his own vomit.

His Cuz got the name of who did it. And how Jericho and his men left the rapist wasn't a pretty sight either.

Muscle bellows, "I was way down yonder by myself and I couldn't hear nobody pray!"

"I heard you, brother," Jericho, who had found him first, says.

He found Muscle bloodied and almost dead, holding on to the bars and crying.

"How they treat you will turn you mean if you're not already mean," Isaiah declares. "Devil'll stand on the sidelines and holler, 'where you headed, young man? Take it easy, no need to work yourself up in a sweat going up the road when you can have more fun going down!'

"Satan's voice'll sound sweet, but if you listen closely you'll see that ugly acting devil's berating you.

"Ugly! Fat with evil! Puffed up with arrogance!"

"Isaiah's signifying!" Muscle says. He recalls one particularly ugly prison guard with a belly sticking out like a portable pot.

The music changes key and Isaiah starts walking up and down the aisles humming.

Isaiah's voice lowers to another register, "But you got your scripture handy. Got your love medicine ready."

Then, still preaching, he sits down in the middle of the pews with the young men. This unexpected flourish startles them. Isaiah snuggles up closer to them. One with them. Puts his arm around Muscle.

"Um-hmm, got your Bible open!" Roosevelt Tate croons. Roosevelt Tate is moved to accent what Isaiah says by running his nimble fingers up and down the organ, in a quick, shimmering arpeggio.

"You get off that highway, turn off the key, park and start thinking about what can be done. Inside your mind you pray."

"God *always* hears you," Roosevelt Tate adds. At the organ, he is still in sync with Isaiah.

"Um-hmm, you start up the motor, turn that jalopy around.

And now it's still not easy, because the devil hears you praying and now Satan's more alert. But still, you turn around and start winding your way toward heaven. I call heaven a place where you begin to love yourself. Up the road, don't you see?"

"Up the road," the chorus of men croons.

"Up the road," Isaiah preaches, "love is in the wind!"

"Up the road," Roosevelt Tate sings with his head tilted back.

"Love is in the wind!" the church chants.

Roosevelt Tate wiggles down and starts coaxing a traditional hymn from the ebony and ivory keys on his organ. With the familiar music, the young men follow a musical memory back to their early years. A time when God was another name for goodness. Back to the time when homemade ice cream was served on the church steps. To a time when love was in the wind.

Isaiah stands up and starts making his way to the door, still preaching. "Lord, take us back to the beginning. Take us *forward* to tomorrow!" Isaiah says after Roosevelt unbends his back from over the organ and lets silence surround Isaiah's words.

"Love," preaches Isaiah, "I say Love, Love is in the wind! Why don't y'all come back next Wednesday and you'll get the next installment. But tonight I want you to think about what we're offering here. Tonight and for the next six days, remember that up the road love is in the wind. And think about what Mama Vennie Walker's asking of you."

"Think about it!" the choir director chants. He rhythmically pumps the pedals to a new melody with a strong back beat.

Isaiah makes the most dramatic exit anybody can remember a preacher making, all the time chanting, "Love! Love is in the wind!"

"Hey, Mr. Jericho, you got time to come listen to this new song?" Roosevelt Tate calls after the door closes behind Isaiah.

As the group approaches, Roosevelt Tate works the organ

pedals until the Hammond throbs with step-stomping energy. Muscle says to Jericho, "That can't be gospel. It's too real!

"Real? Real live!" Muscle says.

"Bad's what it is," Jericho decides.

"Listen up!" Roosevelt Tate croons as his fingers skip across the keyboard and wade deeper into the new song.

The beat of the music rumbles inside their minds, and they can't move away. The music has a hold.

Then Roosevelt Tate opens his throat and sings from some-where rich and deep in his baritone soul.

> *Why, don't you think*
> *Think about tomorrow . . .*

When a mesmerized Jericho leans forward to follow the music that Roosevelt's hands heed, he notices the title and credits inked across the top of the page, "Think About Tomorrow," composed and written by Dr. Abyssinia Jackson.

Roosevelt Tate sings the number with such fervor that the group finds itself listening beyond the beat and heeding the lyrics of the music.

The lyrics call to them in chords that unsettle their steady nerves, twitch their tendons. "Think About Tomorrow." The song hip-hops through their ready minds.

"So this is the battle cry," Jericho says.

"It's not a person they're asking us to fight. It's the devil inside people we'll be fighting. It's mental, then," Muscle whis-pers to the rest of the men.

Jericho nods to the group, and they know they will follow him anywhere.

"Okay, men, we know the enemy. And we're gonna be dan-gerous! Dangerous to the devil!"

They hear the song's message still when Jericho and Muscle escort Mama Vennie Walker down the church aisle with the whole gang stepping in sync, in columns, behind them. They leave the sanctuary steps escorting Mama Walker, and then wheel around the corner.

The hip-hop beat to "Think About Tomorrow" blares, making new waves, etching new grooves in their brains.

J*anet* Lacy blanches when Abyssinia asks her about the mysterious card.

"I didn't see who left it," Janet Lacy claims. "I turned around, and when I looked again, there it was!"

"Do you remember who was in the room?"

"No. It's been a very busy day. Remember, I'm also helping the nurse."

"Yes," Abyssinia agrees. "This must be the busiest day of the year."

Someone has written "Abyssinia Jackson, M.D." in ragged, crooked script on the line provided for the patient's name. "Abyssinia Jackson, M.D.," she whispers to herself. The patient? A slip of the pen? A joke? Or perhaps a play on the expression, "Physician, heal thyself?"

*Who wrote my name and left it for my receptionist?* Abyssinia wonders as she takes the mystery card out of her satchel.

The spaces for day, date, and time are blank. In the scheme of things, it is not something to agonize over. Just something to ponder.

Maybe, she thinks, it wasn't a stranger, but some child accompanying her mother to the office. Perhaps the preschooler kept herself busy by copying the doctor's name at the top of the card onto the blank line.

"Yes," Abyssinia says aloud, "it does look like a child's hand, a child's doodling, or maybe the calligraphy of God."

When she closes the office, Abyssinia clutches the peculiar card, turning it over and over in her hand. What does it all mean?

Finally, she sticks the appointment card in her pocket and heads for the residential wing of the house.

Carl Lee sprawls across the table, reading the football scores in the sports section of the newspaper.

"Looks like we're both too tired to cook dinner. How about breakfast for dinner."

"I'll make the orange juice." He lifts a bag of oranges from the refrigerator, slices and squeezes two dozen into the quart-size pitcher while she mixes the waffle batter in a big crock bowl.

"Want them crisp again?" she asks as she pours the mix.

"As usual."

When the sizzling waffles puff just high enough to raise the top of the waffle iron, she heats the wrought iron skillet, tosses in farm brown eggs, and scrambles the whites and yolks together until she's made a soft and golden soufflé.

"A man-sized dinner," he chuckles as he ladles the ample fare onto the warm plates he left heating in the oven set at a low temperature.

"You're a hungry man," she says, as he chugs down his third glass of orange juice.

"Better watch my pot belly. Older I get, the more I love to eat. Speaking of getting older, I think we ought to adopt soon. Wanna be young enough so I can run across parks, toss a football back and forth to my kid, do outdoor daddy things. Carry our child on my shoulders."

Abyssinia nods. "Should we start on the paperwork next week?"

"How about Monday! Sooner we start, sooner I can be a daddy."

"I just wonder about one thing," Abby says.

Carl Lee tenses. They have been talking about a child for years, and since they have already decided to adopt two, he is anxious about what Abyssinia might now be thinking. "What's that?"

"What'll we name them?"

"Name them?" he says relieved.

He drizzles more maple syrup over the hot waffles.

"What about calling the girl Abby?" he asks.

"Abby," she says and thinks about it a long time as she studies his beaming face. "Abby? No. I want her to have her own identity. She needs her own naming ceremony."

"Okay, I can see that. But have you had any dreams about a name?"

She shakes her head, not one name has visited her dreams. Where there should be a name, or the sound of a name, there is only silence. "No, nothing yet. What about the boy's name?"

"Your call, Abby."

"Carl Lee, Jr.?"

"No, for the same reason you gave, for not wanting a child named after you," he answers too lightly, too quickly.

"And have you dreamed that name?"

"Well . . ."

"Well?"

"I can see it now," he blurts. Then, after a brief pause, he adds, "A son named after me!"

"Then so be it. And we'll probably call him Junior."

The huge grin stretching across Carl Lee's face is all the verification she needs that she has given the right answer.

"Being a junior, he'll just have to fight to claim his place in the world all the more vigorously." Carl Lee's chest sticks way out. "That kind of thing strengthens a young man."

"I wouldn't know about that part," Abyssinia says playfully. "That's definitely your department."

When Carl Lee leaves for work the next morning, she is brimming over with joy at a ceremony for the naming of Carl Lee, Jr. The christening. A baby lifted up to the congregation. Affirmation. With the discussion of the name and Carl Lee's setting up of the appointment with the adoption agency, the soon-to-be-theirs children are more real to her than ever.

For a while she stands and lets her imagination loose, thinking about how the house will sound with little ones in it. The walls will vibrate with growing-up cries mixed with happy laughter. Cries from the childhood pain of cutting teeth, chicken pox, measles, and earaches. She and Carl Lee will attend the little ones with spoons of medication and steaming pots of broomwheat tea. More laughter than tears. Abyssinia walks from the kitchen, hearing a baby girl joyfully beating pots with wooden spoons, then into the living room, studying the hardwood floors where she can already see Junior running, bumping into things as he careens toward the bedrooms. She touches the ivory walls and imagines them sticky and smudged from little fingers. She smiles at the sight of the hallway and doors decorated with crayon scribbles. All the doors would serve as art shows of pin-up pictures and crayon masterpieces. And this one. What early art work would go here? She reaches the cellar door.

Her train of thought shifts from exhilaration to dread. Instead of moving on, she stops. Can't move. Trapped. Then beckoned. Pulled by the secrets down beyond that yet-to-be-scribbled-on basement door.

The cellar. She turns the brass knob and descends into grayness as she heads down the stairs. On the curved landing, she stops and holds on to the banister. Hesitates. Then continues down. Toward the room at the bottom.

Who would suspect that in this House of Light, underneath ground level, she keeps this dark room? A gray chapel. A place void of mirrors.

Even the air vent slats tilt downward, and while air is free to move in and out, only whispers of sunbeams can enter.

Because Abyssinia always refuses to turn on the lamp near the gray sofa, only a muted light slips into the room through the slats, a light just this side of darkness. Just enough shining through for her to write in her notebook:

Here in this room it is warm. And here is my soft couch stuffed with old gray cotton.

I sink into its comfort. It settles around me like an old friend.

I come here to remember the impossible.

Here I tell my songs to be still.

Here I put prayers in the way-back land of my mind.

Here in the gauzy darkness, I scribble forbidden words in my gray journal.

Abyssinia keeps writing, moving down the pages and through the notebook.

When she comes to the end and touches cardboard, she

places the used tablet on a pile and reaches for a new one to take its place.

She pauses to listen to the rain falling softly outside. The rain beats down stronger, making a tinny sound splashing against the vents and rattling them. She returns to her blank book, the color of storms.

> This room is a secret place, an obscure corridor in the bottom of my heart, unreachable except by someone expert at negotiating mazes.
>
> Sometimes when I am down here I forget the promise of the sun. The sun is not evident, how can I miss it? Here is sundown.
>
> I sometimes go so deep into myself I forget Carl Lee. Carl Lee, the Sun. Mama and Daddy, patience and strength.
>
> I have left my wings in a secret sanctuary.
>
> In a house filled with light, I have chained off shadows.

When the new residential section, the "L" part of the house, was first added to the medical wing, the neighbors who helped construct the building pictured this basement as a storage cellar with lots of shelves for jars and jars of canned peaches, spiced pears, and plum preserves.

Abyssinia gives the bulk of her time to Carl Lee, to her patients, to the church, to her music. She allots no time for canning.

> It is Mama who cans and preserves the fruits of these fields.
>
> Mama?
>
> To have the patience of my mother. To be patience.

But I am not.

I can never be.

I thought I had given up all my rights to motherhood.

Yet to my immense joy, soon I'll be mother to two children.

I am afraid.

"**M**orning, Dr. Jackson," Janet Lacy says.

"Morning, Miss Lacy. Who've you got for me today?"

"Schedule's not nearly as busy as last week. You got four returning for checkups. And you have one new patient."

"What's the name?"

"A. M."

"Not a name I'm familiar with."

Abyssinia picks up the list of names. "What's his complaint?"

"*Her* complaint," Janet Lacy corrects as she hands over the first chart.

"Her?" Abyssinia looks at the name on the chart. "You did say A. M.?"

Janet Lacy nods.

"I've heard of boys being called by initials. Unusual for a girl." Abyssinia opens the folder and quickly peruses the patient's answers to the general slate of questions.

"A. M. Hmm," Janet Lacy says. "Something about her eyes. She's your first for the morning. Already in the examination room."

Two young people wait. A young man and the patient, A. M. The young woman's pallor is okay, she notices at first glance. The color reminds Abyssinia of Oklahoma's red clay earth. Her bushy hair is becoming, in the way wild things are beautiful.

A tall young man, with a pair of the mightiest hands Abyssinia has ever seen, stands at A. M.'s side. According to Miss Lacy, a young man with hands like hams had assisted A. M. in getting inside the office and aids her in moving around from place to place. He is a teenager, looks to be about the same age as A. M.

"I'm Dr. Jackson," Abyssinia says. She extends her hand to touch A. M.'s. Icy fingers.

"I'm A. M."

"I'm Wade. Pleased to meet you," her companion adds.

"What seems to be the matter?" Abyssinia asks A. M.

"I can't see," A. M. answers.

"When did this start?"

"About a year ago."

"Did you fall down?"

"No."

"Any illness?"

"Like what, ma'am?"

"Meningitis?"

"No."

"Any other illness?"

"A little amnesia," Wade offers.

"You recovered?" she asks A. M.

"Yes. My memory came back."

"What happened to cause it?"

"Don't know."

"Did you fall down?"

"Not exactly."

"We'd better order your medical records."

"We're not from around here."

"Oh." Abyssinia can see that her line of questioning isn't getting her far. She has to rely on her senses, her training.

She runs her hands through the girl's soft, kinky hair, touching the scalp, searching for lacerations and bumps, looking for a concussion that might affect eyesight.

No bumps or contusions. Squeaky-clean hair, recently washed with coconut shampoo.

Wade turns his back when Abyssinia slips the gown away to further examine the patient.

"Heart rate's good," Abby says as she listens through the stethoscope.

"Now cough for me. Great. Lungs clear.

"Pulse is fine."

The young woman shrugs.

"Try not to blink," Abyssinia says as she directs an optical beam at the young woman's pupils.

"Now follow the movement of my left hand."

"I can't."

Non-responsive, Abyssinia notes.

"Could you try to read the eye chart for me?"

"Try? Won't do any good," her voice quivers. "Told you I can't see."

Wade nods sympathetically.


That evening, Abyssinia recalls her first impressions of the youth to Carl Lee.

"Something's not quite right," Abyssinia says.

"What was your diagnosis?"

"I wrote 'Medical complaint: blindness' on her chart."

"But that's not what you really think, is it?"

"You're right. It's what I wrote, but if she's blind, I am. And, as you know, I have twenty-twenty vision."

"Strange case."

"Haunting, really," Abyssinia says. "Reminds me of an Austrian doctor I read about in med. school."

"Who?"

"Dr. Franz Anton Mesmer."

"Did he have a patient like A. M.?"

"There was one case dealing with a young woman who couldn't see. Much written about."

"This Mesmer. Could he look at her?"

"'Fraid not. He lived during the eighteenth century. Believed in spiritual healing. Mesmerized his patients."

"How'd he diagnose the patient you're talking about?"

"Called it hysterical blindness. Modern term is psychosomatic blindness."

" 'Course," Carl Lee says. "Call some woman hysterical nowadays, you'd be the one hysterical."

"Interesting take on sight and vision."

"Mesmer. Mesmerize. How old is this A. M.?" Carl Lee asks.

"Teenager."

"What's she look like?"

"Attractive. Fine physical shape."

"What do you mean by fine physical shape?"

"Small but strong with firm, developed muscles, as though she's used to exercise. And her lungs are clear, as if she breathes clean, fresh air."

"You sure there's nothing else wrong with her?" Carl Lee asks.

"No. Not that I can see."

"Well, what do you suppose might be her problem?"

"I don't know. She sent me scurrying for my medical books, and when I couldn't find a plausible diagnosis, I referred her to an eye specialist. He saw her this afternoon."

"What was his opinion?"

"According to him there's no physical reason she can't see."

"What has fixed her so?"

"Maybe she's just downright stubborn. Willful . . . But that's not fair. Anyhow that's too easy."

"You look sad," Carl Lee says.

"Makes me want to cry."

"You're not one to cry over your patients."

"No, I'm not. Gets in the way of treatment."

"Why's this one different?"

Abyssinia shrugs.

"Where'd she come from?" Carl Lee asks.

"I don't know. And her chart had no address. A husky boy leads her around."

"Sounds like a jock."

"I've invited them over for Sunday dinner, if it's all right with you."

"I'm as fascinated as you. And I'll get the chance to talk to an athletic young man!"

"Talk to *him*? This is about *her*!"

"Well, it'll make them both feel more at home."

Abyssinia shakes her head. "I do believe most men were born with a jocky gene."

"You might have a point, honey. Anyhow, I can't wait to get cooking in the kitchen. Now what kind of gene is that?" He flashes his "gotcha" attorney smirk.

"What's our daughter fixing?" Strong asks as he and Patience begin walking the short distance to Carl Lee and Abyssinia's house next door.

"Whatever it is, you know you'll like it," Patience says.

"Carl Lee'll be . . . how do the kids say, kickin' it in the kitchen. So I know every pan's in good hands. A man makes all the difference!" Strong answers.

"And I'll try not to eat too much," Patience says.

"More you move your lips, more pounds on the hips," Strong, who pinches her playfully, declares. "Don't nobody want a bone but a dog, and he'd rather have meat."

"Strong, Strong, Strong, why don't you quit?" Patience says, not really wanting him to quit. "You know I got to watch my weight."

Strong pats her on the rump. "I'll watch it for you, baby."

"Abyssinia'll be rationing the salt and cutting down on the fat. She got ways to make a meal still taste good. Spices!"

"Pinch of this. Pinch of that. I know all about it. Look at me. I'm the Barbeque King. So I know they're not fixing barbecue. They need to let me know in advance what's on the menu! Do I ever not tell guests we're having potato salad and greens when I invite folks over? No. You'd think our daughter would give us at least a preview," Strong says. "I can hardly wait!"

"Any time anybody mentions food, Strong, you're ready to pay a visit. If I'd told you some church you didn't go to was feeding folks tomorrow, you'd be stepping over there peeping in the pots."

"You got that right," Strong says. "Anyway, I need to check out all these churches' meals. Abyssinia and Carl Lee have been contributing to the homeless programs to feed the poor going on several years now. And I need to make sure these church cooks know how to burn!"

"It's in the Bible," Patience declares. "Nobody in God's world should go starving and hungry."

Then she gives him a lesson on the two fishes and the five loaves of bread.

He is holding her hand and smiling. He could recite the entire Biblical chapter of Luke to her, but he doesn't. He's too busy listening to her sibilant voice. The sound still touches him and makes him feel alive. He marvels at the wonder of her, even after all these years.

"God sent us a beautiful day," he says as he stops and looks down Loganberry Road at the smoke puffing from chimneys. Here and there whooping children ride sleds. Then he takes Patience's arm and they move on. The faint fragrance of savory cooking wraps around Abyssinia and Carl Lee's house, beckoning like a warm fire.

"Well, I could close my eyes and just follow my nose!" Strong jokes.

Inside their house, Abyssinia and Carl Lee are completing the preparation of Sunday supper, chopping and mixing onions and garlic for a sauce to go over the stuffing for the poultry.

When Carl Lee pours apple cider in the bubbling brew, the doorbell rings.

"I'll get it," he says.

"Abyssinia, honey, it's your parents."

"Can see we got here before the youngsters. What're their names again?" Patience asks.

"A. M. and her boyfriend, Wade," Carl Lee says.

"Hope we're not too late to help," Patience says as Carl Lee takes their coats.

"No. You're just in time. And we don't need any help. We've got it covered," Carl Lee says proudly. "You're our guests today."

"Nothing puts a smile on my face like seeing a man in an apron!" Patience says.

Strong thrusts his nose up and sniffs the delightful aroma. "What tempting tasty's turning in the oven?" he croons.

"That's just where I'll be, in the kitchen basting *something tasty* in the oven," Carl Lee teases. He winks at Patience, his collaborator in keeping up their ritual of surprising Strong at every Sunday dinner they are invited to. "Make yourselves at home."

After plates and silverware are on the table, Abyssinia and Carl Lee join Strong and Patience in the living room, admiring the new fallen snow collected in heaps on the window ledge. Sunbeams illuminate the snow, and it sparkles in the chill light.

"That must be them," Patience says.

Their eyes follow the path of white snow to A. M. and her boyfriend, Wade, walking down the snowy road toward the house. Just as the two young people turn the latch on the gate, Strong starts talking strange.

"It's Grace. Oh, my sister, Grace!" Strong cries.

Aunt Grace and her two sons died in an earthquake, so Patience, Carl Lee, and Abyssinia just look sadly at Strong. Will he ever recover from the loss of his only sister?

Then Carl Lee follows Strong's eyes and gets a good look. Carl Lee is motionless, his eyes glued to the young woman. "Abyssinia," he gasps. "Look!"

$A$byssinia follows Carl Lee's gaze, and Patience follows Strong's. "Sure does look like Grace," Patience says.

Now Abyssinia sees what she failed to notice before.

"Amber . . . Amber Marie . . ." Abyssinia whispers to herself at the same time Carl Lee is mouthing the name. A tremor shakes Abyssinia's body until she is limp as a dishrag. A. M. is Amber Marie.

Abyssinia is rooted to the floor. Carl Lee, used to more action—walking or running—when he is disturbed, leaps to open the door.

At first, nobody knows what to say when A. M. and her boyfriend enter.

Amber listens for words of welcome. When she doesn't hear any, she huddles apprehensively under Wade's protecting shoulder.

"Are we late?" Wade asks nervously.

"No," Carl Lee manages to say. "You're, you're on, on time, right, right on time."

"We . . ." Patience stops and starts wringing her hands.

"We're glad you're here," Strong says in a shaky voice. "We're Dr. Jackson's parents. For a minute I thought . . . You're a spitting image of . . ."

"And I'm Carl Lee, your . . . her . . . Dr. Jackson's husband," Carl Lee adds.

Wade is worried, for nobody has shaken hands. Everybody seems upset.

"Where is she?" Amber asks. "Where's Dr. Jackson?"

"I'm here," Abyssinia mumbles, her knees buckling. "I'm right here."

"I didn't hear you come into the room."

"I've been standing here all the time. I saw, saw you before you got, got to the door," Abyssinia says.

"A. M., you . . . You look so much like . . ." Patience begins.

". . . Like my sister Grace," Strong finishes.

Abyssinia opens her mouth, closes it, and then opens it again.

"A. M." Carl Lee utters the initials, turns them over in his mind. "A. M."

Abyssinia speaks up, "A. M.? A. M., are you? Are you Amber?"

"Amber!" Patience says. "Amber, our niece?"

"No wonder she looks just like Grace!" Strong says.

A. M. sighs as a single tear scrolls down her face. The tear makes a small puddle. *How could I, how could I be so indelicate?* Abyssinia asks herself. She sits down before she falls down. A. M. doesn't speak for a few moments.

Finally she answers, "Yes, I'm Amber."

"And I'm Amber's boyfriend, Wade Dewberry. I live across the road from her in California."

Amber, her head bowed under Wade's sheltering shoulder, nods. An anxious expression tears up her face.

Abyssinia's impulse is to run to her and hold her in her aching arms.

Wade goes on. "Abyssinia, I mean, Dr. Jackson, for some

reason Amber thought you were the only one who could heal her."

"Go on," Abby whispers.

"It's been a long struggle. She had a spell with amnesia after the earthquake."

"Tore up everything, that earthquake," Patience comments.

"And of course, you know about her problem with her sight."

Abyssinia nods, eyes still glued on Amber.

Wade takes a deep breath and continues, "There was one thing especially that she had forgotten. She had forgotten the day she discovered your letter to the Westbrooks in their attic."

"Letter?"

"The letter you wrote years ago."

The revelation hits Abyssinia like a ton of bricks. How could she have predicted that Amber would find that letter? "My God!" Abyssinia whispers.

"It was dated fifteen years ago. I was the only person she shared the secret letter with," Wade says.

"What secret letter?" Strong wonders.

"Wait," says Patience, "let him finish."

Wade swallows. "And the return address was Abyssinia Jackson-Jefferson."

Amber continues in a trembling voice. "When I read it, I, I, I ran away."

"You ran away?" Carl Lee asks.

"Into the woods to be alone."

"I see," Carl Lee says.

"Do you?" Amber asks. "I couldn't understand any of what it meant to me as a person. I didn't even know who I was. Amber Westbrook or Amber Jackson-Jefferson."

"What?" Patience says.

"She's our daughter," Abyssinia answers.

"Daughter!" Patience says. For one of the few times in his life Strong is dumbfounded.

"I can see how my letter, finding it like that, must have confused you," Abyssinia says.

"Confused? Nobody bothered to tell me anything. I was *hurt*," Amber says.

"Excuse me. I'm sorry," Abyssinia murmurs in an unsteady voice.

"Excuse you! As though you accidentally stepped on my toe?" Amber bawls.

"We . . ." Carl Lee begins.

But Amber doesn't seem to hear Carl Lee. She looks directly in Abyssinia's direction and says icily, "You! You gave me away! Might as well flushed me down a toilet stool or thrown me in a trash can!"

Abyssinia's whole body numbs at the force of Amber's statement. She can't move her mouth to respond.

"Why?" Amber asks.

Abyssinia is silent.

Wade continues, "I've thought about it a great deal, Dr. Jackson. And I wonder if the pressure of the letter was behind her desperate need to find you. Her grandfather, Papa Westbrook, thought you were Amber's first cousin."

"We thought so too," Strong sputters, clearly confused.

Wade continues, "He thought it would be unethical for a doctor to treat members of her own family, and he thought you might have felt the same way. And so Amber decided to come here without telling him and without telling you who she was."

Amber speaks, "I wanted to be healed. You haven't done

that," she says in a frazzled, accusing tone. "You don't even know what's wrong with me!"

"That's true," Abyssinia says. "I don't."

"But you're an M.D."

"Doctors don't know everything. I don't know everything. I wish I did."

The bald truth of Abyssinia's answer shocks Amber. A nervous tic flickers at the corner of her right eye.

"It took a lot of courage to come all the way out here to Oklahoma," Strong says to Amber.

"For nothing," Amber says with as much regret as sadness. "I don't know if it's courage or not. I know that this is very hard for me."

"Yes, I see it is," Abyssinia says, breathlessly.

Amber asks Abyssinia, "Tell me, why'd you leave me when I was a baby? Why'd you give me to Mama and Daddy? I mean Aunt Grace and Uncle David? I'm so mixed up—Mama, Daddy, Aunt, Uncle—I don't know who to call what anymore."

"Of course," Patience says bewildered by the events unfolding around her. "Grace and David were the only Mama and Daddy you knew."

"You don't understand," Amber sighs as she turns to where Patience's voice comes from. "Everything's topsy-turvy. All these people. All these names feel so funny in my mouth."

"This is new to us too," Patience teeters on the verge of collapse. She can't separate anything, can't tell if she is happy or sad.

Amber hesitates before she speaks. "Grandma? Grandpa?"

"Yes," Patience and Strong, standing together, answer.

Then Amber turns to Abyssinia and Carl Lee and simply repeats, "Why?"

Amber's eyelids tremble. She squeezes Wade's huge hand so hard Abyssinia thinks she is going to break it.

Abyssinia speaks, her voice shaking, "We gave you up because we thought it would be easier for you."

"Is that the only reason?"

"No . . . To tell you the truth, we thought it would be easier for us too. But I found out later, nothing this important is ever easy."

"Why, we would've kept her for you," Patience says, amazed that Carl Lee and Abyssinia had not considered leaving Amber with them when giving up this child so long ago.

"We could've kept her for you and for us," Strong booms. "She would've been told you were her parents. You could've seen her on school breaks, you could've had her with you all these many years."

"Could've," Amber whispers. Everybody pauses to think about that word. What it really means. Something irretrievable. Their minds can't linger there. "Could've."

"Don't you both remember?" Abyssinia asks. "The heart attack? Daddy, you lay gravely ill at the time."

"I would've risen off my death bed for this child," Strong says.

"Abyssinia did rise up off death's bed," Patience says in defense of their daughter. "Giving life is a death defying act."

Strong says, "Your grandmother's more qualified than I am in that department."

"We felt . . ." Abyssinia struggles to work her way out of the emotional snowstorm. "We felt then that every tub must stand on its own bottom. We were trying to be so grown-up. And it was hard. Just married."

"And so far from home," Carl Lee adds.

Strong tries to help explain to Amber. "They went away to

Tennessee, where Abyssinia attended med. school and Carl Lee studied law."

"What? Their education was more important than I was?" she asks in a voice dripping with icicles. Abyssinia slumps, smothered under the blizzard of snow flurries blinding her thoughts.

The silence thickens all around the room.

Amber directs her next piercing words toward Abyssinia. "And so you gave *me* away?"

"We did," Carl Lee says, flinching. "But . . ."

Everyone shivers, feeling Amber's sadness building and building. An iceberg. It is so huge that they can't get around it.

"You didn't want me!" she yells.

"We did!" the whole room shouts back.

"You stopped trying! You gave me up!" She bolts, blindly careening, away from Wade.

Before Abyssinia can digest this accusation, she sees what is coming next.

"And you don't want me now!" Amber screams. In her delirium, like a delirious bird, she speeds toward the door.

"No!" Wade yells, already in flight to stop her.

But he is too late.

Amber flies outside. No coat, no sweater, not dressed for Oklahoma winter, and running blind. While they have been arguing, blaming, and defending the past, the weather has turned mean.

"Lord, no!" Abyssinia screams as she gauges the temperature. "A blizzard!"

Everyone rushes out trying to catch Amber. So recently arrived from California, she does not understand how treacherous a blizzard can be. How the air can be all right one minute and deathly to breathe the next.

"Stay inside!" Abyssinia warns her parents, who know they are not able to dash through this hazardous coldness.

Carl Lee sprints ahead. He thinks he sees Amber, a ghost running up Loganberry Road.

"No, she turned," Abyssinia, catching up, says. But after a few moments she finds it remarkably difficult to see just where she thinks Amber has turned.

The snow flies. Carl Lee slips and slides on the bricks. He feels no pain. He uses his fall to figure out what might have happened to Amber. Could she have fallen?

Panic guides Wade's feet.

He runs up and down looking between houses, behind thickets blanketed with snow, yelling, "Amber! Amber!"

How many minutes?

The chill cuts into their bones.

Now that everything is so swamped with snow, nothing looks familiar to Wade. It is a new landscape. Where is everything? He has lost his bearings and he is losing strength.

"Amber! Amber!"

Maybe she is buried along with the city under a tomb of snow.

"Stop! Stop!" Abyssinia says. "Just give it a second." She puts her arm up to her head. "She couldn't have gotten far. She would've slipped and fallen by now. She wasn't wearing the right shoes to get far."

"Let's backtrack," Carl Lee says.

And they do.

"That bush doesn't belong there," says Abyssinia.

The bush turns out to be Amber. She had traveled only one block before she collapsed and got covered with snow.

Carl Lee picks her up and carries her back inside the house.

"Oh, dear God," Patience says, sinking down as she holds on to Strong's legs. "The child's dead."

When Amber regains consciousness, she can feel the room spinning around her. She moves her hands and feels the soft, firm contours of the couch supporting her. Sighs of "Oh, she's coming to" and "Thank goodness" whirl around her head.

It seems like an eternity since Abyssinia said Amber was all right and Wade lifted her onto the sofa.

But it is only a matter of minutes. She inhales deeply and tries to sit up.

"Be still a little longer," Abyssinia says.

"What happened?" Amber asks.

"You ran out into the snow," Abyssinia says.

"Trying to run away," Amber says, now remembering.

"You're okay," Abyssinia says. "I checked."

"You gave us quite a scare. Should've known you were all right. You've got a hard head, Amber," Wade says trying to ease the tension.

"You always did say that," she answers too seriously.

"You didn't think we wanted you," Carl Lee says, reminding Amber of her worries, wanting to let her finish hearing what she needs to hear. What she has come this far to hear.

"We wanted you every day of your life," Abby says. "Every time we decided to go to California and bring you home, Grace and David told us that the time was wrong. Grace cried so dejectedly, the sound cut right into my soul. 'It's Christmas,' she'd weep . . . 'All Amber's gifts are under the tree.' "

Carl Lee takes up the thread, "Another time David complained, 'It's her birthday, for Christ's sake. We're giving her a slumber party.' "

"We felt that if we moved you, we'd be hurting you. And we didn't want to do that," Abyssinia says.

"You, you gave up. You gave me up."

Abyssinia can't find an answer to that.

She calls Dr. Jones, who agrees to stop by and talk with Amber.

"Many were the nights we cried over that long-ago decision to leave you."

Abyssinia kneels down beside her. She doesn't know if she has strength enough to breathe, let alone speak. "Amber," she says, "we can't change the past, but would you help us do something about now and the future?"

"Our granddaughter," Patience says. Hope shines like tomorrow in her eyes. She has prayed so many nights for a grandchild. This has to be heaven on earth.

"Amber Marie," Strong says, relishing the name in his mouth. Here is flesh and blood. My *granddaughter*, he thinks proudly. And yet, Amber is decidedly her own person.

When Abyssinia finishes checking Amber's pulse, she asks, "Think you can walk around a little now?"

"Amber can do anything," Wade says.

"Except see," she reminds him.

He takes Amber's hand and guides her from one end of the room to the other.

Carl Lee, eyes still on Amber, asks, "How did you get all the way here from California?"

"We came by Greyhound," Wade says.

"Where are you staying?"

"In Papa Westbrook's empty house."

"That'll never do," Carl Lee says. "That old abandoned place's been locked up for more than a year now; everything must be crumbling with dirt and dust."

"And it's too far. Way down at the bottom of Loganberry Road," Abyssinia says.

Patience agrees. Anywhere would be too far, now that Amber is right here in this room.

"And the cold, why there's no heat."

"Wade chopped some wood and we made a fire," Amber says, feisty, as she rounds the couch holding on to Wade's arm. Just reclaimed her consciousness, still a little dizzy, yet still voicing her independence.

"That's enough walking," Abyssinia says. "Amber, you can rest again now."

"You can live closer in, with us," Carl Lee offers.

"That is, if you'd be comfortable with us," Abyssinia says.

"We could give it a try. Amber, what do you think?" Wade asks as he helps settle her back on the sofa.

"I'm not sure . . ." Amber says.

"We know how you must feel," Carl Lee says.

"No, I'm sorry, you can't know how I feel."

"If you're uncomfortable here, you can stay with your grandparents." Abyssinia kneels beside her. She'll take even a small victory.

Amber laces her hands and cups them over her crinkly hair. It takes her awhile to answer. "My grandparents wanted me. They would've taken me."

"Anytime," Strong says.

Patience rocks back and forth, ankles folded, and dabs at her smarting eyes with her handkerchief.

Strong puts his arms around Patience and continues, "It would make your grandmother and me so tickled if you would stay with us. But we can't be selfish. Your mother and father want you too. We'd be satisfied if you visited us once a day. Once a day! Shoot, once a minute! In other words, everybody wants you. Maybe you could think about it a bit?"

"Please?"

Amber holds out her hands and feels her way through empty space toward where she hears Abyssinia's voice. She touches Abyssinia's face, moves her hands across it. She reads the longing there.

Everybody waits.

Happiness, anger, and grief follow one another in patterns of shadow and light, flashing storm and sunshine across Amber's mouth.

"It'll be good to have you here with us, Amber," Abyssinia says as Amber lowers her hands from Abby's face.

Amber smiles, frowns, sighs. And she is speechless. Too much in one day.

"We'll see how it goes," Amber finally says.

"Good," Strong says. "And since Abby and Carl Lee only have one spare room, Wade, you can stay at our house."

Amber's relieved she's found her natural parents, Abyssinia hopes.

*Still angry because we gave her up at birth,* Carl Lee knows.

Grieves. For her lost California family and for all the lost years when she could have been with her Oklahoma parents.

They sit down at the dining room table as strangers. They sit down at the table as family.

"Daddy, would you please say the blessing?" Abyssinia asks.

"Dear God," Strong begins, "thank you for my family. We are reminded today that you hold time in the perfect palms of your hands. We thank you for allowing Time to stop by here and pause with us this afternoon. We know that healing takes time. We pray you will lend an ear to our plea for the healing of our family. For the healing of Amber. And we thank you for sending Amber our way. I'm so pleased that you've let yesterday, today, and tomorrow sit down at a family table together. Amber is one of tomorrow's children. Her parents stand solidly in today. And I'll soon be one of yesterday's people. Again we thank you for this meal, may it bind the generations. Bless the hands of the two cooks who prepared this bounty. Bless this family. In Jesus' name. Amen. Pass the cornbread, please."

Everybody digs in.

Carl Lee smiles when he notices that Wade has eaten three helpings of candied yams and mustard greens.

"Healthy appetite. You remind me of the kids I coach on the football team. Play any sports?"

"How'd you know? I'm a wrestler."

Amber is quiet. And so is Abyssinia, who keeps looking at Amber to make sure she is okay.

Patience just keeps beaming and passing bowls of food, as though she's just discovered oil in Oklahoma. "You didn't hold back on the fat this time," Patience says. "Or the salt either. It's not Christmas or Thanksgiving. How come?"

Abyssinia shrugs. "You're right, Christmas and Thanksgiving are exceptions." But she doesn't know the full answer. She knows she wanted this meal to be a celebration, even before she knew what she'd be celebrating.

The smoked goose with chestnut and cornbread stuffing is delicious, but the meal, finished with moist sour cream pound cake, has its clumsy pauses. Often, each person stays lost in thought. After dinner, Amber rests again on the couch while Patience, Strong, and Abyssinia ready the guestroom. They dust, mop, polish the hardwood floors, and change the already clean bed linen.

"We're going to Papa Westbrook's house and move the stuff," Wade explains to Amber before he and Carl Lee leave out the door. "With a meal like that under my belt why I could move the whole town of Ponca City!"

"I don't know about all of Ponca City, Wade, but could you move my flute over here?"

He nods, knowing full well that today there were moments when Amber's fingers ached to touch her flute. Yearned to play the scales and chords to alleviate her suffering. Longed to play melody as she meandered along this difficult labyrinth. That sleek silver instrument, beautiful just even to look at, is the first thing he'll lay his hands on when he and Carl Lee go to Papa Westbrook's house.

When they return with Amber's belongings, the first thing Wade does is present Amber with the gray case holding her silver flute. She unlatches the catch and lifts out her instrument.

"Thank you," she says in a hushed voice as she strokes and caresses it.

"You all sure know how to travel light," Carl Lee says as he goes to hang Amber's few almost-summer-time clothing items in the guestroom closet.

"We tried to bring only what mattered," Amber says.

"Well, it's been quite a day," Wade says to Amber. "Rest well, I'm going next door with Grandpa Strong and Grandma Patience."

"See you." Amber kisses them all good-bye.

After they leave, Abyssinia says, "Your bath's ready, Amber. I'll help you in and out of the tub."

Amber says to Carl Lee and Abyssinia as they tuck her in

bed, "Well here I am. Never thought I'd be a guest in my own parents' home."

That night Carl Lee and Abyssinia talk on into the wee hours of the morning about Amber and about her blindness.

"I wanted to kiss her goodnight."

"And give her a hug," Carl Lee says.

"We have to go slow."

"We have to move fast."

"Fast enough to make up for lost time."

"Slow enough to give her time to trust us."

"Time," Abyssinia says.

Carl Lee figures, "I'm afraid she's still holding it all against us."

"And yes," Abyssinia admits, "she's right. At one point we did just give up."

Abyssinia remembers the electric charge she felt when Amber touched her face. A touch she has missed for fifteen years. Her throat aches from the constant strain. "Will it ever get right, Carl Lee?"

Isaiah makes an emergency appointment with Abyssinia at the House of Light.

He gets off the scale, and she pens his weight into his chart. "Perfect," she says. "Blood pressure?"

"Steady and rising," he says.

"Why's that?" She can feel something coming. Felt it when she walked in the room.

Then here it is. "Getting ready to do something that's kind of revolutionary," he confesses.

"What's that?"

"Join the Police Department."

"What?"

"What do you think?"

"I don't know . . ."

She listens to herself, waiting for her instincts to take over. "You don't look like a police officer." She smiles.

"Wrong suit."

"That's not what I meant."

"What did you mean?"

"Guess we're all alike, even in the wrong ways. I mean you don't look like a White policeman."

"A pig?"

"I know we think it's them against us, but I wonder."

"About what?"

"I think it's about stereotypes."

"Stereotypes?" Isaiah repeats.

"I've met more than one good White police officer."

"How do we separate the good from the bad?"

"That's a hard one," she admits.

"What do you think it's about?"

"It's about stereotypes and it's about status."

"What do you mean about status?" he asks.

"If the rotten ones think you're somebody, they won't hassle you. If they know you aren't, they will."

"Not sure what you're getting at."

"It's just that some power happy police beat up and kill poverty-stricken White folks too."

"Yes and call them white trash. Their own color. Read about such a case in this morning's paper. Fellow so intoxicated he couldn't walk a straight line, stinking drunk. Handcuffed him, took him to jail, and pounded his head against the bars. They found him early this morning beat to a bloody death." Isaiah frowns.

"Tragedy in black and white."

"Evil," Isaiah says. "I know it well."

"If they'd brought him here, I could have helped him," Abyssinia says.

"I know."

"How do you heal the hurt that words cause?" Abyssinia wonders. "Trailer trash."

"Hillbillies." Isaiah shakes his head.

"Billy clubs."

"It's just that when it comes to Black people, dark skin is a shortcut to disrespect."

"An added cue."

Isaiah stands up. "I'll remember that. I'll be seeing it close up, first hand. I hope I can make a difference."

"It's important to try."

"I'll do all I can."

Abyssinia cautions, "Isaiah, visit me often to check your stress level. You'll be going into a pressure cooker."

"Good morning, Amber," Abyssinia says.

"Hi."

Amber doesn't talk much. This morning she drifts silently, ghost-like from room to room. Feeling her way through the kitchen. Finger-walking from the counters to the sink. She stops and turns right.

She opens the refrigerator door. Fresh squeezed orange is the flavor she craves. She reaches to the top shelf, pushes aside the pineapple carton, and then deftly clutches the handle on the pitcher of orange juice chilling next to the bottle of liquid cranberry. She does this without hesitation with an acute sense of smell.

*Amazing ability*, Abyssinia thinks, watching, trying to be as still as she can be, trying not to disturb Amber's concentration. She savors watching every move her daughter makes.

Then Abyssinia and Carl Lee start breakfast.

After downing her orange juice, Amber ambles through the house. She stands under the ticking clock in the hallway and swallows its sound. In the living room, she touches the keys on Abyssinia's piano and her face lights up. The corners of her mouth turn up, followed by a girlish giggle. She walks across squeaks in the hardwood floors. Memorizes the loose planks. Each room has its own resonance.

She especially appreciates the smells drifting from the kitchen, where Carl Lee and Abyssinia are cooking her favorite waffle breakfast. She lingers over the plate, moving closer to sniff the dark maple syrup. For lunch, she chooses an apple, a tuna sandwich, and a tall glass of milk. When she crunches down into the delicious red apple, her cheeks crinkle into dancing dimples.

"Amber, would you like to see?" Abyssinia asks late that afternoon when the two of them are alone tidying up Amber's bedroom.

"What do you mean?"

"I mean really see."

"See?"

"Oh, I just thought we could talk about this blindness . . ."

"No!" she blurts. Her voice feathery, flying far away.

"I just . . ." Abyssinia tries again, and then hesitates, realizing that talking to Amber about her eyes is the last thing she should be talking to her about. She stops fluffing the soft pillows and wonders what to do next as Amber slumps down at the foot of the bed, her arms wrapped around her waist.

Wade isn't there, so Amber hugs herself and rocks.

When Abyssinia moves to give her a motherly embrace, Amber's face crumples and she jumps up off the bed, backs away, and trips over her flute case.

Abyssinia wonders how much more any of them can take. She is close to the edge. Wanting so much for Amber. Wanting so much for her family. Wanting so much for herself. She feels dizzy, out of touch with her instincts. She leaves the bed unfinished, stands still thinking, then says, "It's all right, Amber," and leaves the room.

A few minutes later, she hears "The Afternoon of a Faun" drifting from the guestroom. The flute!

When she stands at the doorway, she sees Amber cradling the silver instrument, her eyes closed as if to listen better, her lips puckered into the shape of a bow, her elbows rising and falling, her flying fingers in control of this one part of her life. Her body waltzing with the music, swaying with each breath she blows.

The flute makes Abyssinia recall green trees and spring. Turns cold shadows into flames from a toasty hearth.

A cardinal call. A gentle north wind careening down from a sky carpeted with stars, turning the moon into a giant pearl. This is what Abyssinia feels.

What Amber feels: When Amber touches her flute, partitions between her divided world fall down. Amber, lost in the music, lets her memory rise, escaping in time with her breath through the flute. Talking to God. She remembers stars scattered over the midnight sky as she blows.

Fingers fly, dimples deepen as she blows. And she is wading into the water, remembering the pearl moon. The way Grace, her stand-in mother, organized her pots and spices and herbs hanging from the ceiling, the way she smelled when she leaned over to kiss Amber goodnight, so many lavender goodnights.

When she stops, it seems she has been playing a long time, a stretch of eternity.

She gently lays the flute back inside its cushioned case. Carefully, the way you handle a thing of enduring value. Precious. Priceless. Abyssinia is so touched that tears glaze her eyes.

She moves away from Amber's doorway and goes into the living room, sits down at the piano, and begins playing "Tomorrow's Children."

As she is finishing the introduction, she hears Amber quietly walk into the room and stand behind her listening.

Amber murmurs, "That's beautiful."

"Stay," Abyssinia says. Amber sits down beside her and listens as Abyssinia sings the entrancing lyrics.

Then just as the song is ending, Amber slips away. To her room, Abyssinia assumes. She plays another song, "Let Us Break Bread Together." Then another. Then her inner clock tells her it is time to prepare dinner.

Abyssinia looks at the clock, aware that Carl Lee will be home any minute now. She is walking toward the kitchen to pop the casserole in the oven, when she notices the door to the basement is open. Fear reaches out its glacial fingers. Nobody is allowed to go down there. Panic overcomes her. She can't think clearly. A blizzard storms through her head.

"Who?" She whirls to the open door at the top of the stairs.

"Get out from down there!" she demands in a scared voice.

But nobody answers.

She starts down the cellar steps on wobbly legs.

She sees the light coming up from the cellar, a cold laser.

"Why's the light on?" she wonders.

She panics and starts running.

As she nears the halfway mark of the steep stairs, she trips. Falls, tumbling, still calling in an agitated voice, "Get . . . out . . . from . . . there!"

And she is falling through a red, bruising light.

Carl Lee, just home from work, hears the echoed "Get . . . out . . . from . . . there!" followed by a thud, and comes running.

"Abyssinia! Abyssinia!" he calls.

No answer. He quickly negotiates the stairs. At the bottom, he picks her up.

"Are you all right?"

Abyssinia, fully conscious, is in such a rage she can't answer.

Carl Lee stares, helpless, at her. Out of the tornado of Abyssinia's fear, she sees the shadow crouching in his eye.

"Get away from his eye," she warns the shadow.

Carl Lee carries her into the main room of the cellar, into the dark room that is no longer dark. There in the center of the room, next to the sofa, stands Amber reading one of Abyssinia's gray notebooks.

"Who told you . . . you could . . ." Abyssinia begins. "How, how dare? How dare you!?" she tries again. "Who gave you the right?"

"Nobody," Amber says. "Nobody." Tears tremble, like melting snow, down her face. "I can see," she exclaims over and over again. "I can see!" And she looks down again at the notebook.

"See!" Abyssinia gasps, as Carl Lee grips her arm.

Amber looks up from the page at Abyssinia. Amber's keen glance pierces through every part of her mother. Her eyes, her hair, her body, and her soul. The notebooks have explained how desperately Abyssinia had wanted Amber all along.

"I didn't mean to intrude. I thought it was just a book . . . I didn't know it was your personal journal, and then I opened it . . . and then I started reading, and I, I, I couldn't close it."

"See?" Abyssinia says weakly.

"Amber," Carl Lee says, holding the shaken Abyssinia, "not even I have read Abyssinia's diaries."

"See?" Abyssinia is trying to understand what is right before her eyes.

"She didn't mean to invade your privacy, Abby."

"Oh, I'm truly sorry, I didn't . . ."

Abyssinia struggles to reconcile Amber's miraculous ability to see with her feeling of being naked.

"I feel like my most private thoughts are no longer mine, like they're exposed before the world."

"You're right," Amber says. "I am sorry I intruded, but I didn't feel sorry at all while I was reading. Just relieved that I'd unearthed how you really felt about me. I found my lost world."

"It's all right," Abyssinia finally says. "I'm all right. Didn't you hear me earlier when I called down and asked who's there?"

"No. I didn't hear anything. I was so enthralled . . ."

"Oh, I see."

"I know you do," Amber says sympathetically.

Then Amber turns to look at Carl Lee and remembers other passages she read. She understands his years of longing for his daughter. For her. For Amber.

"May I read a little of it out loud? It seems even more real to me if I can hear it."

"Is it okay, Abby?" Carl Lee asks, intrigued.

"I think so. Which part, Amber?"

"There are so many," she says as she carefully turns the pages. "Can I just pick one?"

Abyssinia nods.

Amber thinks of the journal excerpt that made her begin to understand both her natural parents.

She begins to read:

When we drove up to the house under the chinaberry tree, Grace and David ran out to meet us, as though the word had ridden on the wind before us. Gladness played like a golden light on Aunt Grace and Uncle David's skins, a patina of sunshine danced on their faces as they took our new baby from my arms.

Instinctively, Carl Lee reached for the child, but now Grace and David were cooing over her.

Around the cottage, pine trees and chinaberries filtered the light from the setting sun and threw down a gift of lace designed by the open places left by the leaves and branches of the trees.

In the nursery that Grace and David had prepared, we counted the baby's fingers, her toes. What a perfect jewel.

"Amber," we kept repeating.

"A jewel, our Amber."

We rested up for the long journey home. It was all we could do to keep from changing our minds. Only the terror in Grace's eyes kept us to our sad promise.

We rode the train back to Tennessee.

The after-birth pains were the worst kinds of cramps.

Sitting up, I listened to the clickety-click sound of the steam locomotive speeding us to Nashville and judged we had reached top speed by how fast the smoke from the train rolled by our window. At times the whistle and clang of the train sounded like a lost baby, mournful, wailing.

Chastened by the sacrifice we had made, we prayed deeper in our hearts. We prayed that the love of Grace and David would sustain this child we had carried through the dark fire, through the water, and on into the light of life. We prayed they would care for her in the way we thought she needed until we got her back.

A melancholy shadow disturbed our world. It had sounded so possible when we planned it. I would give birth in the hospital, and then we would leave the child with Aunt Grace and Uncle David. But it had not been that easy.

The next day on the train, I slept for long periods, soothed by Carl Lee's touch and the click-clack of the train wheels traveling down the track.

When the train pulled into Nashville, a deep white snow had covered the town. In places the trunks of hickories, red oaks, yellow poplars, and tulip trees dimpled the snow. The leafless trees, absent of the colors that their names boasted, extended branches bending under heavy snow.

These were the very shadows of winter haunted by brown and gray trunks, unable to move their tree arms under the cold coat of snow.

The weight of a child, loaned out and missing from our life, burdened our days.

Carl Lee was right. You cannot loan out a child, the way you loan out a book from the library.

Now Abyssinia, Carl Lee, and Amber stand in speechless wonder, gazing at one another. A flood of a thousand emotions overflowed from the room and illumined the entire house.

The deacons and brethren who walk up the hill to church this Sunday are attired in their usual wardrobe best: traditional suits, hats, and ties. However, Isaiah Spencer sports a spiffy blue uniform.

It reminds the older brethren of when they had been enlisted men in the armed forces.

"How do you like being a law-enforcement officer?" Strong Jackson asks.

Isaiah answers, "I'm a human reminder to the police department. A vocal reminder. Every day I tell my fellow officers that their mission is to uphold the law and to protect the citizens. All citizens. And, yes, Strong, I'm watching your black back and theirs."

"It's not a contradiction, then?"

"What do you think?"

"I know you know why and what you're doing," Strong Jackson answers. The men who frequent Strong's Better Way Barbershop nod and step on into the sanctuary. "And he'll be going to college part time. Smart man!"

Maggie Peppermill and her friends talk as they move on up the hill.

"Vennie said we'd better be here. And when she calls, you

257

know we got to go," Maggie says to her day-working women friends.

"Thought I'd stay home today," one friend says, "but here I am."

"Me too," Maggie admits. She and her group usually always come to church for regular service, but they sometimes stay home and sleep in on youth day, saving their energy for the night service.

"Would you look at that?" says Maggie Peppermill, who trains her eyes on the entry walls covered with framed photographs of Mama Vennie Walker, Maggie Peppermill, and a host of founding members. "So that's what the young men were doing with those cameras! Humph! Humph! Humph!" The church house is packed.

"Welcome," the minister says. "So glad to see so many of the faithful this blessed day that God has given us."

Everybody amens him on.

"Praise the Lord," the ushers in the aisles echo.

"Yes sir!" the women of the sewing circle respond.

The minister preaches on the generations.

"Every child is a child of God, and so already a member of His family."

"That's the truth," the church responds.

"But we become so gratified when we see individuals reunited.

"We see God's plan in their lives and therefore in all our lives.

"This morning we celebrate the reunification of Dr. Abyssinia Jackson and Attorney Carl Lee Jefferson with their daughter, Amber."

"Amen," responds the congregation.

"And now we'd love to hear Dr. Jackson come to us in her own way."

Roosevelt Tate tickles the keys of the organ, then stops, and lets the blended voices of altos, sopranos, basses, tenors, the choir members of all colors of skin, swoop and dip up and down the chords.

"*Abyssinia!*" they sing.

Abyssinia comes to the podium and begins to speak softly.

"First giving honor to God, to the minister, to the church, and to my family. Now made richer by one blessing of a child: Amber.

"My family belongs to God's family.

"We are members of a heavenly family."

"Amen now," a choir member responds.

Abyssinia continues, "Every family has ups and downs, trials and tribulations."

"Tell me about it!" somebody moans.

"My family is no different," Abyssinia whispers.

"Abide with us in our search time, in our sad time, in our coming together time. And today in our happy time."

"Hallelujah!" Vennie Walker shouts.

"I thank you for your understanding. And for your compassion."

"Thank you. Thank you. Thank you," the choir claps.

"Remember," Dr. Jackson says. "Keep a hug in your heart. Keep a light burning for me and for mine."

The minister helps Abyssinia to her seat, then says, "By now you've all heard the story, passed, I know, down the line from telephone to telephone."

Sprinkles of guilty giggles rise from several corners.

"Gossiping's all right. It's part of the human condition."

"Tell it!" Maggie Peppermill says.

"Today's a good day to acknowledge all Dr. Jackson's done for our community by taking part in her happiness. By celebrating Attorney Jefferson's delight."

"Amen," Pearline says as she cradles her twins in the choir stand.

"And let's not forget the contentment felt by Patience and Strong Jackson either. He's been crowing for days!"

"And well he should."

"Ain't God good?" Zenobia, right next to Pearline, asks.

"We're looking at tomorrow's people," the preacher says.

Abyssinia looks over at Amber and gets a glimpse of tomorrow: Amber is a full-grown woman, a powerful attorney, leading a legion of women in the on-going battle for equality and respect. The calendar keeps turning until she sees Amber, a Supreme Court justice, sitting as one of the twelve judges.

Next she looks out into the congregation and focuses on Isaiah. Although he is dressed in a regular police uniform, she looks into the future and sees him receiving his college diploma, sees him decorated in his captain of the Ponca City Police Department regalia. She looks further into the future and sees a statue of him, surrounded by teenagers, those to whom he has dedicated his life and has successfully protected.

The minister continues, "But if you ask these young people, from their point of view, they'd say, 'Rev., we're today's people.' And they'd be right.

"This service, then, is dedicated to the generations."

First, pre-kindergarten through early elementary school levels of the youth choir sing, "This Little Light of Mine, I'm Gonna Let it Shine." Everybody cheers them on. Jericho and the young men from Isaiah's Wednesday night group put some extra *oomph* into their claps.

The tough young men wear chiseled expressions on their

faces, part of what is known as attitude. The dreadlocks crowning their heads become magnets of attention.

"What's it like wearing dreads?" Amber asks as she finds her seat on the other end of the row.

"You got to tend to it like it's a animal," Muscle says, eyeing her with a rakish, slow grin.

Zenobia and Pearline study this distinctive hairdo they have certainly seen throughout the neighborhood, hairstyles so different from the traditional cuts of the youth ushers patrolling the aisles this Sunday.

"Listen up! Before we start singing," Jericho says as his group takes their turn at the microphone, "I want to let you know how glad we are to be here. Hey, we here to represent!

"By word. By music. By looks!

"I see you eyeing this hairstyle! We wear our hair the way God made it. Anybody got a problem with that?"

"Way God made it," the minister echoes.

"We wear it this way because we don't believe God made a mistake. We represent how God created us. What's moving is what's grooving! The music. Listen up!

"And no. We not into dope. Gave up the smoke after Brother Isaiah showed us that some of us just can't handle it. Mess up your thinking worse than drinking. Find yourself sitting and staring into space. Look up, you lost your place. In your mind. In your time!"

The congregation murmurs its understanding.

Roosevelt Tate helps Jericho along.

"Now, Church," Roosevelt says, adjusting the microphone hanging over the Hammond, "get ready to hear some of these grooves that Jericho's prepared for you, one of which was composed by none other than our own Dr. Abyssinia Jackson. Jericho . . . ?"

"Say Amen, somebody," Mother Vennie Walker calls.

"Amen!" the congregation responds.

"We here today, thanks to Brother Isaiah," Jericho continues, even as he remembers, from his early childhood days, the scrutiny of the ushers, deacons, missionaries, and ministers who have come to support whatever they find that is spiritual, positive, and good in the young.

"Well?" the minister croons.

"And this next song is a special tribute to Mama Vennie."

Muscle nods and raises his arms in salute to Vennie Walker and to the beautiful Amber, sitting behind him in the choir stand. Wade squirms, a little jealous.

"Peep this."

Roosevelt, who has learned so much from the hip-hop rhyming group, tickles the glistening keys on his Hammond organ, jumps into the notes while still standing, then sits down and hunches his jiggling shoulders in time, pacing a vibrant music.

His fleet feet pump the pedals and the organ rumbles with power.

People sit up, forced to pay strict attention by the demanding beat.

The organ calls with dexterity.

The drums and bass respond with depth.

Call and response. Survival music, Roosevelt figures, very much the way blues, jazz, and gospel kept a stolen people in touch with their spiritual heritage, passionate about their own worth, kept them joyous and singing anyhow. The dynamic verses erupt in can't-be-avoided, in-your-face lyrics. The sound, huge, explosive. With hips and shoulders engaged, the Wednesday night men peal out a glorious musical message. They sing "Think About Tomorrow" with such thunder, adding rap chords to such appealing gospel poetry, that even the older folks sway, tapping their feet in the pews, in the spirit as the group flows to the words running rampant.

"My man's got attitude," Amber says. She delights in Muscle's rhythmic arm-waving salute to Mama Vennie and Jericho's free-to-be-me stance.

Abyssinia leans forward to take in the young men's moving hair, dreaded and locked so artfully. Then she closes her eyes and listens for something running under and through the notes.

The stained glass windows pulsate in response.

The sound rushes right through the building from the choir stand to the back pew, throbbing like a human heart. Zenobia, sitting next to Pearline in the choir stand, feels her heart skip. Abyssinia nods. She has found the shining thread she is listening for.

Amber and Wade feel the energy, God-filling, so vastly God-filling that all four walls, tapestried with images of Christ and the ten commandments, sway with the beat of rapture-powered rap.

When Amber and Wade stand at the microphone to present their song, they first pay tribute to Jericho and his group, who peep them out, waiting to see what they are about.

"Better not be lame," Muscle quietly quips. He is hawkin' Amber with sensual masculine interest.

"We wanna acknowledge the new singers." Amber turns toward Muscle and Jericho. "Hip-hop artists with brilliant minds."

"Endless rhymes," Wade says.

"Mad phat!"

"Flippin the script."

"Quick and thick," Amber chants.

"Parlayin and loungin'."

"Kickin it," Amber croons.

"Emceeing Poetry Preachers!" Wade finishes.

Amber and Wade's rapid-fire critique connects rotating rhythms and scintillating changes paralleling hip-hop. Jericho beams, the cast in his right eye shimmers.

"The Amber girl sees what's right before her ears," Muscle quietly chuckles, still jockin'.

"Wade's got skills, too," Jericho acknowledges.

" 'Bout something," Muscle admits.

In that binding moment, Jericho composes rhymes and rhythms in his head. His brain busies itself creating challenging, soul-supporting lyrics.

Roosevelt Tate ripples chords that keep the Jericho beat jumping under Amber and Wade's tribute to the genius of Jericho's group. Now he smoothly segues, augments the sound and changes the key into Amber and Wade's upcoming song.

Roosevelt's transition, effortlessly eased into without pause, impresses Abyssinia. Roosevelt has found the link!

Wade holds a cello between his knees. Then he begins fingering the strings on the cello's neck with deft, left-handed agility while his large, right hand guides the bow across the four strings lacing the cello's belly with hesitant and hurried pressure.

By the time Amber pulls the flute to her lips, Abyssinia knows what she's always known, that what is beautiful multiplied times one is exquisite multiplied times two, is exponentially superb. Today, Amber's playing is even more powerful than she remembers it when she first heard her flute notes drifting from the guest bedroom. Today the scintillating, lyrical beauty of the music glues Abyssinia to her seat and takes her traveling out of herself, so lost in the music she forgets she is supposed to sing with the pair.

*Amber came all the way from California to play me my song,* thinks Abyssinia. *Remarkable. A song for me. A song for Abyssinia. A healing song. Composed by my child.*

Amber and Wade presented her with the music and asked her to write the lyrics. Abyssinia had titled the number "Sacred Mountain, Sacred Tree, Sacred River that Runs Through Me."

When Amber and Wade finish the instrumental introduction to Abyssinia's song, Carl Lee reaches for Abyssinia's hand and the two join the young people around the microphone. Abyssinia lets the lyrics to the first verse ring out:

> *Trinity: Mountain, tree*
> *Light possibility*
> *Light, illuminate the mountain,*
> *Light, green the tree*
> *Light, beacon over the river*
> *Light, fall down on me*

Carl Lee dips in:

> *Light possibility*
> *Trinity*
> *Mountain, river, tree*
> *Light possibility*

Abyssinia continues,

> *In the red river of my veins flows the soul of me*
> *In the forest of my mind there grows a tree*
> *In my passage through time, I've found mountains to climb*

Then she and Carl Lee together claim the next lines,

> *Trinity*
> *Mountain, river, tree*
> *Light possibility*

The song reminds Abyssinia of all that nature has placed around them. She remembers picking Oklahoma wild flowers, leaning against the trunks of trees, drinking in the quiet sky.

> *Trinity*
> *Mountain, river, tree*
> *Light possibility*

The delivery by the four opens up a spiritual space for the entire church. What is gift multiplied times four?

Mama Vennie Walker closes her eyes and rests in the abiding place deep within each listener.

"Man, oh, man!" Muscle confirms. "Doctor got pipes!" Even while he is chuckling, he feels the inner God move in him, and he becomes quiet, too, listening.

After announcing that Amber and Wade will soon be returning to California, the minister intones the benediction: "May the good Lord watch and keep thee . . ."

Wrapped in their woolen scarves, fur-lined gloves, and thick coats, young, middle-aged, and old cluster in separate groups outside the sanctuary, trying to understand just what has happened in the church. The young adults squeal with delight when Jericho and his men exit the tabernacle. One young woman swoons. Her laughing friends catch her. The teenage contingency waves at Amber and Wade, the way they wave at gospel stars.

"Have a safe trip to California!" they cry.

Amber and Wade walk in step with Abyssinia and Carl Lee, who follow behind Patience and Strong. The older congregation members, anxious to get home to warm winter fires, appreciate this new family, at least new to them. Abyssinia is theirs. Yet they are happy to share her and bask in her and Carl Lee's new-found family bliss.

"I know how it happened," Maggie Peppermill says to a group of her gray-haired missionaries who rub their gloves together to stay warm.

"How what happened, Maggie?" one of the matriarchs asks.

"How Amber got conceived."

"Now wait a minute. You couldn't've been there."

"No, I wasn't there when it happened but I remember what happened that led to it."

Now everybody is interested.

"What?"

"Think back to the wedding."

"Beautiful wedding."

Maggie continues, "I remember her Aunt Grace all distracted. Her mind on that California husband of hers, I guess."

"True, but what's that got to do . . ."

"Everything," says Maggie Peppermill.

"Still, I don't see how you could know . . ."

"Plain as my face. That Grace! The woman forgot to put Abyssinia's overnight case in the honeymoon trunk. Sent those children off full of love without the little personal stuff Abyssinia needed, not even a night gown, and when passion came stepping 'round that honeymoon night, I know what happened. Birth control? Mother Nature took control. Mother Nature, now that's some kinda do-what-she-wanna-do woman!"

Abyssinia and Carl Lee, who have stopped to speak to Mama Vennie Walker, overhear Peppermill's assessment of how Amber came to be. They smile in spite of themselves.

They remember that honeymoon night.

A wedding is enough to ruin anybody's wedding night, she had thought after their tiring drive from Ponca City.

"No, not just a wedding. Aunt Grace," she gasps, thinking of the forgotten overnight bag with the birth control compartment.

*That night she says from the bathroom, "I'm coming through, Carl Lee. Your turn."*

*When she enters the room she notices he has drawn the drapes so that the lamp bathes everything in an airy twilight.*

*He keeps staring at her wrapped in the simple towel that has the hotel's name embossed across the bottom; he can hardly take his eyes away.*

*To lighten the moment, they wink at each other.*

*Smiling, he backs into the bathroom. In a minute or two she hears him singing in the shower. By the time the shower stops she is already sound asleep between the cool sheets.*

*When he comes into the bedroom, he hears her purring, her sleeping breath rising and falling gently.*

*"I don't believe it," he says, sinking down on the edge of the bed.*

*He swings his legs up and gets in, pulling the sheet up to his chin.*

*She murmurs something as he snuggles close to her, smelling the lavender fragrance of her bath.*

*Aching with wanting her, he falls asleep.*

*About three in the morning they both wake up, and the ache is too much for them.*

*He turns to her and kisses her with all the years of love that have been building between them.*

*There is no stopping the passion. It is all in the room.*

*In his hands.*

*In the flashes of fire jumping and skipping blue flame down through his mind.*

*She returns him passion for passion. Kiss for kiss.*

*She comes to his heart dressed in openness.*

*A bouquet of lavender twined in her hair.*

*The taste of apples in her throat, in a room mirrored bright with candles throwing arrows of amber everywhere. She thinks she hears peach trees singing the secrets of chee-chee birds. She comes to his heart with June tumbling through the sky.*

Of course, Abyssinia and Carl Lee remember. Now, after saying goodbye to Mother Vennie, they pause and listen to the rest of what the older women have to say.

"What I wanna know," one of Maggie Peppermill's friends says of Amber, "is she or is she not beautiful?"

"She is," they all chime.

"And smart," Maggie Peppermill says. "Told her to stop by my house and read me my *Ebony* magazine."

"What'd she say?"

"Said they're both coming."

"Now why didn't I think to ask her?"

"She and her boyfriend. Umph! Umph! Umph! That boyfriend so handsome makes you wanna holler hallelujah!"

"Now, Peppermill, you know you too old to be grinning at that young man."

"Look, I said I was born again. I didn't say I died. Long as I live, I'll keep on looking."

Abyssinia and Carl Lee are still smiling about Maggie's sense of humor when they rejoin their family. Patience, holding onto Strong, carefully negotiates the ice-slippery street. "I never thought I'd see the day I'd hear hip-hop in my church house," Strong says.

"... And the children, looking wild as the Africa we see in that geographic magazine, dancing wild as Africa on television," Patience says, steam puffing out of her mouth.

"Hear it blasting from car windows," Strong says, remembering the assault on his ears. "They need to turn that mess down!"

"When we were that age they said all kind of stuff about our music," Patience reminds him. "Called it the devil's music. Wasn't the devil's music no how! Something African going on. Why give the devil the credit? It was ours."

"Well," Strong admits, "you got a point. I liked Jericho and their music. Can't say I like *all* that ugly noise flying out of those rolled down car windows. Down right disrespectful, some of it. If I'd said some of that stuff, my Mama'd be making a new door through the house wall, and I'd be knocked out and laying mangled and crippled in the road. Tell you somebody crooked's behind this mess. Words ain't right. Now Jericho and his group, they headed in the *right* direction!"

"That's fair enough," Patience says, "headed in the right direction because they're heads on right."

"Now my granddaughter," Strong boasts, his voice rising. "Even Jericho's men liked her and her music. That made my day. Amber's flute and Wade's cello . . ."

"And Amber, she appreciated their vibes," Abyssinia says.

"So cool it was bad," Amber grins.

"When it comes to today's Sunday concert, I can't say I heard it all. I have to say I've heard some more," Patience agrees.

"Well 'Trinity' *was* exceptionally exquisite," Strong comments. "And everybody says so."

"Muscle called it 'revolutionary,' " Wade, who cherishes both compliments, says. What he didn't add was that Muscle, in man to man language, had also complimented Amber, in recognition of her beauty. He is sprung on her. While clutching his left chest Muscle had said to Wade, "Your woman's a heart wrecker! I'd like to be the spoon in the hot tea she stirs any day!"

Wade had grinned back in appreciation, understanding what the envious Muscle could only know by getting to know her. Amber is his girlfriend, but she is not his. Amber is her own woman.

"She's a honeycomb all right. Me, I'm just the bee," Wade says as he struts away.

Together, for several evenings, Abyssinia and Amber read the gray notebooks, so filled with anguish and love for Amber. They read. Sometimes alone. Sometimes to each other, taking turns.

When Carl Lee reads passages again, his soul stops awhile and rests. As he closes the journal's cover, Abyssinia sees the shadow leak out of his eye and trail down his golden face.

"Oh, Carl Lee," she whispers as she kisses away his tears. "She came back to us, Carl Lee. She brought *herself* all the way home to Oklahoma."

"And now this afternoon she's taking herself on up out of here," he answers, lines deepening in his forehead. "Leaving us down here in Oklahoma and going back to California," he moans, but there is release in his tears. They have received more than they need from this brave young woman who is their daughter.

When it is time, Abyssinia and Carl Lee drive Amber and Wade on the long ride to the airport.

After Amber and Wade pick up the flight tickets, they stand in a circle and look at each other with yearning.

They hesitate, not wanting to part. "Whenever you want to stay here, Amber, you just let us know," Abyssinia says.

"Go ahead," Wade says, seeing how their arms ache to hold each other.

Abyssinia hugs Amber so tight they can hear each other's

hearts thunder. Amber, legs gone suddenly limp, hugs Abyssinia back. Then it is Carl Lee's turn.

After that it is easier. Three-way and four-way hugs that include Wade.

"Wade, thanks for helping us come together," Carl Lee says.

"You're welcome. Thanks for the hospitality."

Amber and Wade turn toward the line of passengers now handing their tickets to the agent, who tears off the stubs.

"I'm sitting by the window," one passenger says to his companion.

"Time," Wade says.

"Be back soon," Amber promises.

Abyssinia and Carl Lee sigh as they all start the short but long journey toward the smiling airline agent waiting at the departure gate. "Soon," all three, Abby, Carl Lee, and Wade say, as they echo Amber's teary response.

"Call us the minute you hit the house," Abyssinia says.

"And give Papa Westbrook our best," Carl Lee adds.

When the ticket collector checks her watch against the departure time and the loudspeaker announces, "Last call," Abyssinia holds Amber's face in the palms of her hands and whispers, "You've made me so proud, Amber. You've blessed my life."

Wade pulls Amber away. It is not easy. An invisible cord of steel runs from mother to daughter.

Carl Lee holds onto Abyssinia.

"I want to go . . . with her," Abby says evenly, her whole body pointing toward the gate.

"Next time," he says.

Then the gray steel turns to flexible ribbon, relaxes the cord enough for the two women to part.

Amber and Wade are the last reluctant boarders.

As Amber turns around to wave one last time, Abyssinia calls, "I love you."

"I love you back," Amber sings.

After the jet pulls away from the gate, after it has taken to the air, Abyssinia sighs, "There she goes."

"That's why you couldn't come up with a name for the girl. We already have her."

"Yes," Abyssinia agrees, as they turn toward one another. "Amber and Carl Lee, Jr. Child and child-to-be."

Carl Lee asks, "Abby, you want to know something?"

"What?" she whispers.

"When you saw Amber could see," he says, "I saw a shadow leave your body."

"Shadow?"

They stare at each other, understanding that shadow gives up its hurt when healing light touches it.

Amber has led Abyssinia to her light, led Abyssinia and Carl Lee to their light, to a New Testament, the testament of compassion. If you ask Amber, she will say it is Abyssinia and Carl Lee who have led her to hers.

Abyssinia glimpses tomorrow through a shimmering globe of the planet. The glow spreads on out to the universe. It blesses images. It blesses her life. She stands awaiting possibility, still holding Carl Lee's hand, listening in the twining light as it plays tag with the wind in the trees. The light whispers its question.

And Abyssinia answers.

"Yes."